THE ICE MAIDEN

B.D. SMITH

BLACK ROSE writing™

The final approval for this literary material is granted by the author.

Second printing / First Hardcover printing

This is a work of fiction. Names, characters, businesses, places, events and incidents are either the products of the author's imagination or used in a fictitious manner. Any resemblance to actual persons, living or dead, or actual events is purely coincidental.

ISBN: 978-1-61296-862-9 (Paperback); 978-1-944715-91-5 (Hardcover)
PUBLISHED BY BLACK ROSE WRITING
www.blackrosewriting.com

Printed in the United States of America
Suggested Retail Price (SRP) $17.95 (Paperback); $22.95 (Hardcover)

The Ice Maiden is printed in Adobe Garamond Pro

THE ICE MAIDEN

PROLOGUE
THE FOX

Winter had come early to central Maine and the ice was a good foot thick in many places by the beginning of the ice-fishing season. Under a gibbous moon, clusters of fishing shacks were scattered across Sebec Lake, and snowmobile headlights carved occasional slow arcs through the January night. At about eight-thirty, Gary and Maureen Griggs left Greeley's Landing on the south shore of Sebec, heading for their shack west of the narrows. There were other public boat ramps on Sebec, but because of its proximity to Dover-Foxcroft, the county seat and largest town in Piscataquis County, Greeley's Landing had been the lake's major access point for boating and ice fishing for more than a century.

Gary had caught a few good-sized lake trout and salmon a few days earlier, and with a fresh pail of emerald shiners he had high hopes for another good night of fishing. Riding behind Gary on the snowmobile, his wife Maureen encircled his waist with her arms and tucked her hands up under his coat for warmth. They made good progress north up along the shore, past the shuttered shoreline cottages on their left. The ice was snow-covered and there was little wind.

As they turned left and passed through the narrows, with the dark forest closing in on both sides, Maureen suddenly squeezed Gary's ample belly and called into his ear.

"What's that rusty red thing ahead, off to the left?"

Gary slowed and turned the snowmobile toward the dim red shape in the distance. As they got closer the snowmobile's headlight lit up a red fox, far out from shore, standing with its head down, intent on something on the ice. Gary had been delivering propane for Robinson Oil, out of Dover-Foxcroft, for almost twenty years, and he had seen plenty of red foxes rushing across the road in front of his truck during that time. They could also occasionally be seen during the winter months running across the frozen lake in the daytime. But he had never seen one on the lake at night, or standing still, like this one.

"Maybe it's nabbed a fish from one of the ice shacks," Gary thought as they approached the fox. He expected it to run as soon as the headlight hit it, but the fox continued to gnaw at something on the ice as they came closer. A rabid fox had been reported earlier in the fall up around Willimantic, at the western end of the lake, and just as Gary decided to veer off out of caution, the fox turned and ran into the darkness toward the safety of the south shore.

"What was it doing?" Maureen asked as the snowmobile reached the spot where the fox had been standing.

"Not sure," replied Gary. Getting off the snowmobile, he walked into the headlight's beam, puzzled by what he saw on the ice. Two planks had been laid side-by-side, flat on the ice, and in the narrow gap that separated them, what appeared to be four white sticks protruded up through the snow. The two larger sticks were about an inch in diameter and spaced about a foot apart, with the two smaller diameter sticks each almost touching the larger ones. Gary knelt and saw that the sticks were in fact bones, with the ends gnawed down by the fox, and probably other scavengers before it. Looking closer, Gary saw that low mounds of flesh still encircled the bones at the ice surface, and it dawned on him what he was looking at. Someone's body had been inserted headfirst down through the ice and then held in place by the two boards until the ice refroze. He was looking at what was left of a person's lower legs. Scavengers had removed the feet and were working their way down toward the knees. Gary turned to Maureen.

"Hand me your phone, hon," he said. "It looks like we got a corpse."

1.

BOWERBANK

About eight miles east of where Gary was dialing 911, in the dispersed north shore community of Bowerbank, population 120, Douglas Bateman was watching Monday night football. Tom Brady had just completed his fifth consecutive pass in the Patriots' opening drive of the second half. The sound was off and Doug divided his time between the game and gazing out the window toward Pine Island, located about a half-mile west of his lakeside house. He wondered if the eagle pair that had nested there for more than a decade would be returning in the spring.

The Pine Island eagles had held a special significance for Doug and his wife Beth, as the pair first appeared the same year that they had moved into their north shore home with their newborn son Eric. Each spring the Batemans eagerly anticipated the return of the eagles to Pine Island from their winter range. Once they arrived, Doug and Beth would take turns watching through binoculars for the first glimpse of an eaglet's head above the rim of the nest. When he was four, Eric joined his parents in watching for the first appearance of the baby eagles, and from then on he was always the first to see them – it became a family tradition.

Soon after Eric announced the presence of eaglets in the nest each year the summer sky over the lake would be filled with the fledging's piercing cries whenever they recognized one of their parents approaching with food. Later in the summer Doug and Beth and their son would laugh together at the clumsy first efforts at flight by the young eagles, and their frequent crash landings into the trees on Pine Island. And then, when the young eagles had become proficient, and soared high above the lake with their parents, the Batemans would know that the end of summer was fast approaching. In another month or so the first turning of the trees would mark the eagle's imminent departure.

A year ago last August however, Doug and Beth's world changed forever with the death of their son. Like generations of teenagers growing up in the area, Eric had joined in the summer ritual of jumping off the bridge in Sebec Village, located at the east end of the lake where it narrowed dramatically to form the Sebec River, the lake's only outlet. The bridge spanned the deep pool formed just upstream from a small hydroelectric dam, and on hot summer days the bridge and the cold dark water below would draw dozens of teens, showing off and comparing suntans and tattoos. No one saw Eric jump from the bridge that Saturday afternoon in August, but he was soon missed by the group of friends he was with. His body was pulled from the water later that day, and his death was judged to be another of the tragic accidents that far too often seemed to strike the close-knit communities of central Maine. The blunt force trauma to the side of his head was determined to have been caused by impact with the bridge or by hitting a submerged rock.

Doug and Beth tried to go on, but as the days grew shorter, the surrounding forest grew darker, and winter set in, Beth left the memories and their home on the north shore and moved back to town. At about the same time that Beth moved in with her sister in Dover-Foxcroft, a developer from the Boston area acquired Pine Island and transformed the long-abandoned cottage located close to the base of the eagle's nesting tree into a summer rental. The next spring, for the first time in a decade, the eagles failed to return to the nest. Doug wasn't sure if they ever would.

As Doug turned his attention back to the televised Patriots game, a barking-dog ring-tone indicated an incoming call from his partner Tom Richard. Doug let the call go to voicemail, but reached over and picked up his phone when the unanswered call was followed by a text message.

"Pick up your phone, asshole, it looks like we might have a homicide up there at Sebec."

Doug and Tom were two of the 20 detectives in the Maine State Police Major Crimes Unit. The MCU investigated all suspicious deaths, homicides, child abuse cases, and other major crimes that occurred outside of the state's two largest cities- Portland and Bangor. Doug and Tom both worked out of the Orono barracks, about 45 minutes away from Doug's home on Sebec Lake.

Doug pushed the return call button.

"What's the story, Rocket?"

"A call just came in from the Piscataquis County Sheriff's Office – one of their investigators is responding to a report of a body in the ice. It was called in

8

by someone out ice fishing close to a place called Greeley's Landing. You know it?"

"Yeah, I know it," replied Doug. "Are they sure it's not a prank? They can get drinking pretty heavy out on the lake and sometimes like to have a little fun with the local law enforcement."

"It sounds legitimate. The caller identified himself – a Gary Griggs."

"I know Gary. He's not one to joke about something like this."

"Maybe you should get over there before they fuck things up," suggested Tom.

"Their guys are all experienced. I think it can wait till tomorrow. Let them see what it is."

"I don't know Doug. The deputy who called me said it was a new investigator. Someone from away. He sounded amused."

"Sweet Jesus," replied Doug. "Just what we need – someone eager to make their mark. OK – I will head over there. Ask them to have someone meet me at the boat ramp. I'm 15 minutes away across the lake, but my sled is over in Milo getting a new fuel pump, so I'll have to drive the long way around – should take almost an hour."

Doug turned on the outside lights and stepped out the back door, heading for the garage. His home had started out as a small summer cottage built by his grandfather in the 1940s. Like most places on the north shore of the lake it was for many years accessible only by boat. By the mid-1960s a fire road and electricity had finally reached the cottage, and following his grand-dad's death Doug's father had expanded and winterized it, turning it into a year-round home for his family.

When they took it over following his parent's death, Doug and his wife Beth had in turn made improvements to the main house and added a large barn-like garage. It had room for Beth's Subaru, Doug's 1987 Jeep Cherokee, and a variety of watercraft, including kayaks, a canoe, a beat-up aluminum 14-foot outboard, and Doug's "woodie" – a vintage 1952 17-foot Chris-Craft Sportsman inboard.

Doug's Cherokee pulled up to the boat ramp at Greeley's Landing just shy of ten PM. A Piscataquis County Sheriff SUV and a Dover-Foxcroft Police cruiser were parked in the darkness with their motors running, along with a dark green Toyota Land Cruiser with Michigan plates. Doug admired the Toyota as he got out of the Jeep. He guessed it was a 50 series, probably dating to the mid-70s, and looked to be in great condition.

Two snowmobiles had been unloaded from a trailer hitched to the back of the SUV. Maureen and Gary Griggs were seated in the back of the county sheriff SUV, and a uniformed sheriff's deputy and a Dover-Foxcroft police officer leaned against its' front fender, watching his Cherokee approach. As he climbed out of the Jeep an attractive, athletic woman with short blond hair walked toward him with her hand outstretched.

"You must be with the state police. I'm Anne Quinn, Investigator with the county sheriff's office. Thanks for getting here so quickly – we welcome your assistance in this matter."

Doug glanced over to where the two officers were listening to them, saw their slightly amused expressions, and taking the outstretched hand in his, replied.

"I'm Doug Bateman with the state major crimes unit. Can we sit in your car while we talk?"

Once seated in the Land Cruiser, out of earshot of the two officers, Doug turned to Anne.

"I live in Bowerbank, up on the north shore," Doug said quietly, "so it didn't take me long to get here once I got the call from Orono. I grew up here, went to high school here, and know pretty much everybody, including Jim Torben and Barry Volkman – the two uniforms over there. They're both good men, but like maybe too many people in this community, they have sort of a chip on their shoulder, and it can take a while for them to warm up to people who aren't from around here. You don't even have to be from out-of-state. People from down on the coast are still considered outsiders. People talk, word gets around, and it wouldn't take long for the story to circulate about how you and I butted heads over this case, if it turns out to be a case. I would like to avoid that. If there is a dead body out there in the ice, a suspicious death, a homicide, then it's my case. The MCU investigates all suspicious deaths and homicides state wide except for those that occur within the city limits of Bangor and Portland. We count on and expect the cooperation of local law enforcement, and you have an important part to play in this investigation. We can work together as a team and I will make sure that you get a lot of responsibility and get ample credit in the case. But it's my case."

Anne looked at him and smiled slightly.

"Quite a speech. Sounds good. Where do we start?"

Somewhat surprised, Doug smiled in return.

"Have you interviewed Gary and Maureen," he asked, "and have you been out on the ice to look at the body?"

"I talked to the couple, but we haven't gone out to the scene yet. Apparently they approached within about 30 feet on their snowmobile and he briefly got off to look, but otherwise the scene is undisturbed."

"OK, Good. First thing, let's have Gary take us to the body, and then they can go home. We don't want them talk to anyone about what they saw out here tonight though. We can get a formal statement from them tomorrow. If it does turn out to be a body, a suspicious death, Jim and Berry can go around to the fishing shacks tonight and get names and contact information for everyone out here. Some of them have been drinking while fishing, so it's better to wait till tomorrow or the next day to ask about who and what they may have seen out on the lake over the last few weeks. Barry is Dover-Foxcroft Police and it's not their case, but I bet he won't mind helping on a homicide, if that's what it is. He has probably been mostly doing domestic dispute calls and DUI stops lately, so this will be a welcome change for him."

Anne nodded agreement, and Doug opened the car door, looking back and saying, "OK, let's go – you do the talking."

Doug greeted the two officers and Maureen and Gary by name, shook hands all around, and stood silently beside Anne as she asked Gary to lead them back out on the ice. She instructed Jim to stay with Maureen until they got back in off the lake and asked Barry if he might be interested in helping with the investigation by joining Jim in determining who owned the fishing shacks. Barry agreed, and Anne led the way over to the snowmobiles. Before Doug could ask if she had ever driven a snowmobile, Anne mounted the nearest one, started it up, pulled on a knit cap, and raised the hood on her coat. As he straddled the other snowmobile, Doug turned to Jim.

"This won't take long – 15 minutes at most."

Anne and Doug followed Gary out onto the lake, through the narrows, and they soon reached the spot where Maureen and Gary had found the bones imbedded in the ice. Without getting off the snowmobile, Doug illuminated it with his flashlight and asked Anne.

"What do you think?"

"Definitely human," Anne responded over the sound of the idling snowmobiles. "Paired tibias and fibulas, too small for moose or bear, too big for a dog or other mammal."

Doug turned to Gary.

"You and Maureen can head home, and please keep this to yourselves for now. We'll set up an interview with you for tomorrow."

Gary nodded, turned his snowmobile, and headed back to Greeley's landing.

Anne looked toward the darkness of the south shore.

"The victim's footwear could be around here somewhere if the scavengers haven't carried the feet off. We might be able to track the foxes in the snow."

Doug nodded, extracted his cell phone from deep in a pocket of his coat, and called Orono.

"Hey Rocket, I'm out on the lake with Anne Quinn, the county sheriff investigator, and we have a body imbedded in the ice. Can you call Vasselboro and Augusta and see if they can get a dive team and an evidence response team up here tomorrow, and also contact the chief medical examiner's office?"

"I'll call right now. Wish I could join you on this, but they still have me stuck on desk duty because of that perv."

"Shouldn't be long now Tom. You'll be back out on the street any time."

Despite his encouragement, Doug wasn't all that sure that Tom, his long-time partner and good friend, would be freed from a desk assignment any time soon. Tom's nickname was "Rocket" both because he was rumored to be the nephew of Maurice, "The Rocket," Richard, the legendary right wing of the Montreal Canadians, and because he had a very short fuse when dealing with suspects accused of crimes against children and women.

The Rocket had grown up in the tight-knit Acadian communities of the St. Johns River Valley around Ft. Kent in northern Maine, right on the Canadian border. He had boxed in college and did pretty well in the golden gloves heavyweight division before joining the Navy after graduation, where he served a six-year enlistment in some sort of special ops unit. In spite of all his military training, however, he still displayed a lack of self-control in some situations, and had the physical skills to inflict significant damage in a short period of time. A few months back while off-duty Tom had run across and recognized a suspect in a major child pornography case who had been on the run for several months. There had been no witnesses to the arrest and Tom asserted that the suspect had resisted, requiring him to respond accordingly, resulting in the suspect sustaining a broken jaw, split lip, and bruised kidneys. It didn't help that Tom's long-standing on-and-off affair with the wife of a prominent state politician had recently been made public, and that the cuckolded politician had friends in the state police.

Tom Richard lived in a small mid-century modern home on the Penobscot

River just north of Old Town, a short commute from the state police barracks in Orono. He was never without female companionship, due both to his good looks and outgoing nature, but also because he was such a good listener – a trait that served him equally well when he was interrogating a suspect or sharing a romantic candle-lit dinner with his most recent companion, a visiting professor of French Literature from the Sorbonne. She was charmed by his Quebecois dialect, by his extensive knowledge of the neighborhoods of the Left Bank in Paris, and his ability to truly listen to what she was saying.

After pocketing his cell phone, Doug turned to Anne.

"Let's start the canvas of the ice shacks. We also need to find someone to stay here out on the ice to keep scavengers and curious locals away overnight. I have a few people I can try, and we can ask Jim and Barry if they have any ideas.

2.
BELOW THE ICE

Almost five hours north of Boston and three hours from Portland and the coastal tourist trade, Sebec Lake is beyond easy reach of out-of-state summer weekend cottagers. At just over 11 miles in length and 2 miles wide at its widest point, it also lacks the "destination" appeal of the much larger Moosehead Lake located 45 minutes farther north. As a result, much of Sebec's shoreline remains undeveloped, and the 900 or so year-round homes and cottages, or "camps," that are tucked back in the forests that border its rocky shores are mostly owned by Mainers, along with a few "summer people" who make the long drive each year from as far away as Arizona and New Mexico. There are only a handful of short-term rental cottages on the lake, and the few viable motels mostly border Peaks-Kenny State Park, which boasts great views of Borestone Mountain and one of the best sandy beaches in the state.

Although jet skiers are a weekend irritant, particularly at the eastern end of the lake closer to the dam, lake traffic is light compared to Lake Sebego to the south, and consists mostly of canoes and kayaks, small outboards, and stately patio boats, along with far fewer larger inboards, often pulling tubes of youngsters shrieking with excitement. At night, campfires flicker along the shore, and the sound of voices carries far out across the water.

About 20 minutes south of Sebec Lake, downtown Dover-Foxcroft, the closest town, is the county seat or "shiretown" of Piscataquis County. Up until when they merged in 1922, Dover and Foxcroft had been two separate towns located on opposite banks of the Piscataquis River. Dover-Foxcroft is perhaps best known to the outside world as the home of the "Whoopie Pie Festival," a one day event that brings about 5,000 people into town each year in late June, effectively doubling the town's population. Otherwise there is little in Dover-Foxcroft that caters to the tourist trade. The American Pizzeria Appreciation

Society named it "Pizzatown USA" in 2014 based on it having more pizza restaurants per citizen than any other municipality in the country. And up until the Center Theatre Coffee House opened in 2015, there was no place in town to buy a latte or cappuccino.

Doug Bateman often stopped at the Coffee House in the morning on his way to work in Orono, not just for a latte, but also because his estranged wife Beth now managed it, and his morning stops kept her in his life, at least marginally. On the morning after the discovery of the "Ice Maiden," as she would eventually be called by the media, however, Doug instead picked up a coffee at the Sebec Country Store so he could buy the Bangor paper to see if there was any mention of the body discovered the previous day. After picking up the coffee and paper, he texted Anne Quinn to let her know he was 30 minutes out from Greeley's Landing.

Doug was hoping that there would be no replay of last summer's drama, when Robert Burton killed his ex- girlfriend just south of Guilford, the next town over, and then hid out in the woods for much of the summer. Despite an extensive manhunt by local and state police, and the brief involvement of the FBI, Burton evaded capture for 68 days before turning himself in. He had been sighted numerous times over the summer along hiking trails and back roads, and media coverage had been non-stop. Large digital message signs along the roads into the area warned drivers of the murderer on the loose, and along with every other law enforcement officer within a 100-mile radius, Doug Bateman had suffered through two months of increasingly irritating questions about why Burton was still at large.

The Bangor paper didn't carry any mention of the discovery of the body in the ice, and as he stopped for gas on Main Street in Dover-Foxcroft, Doug was hopeful that word would not reach the media for a while yet. Sitting in his Jeep in the gas station, he glanced out the passenger side window, across the street to the Coffee House where Beth worked, and saw her sitting at the table by the window. "That's strange," he thought, "she usually stays behind the counter." Her shoulder-length blond hair, usually kept out of her way in a French braid, was also down today. Sitting across from her at the table was a man Doug didn't recognize – tall and lean, mid-40s, coat and tie, expensive haircut, dark hair, not a local. Beth and the man were drinking coffee and having an animated conversation involving some documents on the table between them. Just then, Beth looked out the window and saw the Jeep. Doug had always been good at reading her moods, and although she was too far away for him to be sure, it looked like Beth's expression was first one of embarrassment, of being caught out, and then her green eyes flashed with anger.

Doug's attention was abruptly drawn away from the Center Theatre Coffee House by an insistent rapping on the driver-side window. Vern Rodgers, who pumped gas for his uncle, the station owner, was using the clipboard with the gas receipt to get Doug's attention. Vern had been one of the few special education students enrolled at Foxcroft Academy, the local high school, when Doug and Beth were students, and he had worked at the gas station since his teens. Because of his short, stocky stature and an almost total absence of facial expression, along with his surprisingly unpleasant personality, Vern had earned the nickname "The Toad" in high school, and was still often referred to as "Toad" or "The Toad." Wearing his signature greasy ball cap, hooded coat, and lopsided smile, Rodgers was a fixture in Dover-Foxcroft, and a bottomless source of vicious rumor and gossip, usually passed on to him to unfairly smear someone's reputation in town or to provide entertainment to anyone stopping for gas on Main Street. Many a juicy piece of slander passed along from person to person in Dover-Foxcroft would start with the question, "Have you heard the latest from the Toad?" Last week he was informing customers at the gas station that the mayor of Dover-Foxcroft liked to wear women's clothes, and that Gladys Murphy, the wife of the local Anglican minister, had two penises.

Doug rolled down the window and reached for the clipboard.

"You found a body in the ice out at Greeley's," Vern blurted out. "It was Jimmy Hoffa." Avoiding eye contact, Vern continued.

"Beth has a new boyfriend. He's from away. He's staying at the new hotel in the Mill and they have sex."

Doug stared at Rodgers, realizing why Beth had just glared in his direction. He grabbed the clipboard, signed the credit card bill, and as Vern stepped closer to take it back, Doug punched him in the face with a short right-handed jab. He felt the crunch of nose cartilage and Rodgers fell flat on his back on the ice. "Not a good start to the day," Doug thought, heading west down Main Street. Vern was announcing that his wife seemed to have a boyfriend, and the word was out about the Ice Maiden. Soon the news would be all over town.

By the time Doug reached Greeley's Landing the wind had picked up considerably, pushing the wind chill out on the lake down into the single digits. The state police evidence response team van was parked next to a county sheriff's SUV, and Anne Quinn was leaning against her Toyota Land Cruiser looking at her phone. As he approached, she said.

16

"Just got your text. Reception is bad out on the lake, so I came in here to check my calls."

Doug returned her gaze and replied.

"It can get cold out on the lake when the wind picks up."

Anne flashed him a broad smile.

"Oh, it can get cold in Michigan where I grew up too, that's not a problem. But the lake ice is slippery in places – hope you have some yaktraks in your Jeep."

Realizing that Anne had picked up on his inadvertent implication that she might not be prepared for the challenges of working outside in a Maine winter, and had deftly countered with a suggestion that he was not as prepared as he should be, Doug returned her smile and nodded in appreciation. He tried again. "Nice Land Cruiser. That's an FJ55, right? Mid-70s?

Anne raised her eyebrows in surprise at this bit of arcane knowledge.

"1974 – belonged to my dad. He left it to me when he died a few years back – my brothers were not thrilled."

Glancing in through the back window, Doug glimpsed a pile of sports equipment – cycling shoes and helmet, snowshoes, a gym bag and three basketballs.

"Basketballs?" he asked.

"My dad was the basketball coach at our high school and my two older brothers both played, so I pretty much had to pick it up to survive. It ended up getting me a free ride to U of M."

"You played college ball?"

"Point guard," Anne answered, and then changed the subject abruptly.

"So last night Berry borrowed one of the ice shacks from someone he knew and he and Jim moved it over close to the body. They took shifts watching the crime scene. No more fox visitations. Jim thought he heard a snowmobile approach about 3AM, but can't be sure. He didn't see a headlight. Berry is helping the evidence technicians, and he and Jim both asked if they could stay on the case.

Also, I talked to the office of the chief medical examiner and once they heard what we had they decided they didn't need to come up to look at the scene. We got the green light to go ahead and have a local funeral home transport the victim down to Augusta for the autopsy. I called Lary's in town and they're sending someone out in a few hours to pick up the body. Interviews with Gary and Maureen Griggs and the ice shack owners are scheduled for this afternoon. Five ice shack owners have been identified and contacted. One is still unidentified."

Doug nodded.

"Vern Rodgers, who pumps gas at the Irving station on Main Street, just asked me if the body found in the ice was Jimmy Hoffa, so the word is out. I'm not sure how Rodgers found out. Berry or Jim might have let it slip to one of the ice shack owners, or Gary or Maureen might have mentioned what they saw to someone. So we can expect to start getting calls from the media. All calls should be referred to my partner Tom Richard over in Orono. Your dispatcher will have the number. Given the murder media frenzy we had here last summer they will be primed for another big story. Let's hope it's just a normal domestic murder we can close out quickly."

As he finished talking, Anne's phone rang. Answering it, she listened briefly and then handed it to him.

"It's the sheriff. He asked to speak to you."

"Hey George," said Doug, "that didn't take long."

George McCormick, Sheriff of Piscataquis County, replied.

"This could be serious, Doug. Vern Rodger's uncle Lem called and said you assaulted his nephew about an hour ago at his gas station in town. Vern's at the Mayo emergency room now, and appears to have a broken nose. What's the story?"

"I stopped for gas and Vern offered a few local news updates – that we had found Jimmy Hoffa's body out here in the ice, and that Beth was shacked up at the Mill Inn with a new boyfriend. He also mentioned that your sweet wife Martha has two penises. He got so excited about his news that he slipped on the ice and hit his nose on the side mirror of the Jeep. No damage to the mirror though. I offered him a ride to the emergency room but he declined. You should be able to see it all on the CCTV feed from the Center Theatre across the street."

"Very funny Doug. It's Gladys Murphy, not Martha, who has two penises according to the Toad, and that was last week. I already checked the CCTV footage from across the street on the Center Theatre's web site, and you can't see what happened. Your Jeep blocks the view. The top of Vern's head is visible close to the driver's side window, and then he just disappears. I can understand how he could slip on the ice though. He gets pretty worked up over his gossip. He definitely needs to be more careful. But all the same, it might be a good idea for you to gas up at the Shell station for a while."

"Will do," said Doug.

The sheriff then asked.

"How's Quinn working out?"

"Oh, she's definitely going to be difficult."

The sheriff laughed, pleased, and hung up. Anne took her phone back and asked, hard-faced.

"Me? Difficult? What does that mean?"

Doug had forgotten that Anne was standing right there while he talked to the sheriff. He decided candor was the only way out.

"It's shorthand. I've known George since I was a kid. He's my wife Beth's uncle. George and I are both married to smart, stubborn, independent, self-confident women who speak their minds, and we have taken to joking about how we have to deal with 'difficult' women. I don't know you that well, but you seem to fall into that category."

Anne thought about this, and then asked.

"So did you punch this Vern Rodgers guy in the face?"

A large white tent had been erected over the body in the ice, both to protect the forensic technicians from the wind and to shield the crime scene from any curious onlookers. Peter Martell, the team leader of the evidence response team, was standing in the bright sun next to the tent, out of the wind. Doug shook his hand and waited for him to begin.

"We're almost done here, Doug. The ice surface is pretty disturbed by the scavenger activity right around the victim. No human footprints, nothing but fox tracks and a few scats as far as we can tell. The boards attached to the legs look promising, and we will take a closer look at them once the body is removed and we can get them back to the lab.

Our search farther out from the body, however, did turn up a few things. We had the dogs here earlier and they followed the fox tracks back into the woods on the south shore. One of them turned up what looks to be a partial human foot with a fragment of leather covering still attached – maybe a moccasin. We bagged it. The weird thing there is that it looks like the bottom of the foot has been burned, almost charred.

We also found snowmobile tracks coming from the northwest that approached to within about 30 yards of the victim, and then return back the same way. Two sets of footprints lead from where the snowmobile stopped, over to the body. One set shuffles in short steps, the other left distinct prints. They were large boots; maybe size 11s, with a distinctive tread pattern. We should be able to identify the brand. The boots return to the snowmobile, the shuffling set doesn't.

The snowmobile tracks are not well enough preserved to get their exact width. They could be anywhere from 14 to 16 inches, which includes just about every sled manufacturer, and the tread design can't be discerned. We might have better luck finding a clearer print when we follow the tracks back across the lake. I sent the evidence response team technicians and Berry out to trace the snowmobile tracks back to the northwest across the ice to see if any impressions show up, and also to see how far they can track the sled's route."

"When is the dive team getting here?" Doug asked.

"They can't make it today. Two brothers went out on Sebago Lake this morning and haven't returned. A search is underway and the dive team is involved –they think the boys might have gone through the ice. But I don't think we need them. I can drill a small hole in the ice here inside the tent, maybe 10 feet or so from the victim, and snake our fiber optic camera down there to get a good look around. The video will come up on our laptop, which is already set up in the tent. What do you think?"

"Let's do it," replied Doug. "How do you plan on getting the body out?"

"Should be simple. We'll wrap a rope around the exposed leg bones and boards, cut through the ice around them, and then lift everything out as a block. We can then seal the ice, boards, and body all in a body bag for transport down to the chief medical examiner in Augusta."

Peter, Anne and Doug moved out of the sunshine into the shadowed interior of the tent, unaware that they were being observed from deep in the forest on the south shore. Sheltered behind a snow bank and insulated from the cold by a snowmobile suit and balaclava, a solitary figure watched them through binoculars and carried on a conversation with himself in a low singsong voice.

"She was lost. She had lost her way. Drifted from the true path. She came to me and I saved her. Welcomed her back into the fold. A whore. A dirty slut. But now reborn. Purified in the cold waters of Sebec."

Picking up an ice auger, Peter drilled an access hole and snaked the camera cable down under the ice. Anne, Doug, and Pete gathered around the computer screen and Pete turned the camera feed on. As the image from under the ice appeared on the computer, there was dead silence in the tent.

The water was clear and there was a slight current. The shimmering light that suffused down through the ice softly illuminated the body of a young woman suspended head down under the ice, and swaying gently from side to side. She wore a bright yellow sleeveless tabard-like garment of a coarse burlap material that extended to her knees. It was decorated with several bright red dancing devil and dragon figures and was stiff enough that it did not float down around her upper body. A human face appeared to have been painted in the center of the tunic, but was obscured by her hands, which were clasped on her chest and held what appeared to be a yellow wax candle affixed to the end of a long stick. Cords wrapped around her wrists and torso held her in this posture of prayerful supplication. Red flames were painted curling up from the hem of the tabard. A noose hung loosely around her neck. On her head, pointing down toward the darkness of the depths, she wore a bright yellow, three-foot high conical hat, like a dunce cap. It was attached under her chin with a red ribbon and decorated with several smaller dancing red devils. Her legs below the knees were light blue, in stark contrast to her hands and face, which seemed to glow from within with a reddish-pink color. Her long blond hair floated free, forming a bright aura around her face, and she gazed directly at the camera with wide-open bright green eyes.

Doug reached forward and closed the laptop.

3.
THE WEBCAM

Late that afternoon Doug, Anne, and George McCormick, Sheriff of Piscataquis County, sat around a small conference table in an office on the top floor of the county court house that had been set aside for the Ice Maiden investigation. Doug was relieved that they had not ended up next door in the already seriously overcrowded sheriff's 0ffice building, built back in the 1880s. Along with the conference table, the office contained two desks with computers, and looked out on Main Street.

Doug turned to the sheriff.

"Thanks for arranging the office space for us and for assigning investigator Quinn to the case. I know you might get pushback from investigators who have been here longer, but I think we'll work well together. Thanks too for assigning your deputy Jim Torben to the case. I checked with Chief Marcus and he agreed to detail Berry Volkman from the city police to us. So all three jurisdictions – state, county, and city, will be involved. My MCU partner Tom Richard will also be working with us, mostly from Orono. Tom will be fielding media inquiries, handling logistics, and case reports as they come in. He and Anne and I will all be entering information into to the central case files, which are well protected on the MCU secure computer case file system. Only the three of us will have access."

"What's next?" asked the sheriff.

Doug looked at his notes and began working down a long list.

"The media should be on to the story any time now, and hopefully all the bizarre aspects of the case can be kept out of the news. If very much of it gets out what we had going on here last summer with the murder and manhunt over in Guilford will look like a walk in the park. We definitely don't want that. The underwater video footage of the victim has been erased from the laptop hard drive. We have a single copy on a flash stick and it will be entered into the MCU secure case file system."

The sheriff managed a weak grin.

"Let's hope your computer system is secure. I would hate to have it hacked by the Chinese or some pimply-faced teen from Russia who then posts it on the Internet."

Doug continued.

"All media inquiries should be referred to Tom Richard in Orono. The only information we will be releasing for the foreseeable future is that we have recovered the body of a young woman from beneath the ice of Sebec Lake, and we are in the process of attempting to establish her identity. We'll also ask anyone with information to come forward.

The body should be in Augusta by now. I am not sure when the medical examiner will be conducting the autopsy. Anne and I will drive down for that. The body was not in the water that long, so they should be able to get the victim's fingerprints. We'll run her prints and DNA through available databases. If we're lucky we might get a match.

The evidence response team has collected a lot of physical evidence from the scene, so the crime lab is going to be busy. In addition to the multiple pieces of clothing and other items associated with the body - the ankle boards, partial foot, candle, noose, and cordage, they also discovered a large brown hooded robe in a nearby ice fishing shack this afternoon. The person who transported the victim to the crime scene by snowmobile stopped at the shack afterward and attempted to dispose of the robe down through the shack's fishing hole. Apparently whatever the robe was weighed down with came loose and the robe floated back up into the hole. The shack has been processed for prints and other trace evidence and the dive team will be searching the lake bottom under where the victim was found and under the shack to see if they can locate anything else. Once we get the forensics back on the physical evidence, which I hope will start coming in over the next few weeks, we can see what develops there: possibly DNA that's not from the victim, or leads from the different items – the wooden boards, burlap, paints, shoe leather, cordage, and the robe.

On our end, Tom will be doing the search for any reports of missing persons who match the profile – initially statewide and then in adjacent states and neighboring provinces if necessary. Once we have the autopsy report we can put out a more detailed description of the victim. The body is also well enough preserved that we should be able to provide facial photos or sketches if we have to. Identifying the victim is obviously critical.

We also need to find all of the people who have been ice-fishing over the last week on that part of the lake and interview them, including re-interviewing the ones we have already talked to this afternoon. None of them remembered seeing or hearing anything that might be relevant, but they might remember something when we question them again. We also need to follow up on the green ice shack where they discovered the robe: who owns it, where have they been the last week, and have they seen anything?

I also want Anne to interview Vern Rodgers tomorrow to find out where he heard the story about Jimmy Hoffa in the ice. I asked Barry and Jim, and Maureen and Gary, and they all say they didn't mention a body to anyone. So we need to follow up on the Toad's source. If we can pin down when the victim went under the ice we might also be able to find someone who saw something on the roads around the south side of the lake, from Willimantic all the way around to Greeley's Landing. There is not that much road traffic at this time of year."

They talked for another few minutes, and after the sheriff had left their office, Anne asked.

"What about the webcam?"

"What webcam?"

"There's a website that shows time-lapse photos from three or four cameras mounted on different cottages around the narrows. If I remember correctly one looked right out toward the crime scene. After I applied for the job here last summer I went online and looked at the webcams every day for a few weeks while waiting to hear if I was going to get an interview. The cameras take a picture every 30 seconds, I think, and archives of each day's time-lapse footage going back a week or so can be accessed online."

Anne turned to one of the computers, accessed the Sebec Lake website, and started scanning the archived footage from the "Beach Cam" for the last week. It took her less than ten minutes to locate what they were looking for: five frames, 30 seconds apart, taken right before the camera went dark on Saturday night, three days ago.

In the first frame two figures could be seen approaching the camera in the winter twilight. The victim, wearing the conical hat, was bent over and her head was tilted forward. She was being supported by a taller figure wearing a brown hooded robe. The hood extended far enough out in front of his head to cast his face in shadow. The following frame showed the woman kneeling next to a hole cut into the ice. She was holding a long flickering candle in front of her chest, her blank eyes reflected in the flame. The robed figure was crouched next to her and appeared to be attaching the wooden boards around her ankles. In the third image the robed figure was standing again and was apparently speaking to the woman and gesturing with his hands. She had vanished from sight in the fourth image in the series, but her feet could be seen sticking up out of the hole in the ice, held in place by the two boards. In the final frame before the webcam shut off for the night, the robed figure had turned directly toward the camera. His face was still shadowed by the hood of the robe and his arms were stretched straight out from his sides, palms up, as if preying to the heavens, or perhaps indicating the conclusion of the performance.

"Jesus," Anne exclaimed in shock. "He knew the camera was there and would capture it. He planned it all out in advance." She reached for her phone and called the contact number for the Webmaster listed on the Sebec Lake web page. Identifying herself, Anne asked if he could come in to meet with them the next morning, and if the "Beach Cam" archive footage from three days ago could be removed from the website until then. In response to his questions she indicated that the footage was related to an ongoing criminal investigation and that she would explain when they met. The Webmaster somewhat reluctantly agreed, and within minutes the time-lapse footage disappeared from the Sebec Lake website.

Later that night Anne did another web search, this time for "Douglas Bateman, Maine State Police." She found numerous links to stories about cases he had worked, a few alumni hits for the Foxcroft Academy, and several stories about the tragic death of his son Eric. "No wonder he seems so quiet," she thought. "No wonder he and his wife are separated."

4.
ANN ARBOR

The next morning Anne woke to the rumble of her cat Charlie purring loudly. Charles often slept on Anne's pillow; just above her head, and over the years his purring had provided a comforting background of white noise for her slumber. Her small rental house on Autumn Street in downtown Dover-Foxcroft was still sparsely furnished, mostly with second-hand furniture from craigslist and local sales and antique stores. She had found a brown leather sofa in great condition on craigslist from Bangor, and several rustic side tables and floor lamps from the Kamp Kamp Indian store up in Greenville. Chesley's Auction House over in East Corinth had yielded a threadbare oriental carpet and massive oak coffee table, and the antique store located in the old bank building in downtown Dover-Foxcroft had sold her a dark green pine Chifferobe dating to the 1920s.

Anne lay in bed listening to Charlie and realizing again how much she enjoyed waking up alone in a quiet house, without the tension of getting through another day with her ex-partner Kevin. She didn't miss the avoidance and sour interaction that had been part of their long crumbling relationship. They had first met on a beautiful late spring day in Ann Arbor, several years after her graduation from the U of M. She had been eating lunch at Krazy Jim's Blimpy Burger on Packard Street, a campus landmark known for the aggressive rudeness of its counter staff and the best greasy burgers and fries in the state. Sitting at the counter by the window where she could keep an eye on her bike, Anne didn't pay much attention to Kevin when he took the empty seat next to hers. He struck up a conversation between bites of his burger, and didn't seem put off by her Ann Arbor police department uniform. She had been on bike patrol for almost two years by then and it was her last week in uniform before moving over, finally, to the detective section of the A^2 force. Kevin asked a lot of knowledgeable questions about her bike, a Trek Police Edition, and how it compared to Fuji and Smith and Wesson Police bikes. He seemed nice, and they met up for a road ride that weekend in the Irish Hills west of Ann Arbor.

Anne gave up her apartment and moved in with Kevin in the fall, at the start of his third year as an assistant professor in a tenure-track faculty position in archaeology at the U. of M. His responsibilities included both teaching and advising students in the Department of Anthropology, as well as serving as a curator in the Museum of Anthropological Archaeology located up on Geddes Avenue, right next to the dental school. Rarely visited by undergraduates, the museum building was mostly known on campus for the two bronze pumas that flanked its main entrance, which were rumored to roar whenever a virgin walked by. The joke, of course, being that the pumas never roared.

Kevin's tenure-track position was a coveted one, as many universities were well along in shifting over to a more efficient business model approach to higher education that involved the hiring of faculty in adjunct positions on one to three year renewable contracts. Adjunct faculty members were second-class citizens in the academic world. They were expected to shoulder heavy teaching loads and had no job security. Tenure-track faculty, in contrast, could look forward to permanent lifelong employment once they were granted tenure, usually after a trial period of five to seven years of employment. The granting of tenure and promotion from assistant to associate professor rank was by no means a given, however. New assistant professors lived in perpetual fear of being denied tenure, the ultimate humiliation, especially because it came so early in an academic's career and often constituted a lifetime sentence of adjunct faculty positions.

Kevin's tenure review, which then was still two years away, would involve consideration of his teaching record, research publications, success in grant applications, and the level of support he gained from the tenured faculty in his department. Although Anne didn't realize it when they moved in together, Kevin was on track to come up short in all four of these performance areas.

Having taught several courses as a graduate student, to good reviews, Kevin had agreed to the suggestion that he fill in for a professor on sabbatical and take over the teaching of her introduction to archaeology course. He taught the course during the spring semester that he first met Anne. It did not go well. It was only later that Kevin realized that the other faculty had enthusiastically applauded his taking over the course because no one else was eager to try to fill the shoes of the absent professor. Known for her numerous teaching awards, the archaeologist Kevin was filling in for had over the years honed her introduction to archaeology class into an entertaining Indiana Jones-like piece of performance art that was wildly popular with undergraduates and invariably filled large lecture halls. While competent, Kevin's lectures were no match for what students had come to expect, and his audience shrunk by almost half after the first week as students dropped the class in droves. Many of the reviews at the end of the semester were negative, calling the lectures boring and uninteresting. The museum director and department chair were both quick to assure Kevin that he had done a fine job and that no one had expected him to match the professor he was filling in for. He could sense the insincerity of their reassurances, however, and other faculty seemed far too cheerful in their commiserations.

Kevin didn't fare any better with his research and publications. His specialty was archaeobotany, the analysis of ancient plant remains, and he had been initially hired on the basis of his pioneering application of an innovative and potentially revolutionary new way of identifying early domesticated plants through the identification of microscopic starch grains and silica bodies recovered from archaeological deposits. In an apparent breakthrough article published in a high impact journal just before he was hired, Kevin had pushed back the date of maize domestication in southern Mexico by several thousand years. Other archaeologists were now sharply criticizing his earlier study, however, and a number of articles questioning the new technique and identifying problems with Kevin's methods and conclusions were beginning to appear. As a result of this backlash against Kevin's "microbotanical" approach, the two grant proposals he had recently submitted to the National Science Foundation had both been rejected.

Kevin's less than stellar record in teaching, research, and grant applications in turn led to a clear attitudinal shift on the part of his colleagues. Well in advance of his formal tenure review he was viewed as damaged goods. He began to avoid the morning coffee hour at the museum and started holding his office hours at a local pub that was a graduate student hangout. Soon he was providing empathetic advice to disgruntled students and becoming involved in their personal stories of unfair treatment and their complaints against the hegemony of the dominant white males among the faculty. Kevin's increasing involvement with the graduate students and their issues made his final dramatic fall from grace all the more ironic.

For Anne the first indication of what had happened came when she returned to their apartment late one night at the end of April after a grueling day of court testimony in a date rape case to find that all of Kevin's clothes and personal items were gone. He had cleared out in a hurry, leaving behind all of the furniture and other worldly goods they had accumulated together over the past year and a half. There was no note, no explanation from Kevin for his abandonment. After the realization sunk in that Kevin was gone for good, Anne opened the windows in the living room to let in the sweet spring breeze, put on her favorite Regina Spektor album, which Kevin hated, turned out the lights, and lit up a joint. A while later, well into her second bowl of dark chocolate chip gelato, she realized she couldn't stop smiling.

The next day Anne learned all she needed to know. She picked up a copy of the Michigan Daily, the on-campus student newspaper, to read with her morning coffee, and saw on the front page a long story detailing the accusations by three graduate students of inappropriate sexual advances made by Kevin over the last several months. In the atmosphere of political correctness that was sweeping many college campuses across the country, the accused, a white male faculty member, was considered guilty of something even before the facts were fully known. Kevin knew he was finished. He resigned his position in a brief email to the dean, and without any goodbyes, cleared out his office and their apartment and headed out of town.

As Anne read the story about Kevin she was surprised by her reaction to his downfall. Rather than being angry or hurt, she was simply relieved. The long downward spiral of alienation between them had ended. She didn't need to see him again or talk to him to achieve any sort of "closure," a term she thought silly, and she realized she wasn't the least bit interested in where he had gone or what he was doing. That chapter of her life had ended, and for the first time in years she was free to consider where she was headed. Sitting in the Comet Coffee House in the Nickels Arcade, just off State Street, with a latte and the Michigan Daily in front of her, with students streaming by on the way to class, Anne realized her future was not in Ann Arbor.

Kevin's difficult experience as a faculty member and his lengthy late-night accounts of how he had been victimized by the system had opened Anne's eyes about the academic world and how it worked. Her perception of the university had also changed over the past several years as a result of her position as head liaison between the AAPD and the U. of M. Police Department. It had become depressingly clear to her that the university was primarily interested in protecting its reputation. Her rose-colored undergraduate view of the ivy covered walls of academia and its role in the intergenerational passing on of wisdom had been replaced by a colder, harder edged recognition that the university was now a big business. Their overriding concerns were for public relations and the bottom line.

Anne had lived in Ann Arbor for almost a decade but it had never felt like home to her. It was to her a town of transition, of transients, with thousands of students coming and going each year, moving through a temporary world of puffed-up faculty, self-important administrators, and the glorification of Saturday afternoon football games. There was nothing holding her in this town, and with her job experience and education she knew she could move just about anywhere in the country.

Dropping the newspaper in the trash, Anne headed back to her apartment to start job hunting. On the way she called work to let them know she was taking a personal day. It was a warm sunny morning and the trees were just beginning to show the light green leaves of spring. The long gray Ann Arbor winter was over. As she walked across campus Anne felt the way she had as an undergraduate when she had finished her last final exam and the summer stretched endlessly out ahead of her.

She realized she had a pretty clear idea of the kind of town she was looking for, and it was, not surprisingly, a lot like the place where she had grown up. Manistee, Michigan, was pretty far up the west coast of the Lower Peninsula, where the Manistee River emptied into Lake Michigan. It was bordered on the west by Lake Michigan and on the east by Manistee Lake. First settled in the 1840s, it had become the hub of a booming logging industry, with dozens of shingle factories established in the last half of the 19th century. In the late 1800s Manistee boasted more millionaires per capita than anywhere else in the country. Today it was the county seat and had a population of about 6,000. Given its distance from Chicago and southeastern Michigan it was not a big tourist destination, although its white sand beaches, salmon and trout fishing charters, fall deer hunting, and winter snowmobiling did draw outsiders into town. It had been a great place for Anne to grow up, and she loved going back to visit. But her two older brothers, David and Jonathan, still lived in the area and were well-established pillars of the community. If she moved back she would always be identified in relation to them and she had no desire to be forever in their shadow and within range of their brotherly advice and guidance. Anne was looking for something similar to Manistee, but a place where she could make her own way.

Within a half hour of searching online she had seen the job posting for an investigator position with the Piscataquis County Sheriff's Department, and had started to research the town of Dover-Foxcroft. It looked to be a lot like Manistee. It was the county seat and had a deep history as a mill town and in lumbering. It also had about the same population as Manistee, a historic downtown, and a beautiful nearby lake. Anne called the contact number to confirm that the job was still open, and applied that afternoon. After waiting several weeks and checking the Sebec Lake Webcam on a daily basis, she had a phone interview with Sheriff McCormick. Once she had convinced him that she was fully aware of what the job was and what the county was like – large and poor and rural, and he realized that she had grown up in a very similar setting, he invited up for a formal interview. That went well, and her background in liaison work was a big plus since the county sheriff's department constantly had to work with both the state police and the scattered police forces of the towns within Piscataquis County. After the interview Anne stayed in the area, rented a small boat to explore the coves and shorelines of Sebec Lake, climbed Borestone Mountain, drove over to the coast, up to Baxter State Park, and around the Golden Road, and when the job offer came she accepted it immediately.

Anne's cell phone pinged with a text message, bringing her back to her small rental house in Dover-Foxcroft. The Webmaster would meet her and Doug at the courthouse at 8:30, and her interview with Vern Rodgers and his uncle Lem was set up for 9 at the Main Street gas station.

5.

THE PROFESSOR

Anne met Ted Height, the Webmaster for the Sebec Lake Webcam, at the front door of the courthouse and led him to a waiting room off the courtroom for their meeting. Shifting nervously in his chair as he looked at Doug and Anne, Height placed a flash drive on the table.

"Here is the time-lapse footage for the day you asked about."

Anne picked it up and plugged it into her laptop and asked her first question.

"How long do the daily archive files stay up on the web and what happens when they are taken down from the site?"

"They stay up on the site for a week and then I take them down and delete them. "

"So the footage you just gave us would have been taken down and erased a few days from now if you hadn't taken it down yesterday at our request?"

"Yes."

"Have you looked at the footage?"

"Yes, and then I erased it. What you have on the flash drive is the only copy."

"Do you keep a record of visitors to your site, and specifically, anyone who has viewed that day's time lapse footage?"

"No, we don't, but I'm pretty sure you have someone who could generate a list of visitors to the site. It shouldn't be a very long list since the footage for that day only went up on the site three days ago."

"O.K. Thanks Ted. Two things. You can understand why we ask you not to mention the last five frames on the footage to anyone, and if anyone contacts you about the time-lapse for that day, please give me a call. Here's my card."

Height stood up, nodded, and left the room, leaving the door ajar – clearly

32

relieved to be done with his encounter with law enforcement and eager to try to forget what he had seen in those last five frames of webcam footage.

Doug turned to Anne and outlined their next steps.

"I'll call Tom Richard right now and see if it's possible to find out the IP addresses for any visits to the archive webcam footage in the last week. When you finish with the interview of Vern and Lem, we need to drive into Orono to meet up with Tom. He has a set of photos that the crime lab sent over of the items of clothing and other objects associated with the victim. The three of us have an appointment early this afternoon with a former professor of mine at the University of Maine. She has agreed to look at the photos, and given my description of them, she thinks she can be of help."

Anne nodded, and asked.

"She teaches medieval history?"

Doug raised his eyebrows in acknowledgement.

"As a matter of fact, she does. We're meeting Tom at Paddy Murphy's at noon for lunch – it's an Irish pub in Bangor. Great burgers."

Anne arrived for her interview with the Toad a little after 9. Lem Rodgers opened the door to the office of his gas station on Main and immediately lit into Anne.

"This is outrageous. First Bateman attacks Vern for no reason, then the sheriff and the city police won't to do anything about it, and now you insist on interrogating him over some offhand comment he made."

Anne smiled at Lem, a somewhat disheveled man in his fifties with the rheumy eyes and veined red nose of a serious drinker. He was wearing a winter coat that had seen better days, along with red suspenders, an old sweatshirt, baggy pants and work boots. She stepped by him and sat down across the desk from Vern Rodgers, who slouched sullenly with his baseball hat pulled down over his eyes. "He does look like a toad," she thought. Anne introduced herself in a pleasant voice, trying to ignore Vern's strong body odor.

"Vern, my name is Anne Quinn. I'm with the Sheriff's Office, and I want to thank you for taking the time to talk to me. Can you tell me how you found out that there was a body in the ice?"

Vern looked at her from under the brim of his hat, flashed her a lopsided smile, but made no reply. Anne tried again, and this time Vern answered in a high singsong voice.

"Jimmy Hoffa – the Mafia killed him. They found him up at Greeley's Landing."

"How did you hear about Jimmy Hoffa?"

"Beth is fucking that guy in a suit – he's her new boyfriend."

Anne glanced over at Lem who was also smiling now, clearly enjoying this nasty bit of gossip. She asked again.

"Who told you about Jimmy Hoffa?"

"The sheriff told me. He knows Jimmy Hoffa. Doug hit me. He killed his son."

"George McCormick, the sheriff, told you about Jimmy Hoffa?"

"Ayup." Vern replied, smiling proudly and looking vacantly out the window.

"When did he tell you this?"

"At night. I was asleep"

"Was it a dream or did he call you at home to tell you?"

"He left a message here at the gas station. He told me about Jimmy Hoffa." Vern reached across the desk and put his hand on a vintage phone with a built-in answering machine.

Anne leaned forward in anticipation.

"Is the message still on the phone, Vern? Can you play it for me?"

"Ayup." Vern scrolled back through the messages, and finding the one he wanted, pushed the play button. The answering machine microcassette had been used and reused so many times the quality of the tape was poor, and the voice seemed to have been digitally altered, but Anne could still hear it clearly.

"Hi Vern. This is Sheriff George McCormick. I want you to let people know that Jimmy Hoffa was found this morning in the ice up by Greeley's Landing. And thanks Vern. You are doing a great job of keeping the town well informed."

"Does Sheriff McCormick call you often with news to pass on?" Anne asked the beaming Vern Rodgers.

"Nope."

Anne tried again.

"Is this the only time he has called you?"

"Ayup."

Lem was willing to let Anne have the microcassette as long as she promised to buy him a new one. Anne agreed, thinking she could find some still for sale on eBay. You could find anything these days on eBay.

Crossing the street to the Center Theatre parking lot, where she had parked the Toyota, Anne sat behind the wheel and placed the cassette in a zip-lock bag, labeled it, and put it in her pocket. As she reached to turn the ignition key she noticed Beth Bateman standing next to the driver's window. Anne had not yet met Beth formally, but had chatted with her a few times while buying a morning coffee. She rolled down the window.

"You're Anne Quinn, right, the new investigator with the Sheriff's Office? I think we have spoken a few times."

"Yes, we have, and you are Beth Bateman, Doug Bateman's wife. I'm glad we have finally officially introduced each other."

Beth crossed her arms and forced a smile.

"Do you have time for a cup of coffee? We need to talk."

"I can't right now." Anne replied. "I have to head into Bangor in a few minutes. But tomorrow morning would work – how about then?"

Beth nodded and turned away. As she walked back to the Coffee House and Anne drove out of the parking lot, Lem and Vern Rodgers watched from the gas station across the street. Vern squinted and rubbed the dirty glass of the window with the cuff of his sleeve.

"They're blond. I like them. They look like sisters. I think they're sisters. They look the same," he said, slipping his hand into his pants pocket and touching himself.

"Yes they do, don't they," Lem replied, smiling.

A little over an hour later Anne and Doug met Tom Richard for lunch in Bangor. Paddy Murphy's had a corner location and sunlight streamed in the large windows that faced a small urban park. Long and narrow, with a relaxed neighborhood feel to it, the pub had a row of old wooden booths along the window wall and an ornate bar along the facing wall. Anne pointed out a booth halfway down and sat across from Doug and Tom, who both chose to sit facing the door. "Cops," she thought, "hardwired to always watch the door."

Tom Richard could be anywhere from 40 to 50, handsome and casually dressed in jeans and a flannel shirt. The first things Anne noticed about him were his deceptively relaxed smile and his large hands, comfortably folded on the table in front of him. It was clear that he and Doug had known each other for a long time, and they seemed to be good friends.

As soon as they sat down Doug updated Tom on the case, including the web site photos of the murder and how Vern Rodgers had learned about the corpse in the ice. As Anne slid the zip-lock bag containing the microcassette of the call across the table to him she could tell that Tom was taking her measure. She felt a little like a suspect in a local precinct interview room.

"So where are you from?" He asked.

"Dover-Foxcroft."

"No, I mean before that."

"Michigan."

"Where in Michigan?"

"Ann Arbor."

"Oh, where the university is."

"Ayup."

Tom gave Anne a long look, took a sip of his Guinness Stout, and glanced at Doug, who responded.

"I told you she was difficult."

It was the best burger Anne had eaten since Krazy Jim's had closed, and while they ate she opened up and gave Doug and Tom her brief history, from growing up the youngest of three in Manistee, with two older brothers, how similar Manistee was to Dover-Foxcroft, her full ride to U. of M., her years on bike patrol and in the detective section of the Ann Arbor Police, and her decision to start a new chapter of her life in Maine. She could tell that Tom and Doug knew there was more behind her decision to leave Ann Arbor than she was telling them, but neither pushed her for more than she was willing to offer.

Anne had somehow expected that the Professor of Medieval History they were scheduled to meet after lunch would be stuffy and longwinded, maybe with her hair up in a tight bun, a serious demeanor, and reading glasses on a chain around her neck. She certainly did not expect Professor Melinda Blood. She was willow thin, in her mid-50s, with shoulder length red hair turning to silver, a loose sweater over black tights, great legs, a warm smile, and a confident manner. Her office on the University of Maine campus in Orono, a short drive from Paddy Murphy's, was lined with full to overflowing bookcases, and they sat around a massive library table in the center of her office that served as her desk and workspace. Under the table a large dog named Jack worked his way around the three visitors, sniffing cuffs and shoes, checking pockets for the possibility of dog treats. He was uniformly golden rust in color and resembled a large German Shepherd except that he had a broad barrel chest and lacked the slinking hind legs of a shepherd. Jack had met them halfway down the hallway leading to Blood's office, tail up, expectant expression, clearly hoping they might have brought him a treat. Stepping out of her office door Professor Blood had laughed.

"My grad students all know to bring him a dog biscuit. That's Jack – he's a

Chinook – a local Maine breed of sled dog, and very friendly."

After Doug had laid all the photos out on the table, Professor Blood picked each of them up one by one, looked at them briefly, and then rearranged them in a line down the long side of the table. Anne noticed that even before she started to speak the professor had the full; one could say rapt, attention of Tom and Doug.

"I have a seminar in half an hour, so I will give you a quick overview of what you have, and then talk about the individual items. If you want, you can leave the photos with me and I can return them to Tom with a written commentary and some recommended readings by the end of the week."

She glanced up, and Doug and Tom both nodded like bobble heads. Anne wondered if the professor realized the effect she was having on the two men, and had little doubt that she did.

"Someone has made an effort to copy or recreate the *auto de fé*, or 'act of faith;' the public ceremony that followed the trial of heretics carried out during the Spanish Inquisition. Preceded by the Medieval Inquisition, which began in the late 1100s in France and spread to different regions of Europe, the Spanish and Portuguese Inquisitions began in the late 1300s, and offer some of the most detailed and valuable accounts of the efforts during that period to protect the Catholic faith. Keep in mind, the person who did this didn't need to be a medieval scholar, or even know very much about the Inquisition. Everything they would need to know could easily have been found on the internet – descriptions, written accounts, images – everything.

The process leading up to the *auto de fé* would begin with the identification, confinement, and examination of individuals suspected of not holding the true faith. People so accused also often just happened to be in opposition to the power and control of the Roman Catholic Church. Examination or questioning of the accused would be lengthy and often-employed methods that today euphemistically would be called 'enhanced interrogation techniques.'

Quite ingenious and diverse methods of torture were used to encourage the accused to confess their hidden adherence to another faith, with Jews frequently being the primary target. Using specially designed machines and implements, joints would be dislocated or crushed, fingernails pulled, and eyes gouged out. Water boarding was a favored technique. They called it 'the toca' or 'tortura del agua,' and it involved first introducing a cloth into the mouth of the victim and then forcing them to ingest water poured from a vessel so that they thought they were drowning. A similar approach was called 'being put to the question' and called for forcing eight pints of water into the victim's stomach. Those that resisted 'the question' would be asked to answer the 'extraordinary question,' which called for 16 pints of fluid."

Picking up the first photo, Dr. Blood continued.

"Boards like these two, sometimes referred to as 'the stocks,' were clamped together, over and under, and across each leg above the ankles. The soles of the feet of the victim were greased with lard, and a blazing brazier would be pressed up against them. Their feet would at first just be blistered, and then, while a board was placed between the brazier and their feet, the victim was given the chance to confess their guilt for the crimes for which they had been charged. If they refused the board would be removed and the brazier reapplied to their feet. The process would continue until they either confessed or their feet were eventually completely fried.

Following the questioning of the accused heretic a trial would be convened, and when found guilty, which was almost always the outcome, a public ceremony or *auto de fé* would be held. The condemned would be paraded in public procession wearing the elements of clothing shown here in your photos, with the procession presided over by the chief inquisitor, usually a Dominican friar."

Professor Blood picked up the next photo.

"The type of tabard they wore was called a 'Sanbenito.' Usually made of yellow sackcloth, it would be decorated with designs that designated the crimes and punishments of the accused. The depiction of devils, dragons, or monks fanning flames on the Sanbenito would indicate that the heretic was impenitent, and was condemned to burn at the stake. If they had repented before the *auto de fé* however, the flames on the Sanbenito would point downward – 'fuego repolto' – indicating that rather than being burned alive, they would first be strangled and then burned. Sometimes the victim would be depicted on the Sanbenito as well, in the center of the flames. The Sanbenito shown here in the photo is for an unrepentant heretic, apparently a woman, judging from the face centered on the garment."

Reaching for the third photo in her series, Blood continued.

"The convicted individuals would also wear 'Corozas,' three foot high pointed pasteboard caps – like dunce hats, which could also be painted with devils or dragons. Finishing off their outfits, the condemned would have a noose around their neck and they would be carrying a long yellow candle."

Professor Blood picked up the last two photos on the table, which showed the candle and noose. Setting them down, she looked at her watch.

"So I think that's about all I can say that will be of any help to you. We could go into a lot more detail to see if it might be possible to pin down the exact historical context of these items but they appear to me to be a rather generic collection – not specific to any particular time or place within the Spanish Inquisition. My guess is that they are the work of someone who went on line or to the library to get some general information. Given the presence of the stocks one might expect your victim to exhibit blistered or burned feet. The stocks also, of course, raise the possibility of other methods of torture being employed. I would prefer to not know any more details of your case, as I have enough going on right now without images of torture invading my dreams. What did I leave out?"

Any opportunity for follow-up questions was interrupted by a brief knock on the office door, followed by a small group of students entering and approaching the table. Jack scrambled out from under the table to greet them. Professor Blood quickly scooped up the photos and turned them face down on the table. "Here is my seminar group, so we will have to continue this another time. I will get that information to Tom in the next few days, and please call with any other questions."

As Anne, Doug, and Tom filed out Melinda placed her hand on Doug's arm.

"Be sure to call me with any questions, Doug."

Tom caught Anne's eye, smiled slightly, and raised his eyebrows.

Standing in the parking lot a few minutes later Tom outlined his next steps.

"I'll look up the top web sites on the inquisition and see if we can come up with a list of the IP addresses for computers in Maine that have accessed them over the past three to six months. It'll be a huge list, but we can narrow it down by looking for IP addresses that have visited multiple sites. We can then cross-reference the narrowed list with the IP address list for computers that have accessed the Sebec Lake Webcam over the past few weeks. Maybe we'll get lucky.

I'll also let you know as soon as I hear anything from the medical examiner regarding the autopsy, which should be in the next few days, and also if there is any update from the crime lab on analysis of the recovered items or anything on the taped call to Vern Rodgers. I'm waiting on the autopsy results before doing any wider search for missing women. My initial search turned up nothing that seemed remotely promising: an Alzheimer's patient in her 80's that has gone missing in Bath, and the wife of an abusive husband in Portland who has gone into hiding several other times in the last year."

Heading back to Dover-Foxcroft from Orono on Route 15, Doug and Anne were passing through the small town of Corinth when a barking dog ring tone on Doug's cell phone indicated a call from Tom. He put it on speakerphone.

"Good news and bad news Doug. The good news – the autopsy is first thing tomorrow morning – 8AM. The bad news- we had four calls from reporters so far today, including WMTW, the ABC affiliate in Portland, and they are not at all happy with the 'woman in lake, more soon' story line so far. Hopefully we can give them more information tomorrow after the autopsy without giving anything away. But we can't keep the lid on for much longer."

Just as Doug ended the call, Anne's phone rang.

"Detective Quinn, it's Jim Torben. Two things. The dive team searched the bottom under where the victim was found and under the ice shack where we found the brown monk's robe, and didn't come up with anything. And Barry and I finally tracked down the owner of the ice shack. It apparently belongs to Jake Yakholm, who is a nasty piece of work. He's well known in these parts for poaching deer and moose, running illegal trap lines, selling bath salts, and getting into fights at the Bear's Den and the Pastimes Pub here in town. He lives up on the Old Brownville Road close to the reservation."

Anne glanced at Doug, who had overheard.

"Let's pay him a visit. Meet us at the Sebec Country Store," she replied. "Bring Barry if he's around."

Turning north off Route 15 onto the Old Stagecoach Road just west of Corinth, Anne and Doug made good time through Charleston and Atkinson, over the Piscataquis River Bridge, and turned into the Sebec Country Store parking lot a few minutes after Jim and Barry had arrived. Doug suggested that they all go in his Cherokee from there since their sheriff's SUV might not get far once they got onto the Old Brownville Road, which turned into a stream bed after a few miles. They drove north through Sebec Village and over the bridge where Doug's son had jumped to his death, and then just before the Sebec Volunteer Fire Department, turned east on Old Brownville Road. Not long after the turn Jim indicated a narrow-rutted track leading off into the woods and they drove into a small clearing bordered by a rundown cabin, a large barnlike garage, and a small trailer. Smoke was coming out of a stovepipe angled up from the side of the cabin and a beat-up minivan was parked in front of the garage. It looked like Jake was home. Doug looked at Anne and pointed to the garage as the three men approached the cabin.

As Anne turned and started walking toward the garage a large man with disheveled hair, Jake no doubt, emerged from its dark interior. The front of his shirt was blood-soaked and he carried a large-bladed knife in his right hand. Without saying a word he advanced rapidly toward Anne, extending his knife hand as he approached her. His eyes were vacant and looked right through her. Drawing his Glock, Doug called to her to step out of his sight line, but moving her left hand to the small of her back, Anne waved him off as she reached into a side pocket of her jacket with her right hand. A flick of her wrist close to her side extended a black steel baton down along her right leg. She raised her right hand up close to her body, spread her feet apart a bit, flexed her legs, and waited. As the bloodied man with the knife lunged the last few steps toward her the baton flashed down, striking his arm just below the elbow with a loud crack. The knife slipped from his grasp as he lost control of his hand and reached to cradle his shattered arm. Anne had retracted and returned the baton to her jacket pocket before the knife hit the ground.

Barry picked up a dead branch, and using duct tape from the back of Doug's Cherokee, stabilized Jake's arm for the trip to town. Watching the splint being applied, Jim turned to Anne and Doug.

"I think Jake here was in the middle of butchering a poached deer or moose in the barn and we interrupted him. Looks like he's high on something and it pissed him off."

A quick look in the barn confirmed Jim's suggestion. A female moose was hanging by its hind legs from a beam and under it a steaming pile of entrails on the dirt floor indicated that it had been killed recently. Reaching for his cell phone Doug took a few quick photos and then called the contact number for the Bowerbank Volunteer Fire Department.

"Hey George, you know where Jake Yakholm's place is over on the Old Brownville Road?"

Doug listened briefly, and continued.

"Yeah, he's a nut case for sure. He just attacked a county sheriff's investigator with a Bowie knife. Should be spending some serious time in the state pen down in Warren. We interrupted him in the middle of dressing a moose cow. Its guts are still steaming on his garage floor and the hanging carcass is still warm. It's a shame to have it go to waste – might be a great addition to this spring's barbecue and benefit auction for the fire station. Think you can send someone over to get it?"

As Doug hung up, Barry frowned.

"Doug, the Sebec Fire Station is much closer than Bowerbank – shouldn't they get the moose?"

Doug looked genuinely surprised.

"I know that Berry, but I'm not from Sebec. I grew up in Bowerbank, so they get the nod."

Jake was sandwiched into the back seat of the Jeep between Jim and Berry for the ride back to the Sebec Country Store, where he was transferred to the sheriff's office SUV for the trip to the Mayo Regional Hospital emergency room in Dover-Foxcroft. After Doug dropped Anne off at her Toyota in the courthouse parking lot, Anne drove by the Center Theatre Coffee Shop to see if Beth might still be at work. Seeing it was closed, she called the phone number in the window and left a message that she couldn't make it tomorrow morning, and suggested lunch. Anne didn't notice the dark colored van that pulled out of the Center Theatre parking lot and followed her until she turned off on Autumn Street.

6.

THE AUTOPSY

A little after 8AM the next morning Anne and Doug were met by the chief medical examiner, Dr. Mike Bowman, in the waiting area of his Augusta facility. He led them back to the autopsy room, which was brightly lit and smelled slightly of industrial cleaners. A long stainless steel counter containing two sinks stretched the length of one wall. Both sinks had a low front rim, allowing the ends of a pair of mobile autopsy tables to extend over the sink for fluid drainage and cleaning. Visitors were given the option of remaining behind a glass window while viewing autopsies but Anne and Doug joined the medical examiner in donning the protective gear that would allow them a close-up look at the procedure.

Their victim was lying on the closer of the two tables and as Bowman stopped beside it, he pointed to two video cameras mounted above the table.

"We had these installed a while back, and they allow us to record video and my commentary on each autopsy. It saves us time and money, both of which are in short supply these days. If you want we can send you a digital copy of the video record along with our official written report. In a minute, when we begin recording, I will have to ask that you not interrupt. Get my attention if you have a question and I can pause the tape. I will also pause the tape if I have any comments or opinions that I don't want in the official record. Are we ready?"

Doug and Anne nodded, and Bowman pressed a button mounted on the wall above the counter to start the video. He identified himself, referenced the date and time, and indicated the presence of the two detectives.

"This autopsy of an as yet unidentified white female is unusual in that the most important questions addressed in a post mortem exam have already been answered by a series of five photos provided to me by Detective Bateman. Based on these time-stamped images obtained from a webcam, the time and place of death can both be established, and it appears to be a death by drowning and a homicide. The autopsy today will in all likelihood confirm that the cause of death was drowning.

The victim is 5 feet 7 inches tall, weighs 125 pounds, and appears to be in her mid-twenties. The body was submerged in very cold water for about 72 hours after death and as a result it is quite well preserved. The pattern and color of the livor mortis exhibited on the body – the head and upper torso is pinkish-red in color where the blood has settled, while the legs and lower torso are bluish-white – is consistent with death occurring after the body was suspended upside down under the ice. This pinkish-red livor mortis color rather than the dark color usually seen is typical of drowning victims, apparently due to higher levels of oxyhemoglobin in the cutaneous blood.

We recovered an excellent set of fingerprints and have taken blood, urine, and DNA samples for comparison with available data sets and for toxicology screening.

Due to the activity of scavengers the feet and lower tibia and fibula are missing, along with associated soft tissue of both legs. Gnaw marks on the bones are consistent with the observed presence of red fox, *Vulpes vulpes*, at the crime scene. A portion of a left foot was recovered some distance away from the body, along with a portion of a leather foot covering. The leather fragment, along with other items of recovered clothing, were removed and transferred to the crime lab for analysis soon after the body arrived at the morgue. Judging from the size of the foot and the purple nail polish, which matches the polish on the victim's remaining fingernails, the foot appears to belong to the victim. I say 'remaining' fingernails because the nails of the thumbs and little fingers of both hands have been removed. We have taken fingernail scrapings from all of the remaining nails and sent them over to the crime lab. Further observation of both hands indicates that the two distal joints of the fingers that still retain nails have all been subjected to crushing injuries. The injuries are all similar, exhibiting a central circular depression, and appear to have been the result of the application of a thumbscrew."

Pausing in his narrative, Bowman lifted the victim's left lower arm and looked at it closely. Reaching over for a pair of forceps he peeled back the edge of an incision that encircled the wrist and pulled out what appeared to be a section of cordage.

"Missed during our preliminary examination of the victim at arrival is a shallow incision made by a sharp narrow blade that encircles the left wrist.

Placed within the incision is a braided fabric bracelet, often termed a 'friendship bracelet.' It is comprised of three braids of different colors – red, white, and blue I think, each of which is the diameter and texture of a shoelace. It will be transferred over to the crime lab."

Doug missed the next few sentences of Bowman's narrative as he realized where he had seen bracelets like the one extracted from the victim's wrist. Along with penny candy, they were thrown to the children who lined the parade route each Homecoming Weekend in Dover-Foxcroft. His son Eric had pinned a number of them up on his bulletin board over the years, along with ribbons from the frog-jumping contest at the Piscataquis Valley Fair and other souvenirs of growing up in central Maine. Deciding not to interrupt, Doug turned his attention back to Bowman.

"A small tattoo of a male ruby-throated hummingbird is present on the inside of her upper left arm, which will be photographed at the end of our examination. No other distinguishing marks, scars, or tattoos can be observed on any of the extremities. There are circling indentations and bruising around both forearms resulting from her arms being tightly bound against her chest to support a candle. The wire binding was removed and transferred to the crime lab along with the candle.

Turning to the torso, there is a large blood clot in the vaginal opening, indicating extensive internal bleeding, but no external bruising, tearing, or lacerations are evident. A large cross has been cut into the victim's chest and stomach. The incisions outlining the cross are shallow and made with a sharp blade, perhaps a box cutter. The vertical portion of the cross is two inches wide, quite straight, and centered on the torso. It extends from just below the suprasternal notch down almost to the mons veneris. The horizontal axis of the cross is the same width, also quite straight, and extends the full width of the chest. Areolas and nipples of both breasts have been removed. A similar cross has been cut into the back of the victim, with the vertical axis following the spine from the atlas down to the base of the spine and the horizontal axis transversing the scapulae on both sides. Judging from the appearance of the underlying tissue exposed when the crosses were cut, their outline was first incised with a box cutter or similar implement, and the skin inside the cuts was then torn rather than flensed away from the body.

There has been some dental work done –a number of fillings on her lower second molars, both sides, and all four third premolars have been extracted, which when combined with the quite regular teeth, indicates orthodontic care.

We will be taking dental x-rays of course, as well as full body x-rays, to help in her identification. No obvious external evidence of strangulation is evident. There is no external evidence of blunt force trauma to the skull, and her hair is naturally blond. Finally, the eyelids and areas around the eye do not show any evidence of a petechial rash, which if present could indicate either strangulation or drowning. The eyes themselves do not exhibit subconjunctival hemorrhages, another possible indication of strangulation."

Bowman paused briefly and exhaled before continuing.

"The reason being that both eyes are glass. Her eyes were both removed by the killer and glass eyes were inserted in their place. They glass replacement eyes also have been sent over to the crime lab for analysis."

Reaching over and pushing the button to pause the video and audio recording, Bowman turned to the stunned detectives. "There's no real need for you to stick around for the internal examination. I expect to find evidence of aspiration of lake water into the lungs that will confirm drowning as the cause of death, and I also expect to find extensive internal damage to the vaginal canal. Other than that, in all likelihood there won't be anything else of interest. I can call you later today to let you know what I find."

Taking off his face shield and gloves, Bowman turned to them with a stricken expression.

"You have a very sick killer out there. A monster. This young woman suffered through sadistic torture of a level I have not seen in 40 years of practice, and I have seen the handiwork of a lot of sick minds. Whoever did this is an animal who needs to be caught and put down, like a rabid dog."

The drive back to Dover-Foxcroft from Augusta in Anne's Land Cruiser was a straight shot, up Interstate 95 and Route 7, and with light traffic would take them a little over an hour. As soon as they got on the interstate Doug called Tom Richard.

"Hey Tom, we just left the autopsy and have enough now for a statement to be released to the media. You ready? Here goes: The body of a drowning victim, a young woman in her mid-twenties, blond, about 5 foot seven and 120 pounds, was recovered from beneath the ice of Sebec Lake earlier this week. We are asking the public for assistance in her identification. She was wearing purple nail polish and had the tattoo of a ruby-throated hummingbird on the inner side of her upper left arm. Bowman can provide you with the audio and video of the autopsy this afternoon. It should give you enough for a wider multiple state and province search for a missing person match. She's not a pretty sight – he really did a number on her – mutilation of her feet, hands, torso and head, including removing her eyes and replacing them with glass ones.

After a long pause, Tom replied.

"Thanks Doug, I will get right on it – wouldn't hurt to give the TV stations in Bangor and Portland a head shot photo – might keep them off our back for a while. We already have some information back from the crime lab. They don't have much to offer from the analysis of items recovered with the victim. The burlap, paints, cords, rope, and wire are all commonly available from hardware and craft stores statewide. One ray of light - they think they may have good blood and DNA that is not the victim's on one of the boards. We should know more on that in a day or two."

Ending the call, Doug turned to Anne.

"Tom says that the crime lab has come up with nothing from the clothing and other items analyzed, with the exception of maybe blood from the boards that isn't the victim's – might yield DNA. Not a promising start. So far we have a lot of physical evidence, but no real progress. Let's hope we get a quick ID on the victim and good solid leads as a result. So far we got bupkis."

Keeping her eyes on the interstate, Anne responded.

"I agree, not a lot so far. But we do know a few things about our killer – maybe pretty obvious but still important. Judging from the webcam images I think it's safe to assume it's an adult Caucasian male, say 25 to 50 years old. Admittedly, given the racial and age composition of Maine residents, that doesn't narrow our pool of suspects down much. But we also know that he's very organized, very methodical, and put a lot of thought and time into this abduction and murder. He must have planned it far in advance and prepared all of the clothing and other items. A lot of research was also done on the Spanish Inquisition, and he may have left an Internet trail. Along with being intelligent and a planner, he's also obviously very disturbed, and there might be something there – a history of mental illness, if we can find it, that will lead back to him. We also know that the killer has outdoors experience based on his use of a snowmobile. Most interesting, I think, is his very clear knowledge of the local landscape, both natural and cultural. He picked the location of the hole in the ice very precisely, to make sure it was centered in the view of the webcam, and he planned the *auto de fé* ritual with full knowledge that it would be captured and archived on the web. By removing the daily footage from the website a few days early we likely signaled to him that we had found the clue, and I bet he was pleased. He wants us to know some things about him, including that he has local knowledge of the lake and the landscape. He must have known that it wouldn't take long for the the body to be discovered, given all the ice-fishing activity. He didn't plan on the fox scavenging, but that didn't matter much.

The phone message to Vern Rodgers fits in with his performance for the webcam – he's letting us know he is a local, that he's part of the community. He's goading us – telling us he's smarter than we are and can stay just beyond our reach, in the shadows, all the while leaving general clues pointing to his nearby presence, while also planting false leads like the phone message to Vern Rodgers."

Turning in his seat, Doug replied.

"The friendship bracelet Bowman found imbedded in the victim's wrist is another clue that points to him being a local. Red, white, and blue bracelets like the victim's are thrown from floats in the homecoming parade held in Dover-Foxcroft in early August every year. But it doesn't get us far since they are also common in other homecoming parades in towns across central Maine, and there must be thousands of them floating around. My son Eric had maybe a dozen of them up on his bulletin board."

Doug turned to gaze out at the snow-covered landscape as they continued north on 95, and after a long silence that extended over several miles, Anne turned to Doug.

"Doug, I'm so sorry about your son – I lost my father a few years back and it was hard. But I can't imagine what it's like to lose a son or daughter."

"It's been more than a year, now, and it's getting easier, I guess. But I think about him every day."

Doug shifted attention to his iPhone, and they drove in silence for most of the rest of the way back to Dover-Foxcroft, until Anne remembered having agreed to meet up with Beth.

"I ran into Beth yesterday after interviewing Vern and Lem Rodgers, and she asked if we could get together. We're going to have lunch I guess – any idea what that's about?"

Doug smiled.

"I haven't a clue, but she can tell you all about Vern Rodgers. They go way back. He was fixated on her in high school – always following her around and asking her out. He even asked her to the senior prom after I had gone off to the University of Maine. It finally got so bad, he got so creepy, that she had to lodge a formal complaint with the school and the local police. If you have lunch at Pat's Pizza, try the burger – not as good as Paddy's, but the best in town."

7.

PAT'S PIZZA

A cold wind and blowing snow kept Anne and Beth from talking much on their short block and a half walk down Main Street from the Central Theatre Coffee House to Pat's Pizza. They entered through the Allie-Oops Sports Bar side of the restaurant, which was bright and quiet at lunchtime. Four flat screen TVs over the bar showed hockey and basketball games and the walls were decorated with a variety of sports paraphernalia, including football jerseys for the Foxcroft Academy Ponies and the New England Patriots.

As they sat down a quite attractive young woman with short red hair and wearing blue jeans and a red and black checked flannel shirt picked up several menus and headed toward their table. Handing them the menus, she turned to Anne.

"I have a strange question for you. I'm hoping you can settle a bet that I have with my brother who works over at the county jail. So how long is your baton?"

Anne looked surprised.

"I carry an ASP Talon Airweight 21 inch.

The woman turned toward the bar and called out.

"David owes me five bucks." Turning back to Anne, she explained.

"He thought you must use a 26-inch model, being a girl and all."

"No, a 21 incher is a better weapon close in, and as they say, it's not the size of your baton, it's how you use it."

The woman smiled, filed Anne's comment away for future retelling, and extended her hand.

"I'm Katie. If you don't object, I'd like to buy you lunch."

Beth interrupted.

"Lunch? Why? What are you two talking about?"

Katie turned her attention to Beth.

"Guess you haven't heard. Doug and the new county sheriff's office investigator here were up at Jake Yakholm's yesterday. Jake came at her with a butcher knife. He was high on bath salts or meth and figured he would gut her. She let him get in close, the way I hear it, and then snapped his arm like a twig. I don't think he is going to be able to slap women around with that hand much any more."

Beth smiled, understanding Katie's lunch offer.

"Jake has been terrorizing the women of this town since he dropped out of high school 20 years ago. He has a long string of ex-girlfriends and a history of domestic violence, restraining orders, bar fights and bad debts. He's always looking for an argument, for trouble. Things have gotten worse in recent years, with his poaching and dealing with the druggies down in Bangor. He was something bad waiting to happen. I hope he goes away for a long time."

Katie jumped in.

"Sounds to me like we have seen the last of Jake. Attempted murder of a police officer ought to punch his ticket good."

After Katie had taken their orders, Beth looked across the table at Anne.

"What kind of case are you working on with Doug?"

Anne realized the Bangor and Portland papers had the story by now, and that it wouldn't hurt to tell Beth what would be common knowledge in a few hours.

"The body of a young woman was found under the ice up just west of the narrows earlier this week. The state police are looking into it as a suspicious death."

"Is that what you were talking to the Toad about?"

Again, Vern Rodger's gossip about Jimmy Hoffa in the ice was already all over town, so there was no reason to avoid the question.

"Doug stopped for gas a few days ago and Vern Rodgers told him that Jimmy Hoffa had been found in the ice. That was before very many people knew about the body that had been discovered, so I was following up to see where Rodgers had obtained his information."

"What else did the Toad tell him?"

Irritated by the direct questions, Anne replied.

"Mr. Rodgers also said that you had a new boyfriend and that the minister's wife and Sheriff McCormick's wife each had two penises."

Beth laughed.

"Classic Toad. OK, here's a parlor game riddle for you – one of those three statements is true – which one? Was Jimmy Hoffa in the ice? Do I have a new boyfriend? Or do the wives of one of our ministers and our sheriff have multiple penises? The correct answer seems obvious: I must have a new boyfriend, right? Wrong. The most likely correct answer, just between us, is that some of the upstanding ladies in town have two penises. Last week it was the minister's wife, this week, apparently, it's the sheriff's wife. Someone tells the Toad those tidbits and he passes them on. What the Toad doesn't realize and almost nobody else in town, including Doug, knows, is that both these women might well have two penises. Not anatomically, of course, but figuratively. Someone informed the Toad, and the Toad is broadcasting around town, that these pillars of the community have two penises available to them – they are having adulterous affairs. For people who enjoy gossip and nasty innuendo the challenge is to give the Toad something outlandish to pass on, but with the possibility that it's a riddle containing a kernel of truth, like the Jimmy Hoffa in the ice story."

"So the new boyfriend story isn't true?"

"I'm guessing that the Toad or his uncle Lem made that one up on their own, just by looking out the window. They have no doubt seen me meeting with Peter Fisher some mornings at the Coffee House. Peter's an architect out of Portland and has been coming up here over the past few years to work on the mill renovation. He asked me to help him look for a camp to buy on Sebec Lake – preferably on the south shore by South Cove. He was thinking about the old Kenny place but it would take a lot of work – no power or road into it, but great views of Borestone and a beautiful old Victorian home. So he brings in recent listing of places he likes and we talk about them. The funny thing is, there is a kernel of truth hidden in the story. Peter is not my 'new' boyfriend, and I am not romantically involved with him right now, but we were a couple for part of my sophomore and junior years at Bowdoin College, and lived together briefly – so you could say he's an old boyfriend. Actually, I think I saw Doug that morning when he was getting gas across the street. Peter and I were having coffee. Did Doug get a laugh out of the new boyfriend story?"

"Not exactly – I think he broke the Toad's nose."

"I heard the Toad slipped on the ice."

"Well, that's possible I guess. You should ask Doug next time you talk to him. But you won't see Doug getting gas there any time soon. The sheriff suggested he go up the street to the Shell station for a while."

Katie appeared with their lunch, a cheeseburger for Anne and a BLT for

Beth, along with two glasses of Sauvignon Blanc.

Anne picked up the conversation.

"So you and Peter were a couple at Bowdoin. I thought you and Doug were high school sweethearts."

Beth smiled and gave Anne a somewhat disjointed and dispassionate account of her life with Doug, seemingly recounting it from the position of a bystander.

"Oh we were definitely high school sweethearts. Doug was a year ahead of me at the Academy and we started dating the end of my sophomore year. It was your typical storybook teenage romance. We were both athletes. He was the captain of the wrestling team and I was on the track team, and we were inseparable. I was on the pill and the physical attraction was intense. We were in a pheromone–hormone haze for two years - proms and skinny dipping, driving out to the dump to neck and watch the bears, drive-in movies and drinking beer with our friends. It was a dream. But then Doug graduated and headed off for college at the University of Maine in Orono. They had a good program in criminal justice, which is always what he wanted. I thought he would become a lawyer but he ended up following his dad into the state police. It was difficult my senior year, with Doug being an hour away and all the distractions – me stuck in high school and him being in college. But we made it work, and the plan was for me to go to the University of Maine too, and we could move in together and live happily ever after. But then I got a scholarship offer for track from Bowdoin and had to take it – my family was not that well off. After that we just drifted apart – two hours' drive time from campus to campus, different friends, lots of parties and opportunities to meet new people.

Peter and I were a couple for quite a while, but I broke up with him at the end of my junior year at Bowdoin. He started getting too possessive, too demanding. He didn't take the break-up well, kept calling and showing up at my place. Now he jokes about it, says he was my stalker.

After he got his degree, Doug went into the state police and was stationed at the Orono barracks. We ran into each other at homecoming that summer, the summer before my senior year at Bowdoin, and started seeing each other again. We got married right after I graduated, in St. Thomas Aquinas, the Catholic Church just up the street here. Then Eric was born, and when Doug's parents died in a car crash we moved into their place in Bowerbank. We had some good years, but when Eric died, I just had to get out of there."

Beth stopped suddenly, and apologized.

"Sorry for running my mouth like that – I rarely talk about it with anyone. It's all in the past now."

Anne smiled.

"I lived with someone for almost two years back in Michigan, just before I came up here, and then one day he just left. The funny thing is, I was relieved it was over. Maybe that's why I don't talk about it, or even think about it much. You have to keep moving forward, not dwell on the past. So you and Doug are Catholic?"

"I was Catholic, but when Eric died I pretty much gave up on religion. Doug never did have much of a leaning in that direction. Now I guess the endorphin surge I get from working out is as close as I get to any higher level of spirituality."

"Do you still run?"

"No. I was a middle distance runner in college – 800 meters was my race. I tried doing longer runs after college but my knees have not held up well. So now I cycle when the roads are dry and it's warm enough. Otherwise I ride my trainer in front of the TV."

Anne looked surprised.

"People cycle around here?"

"Well, not a lot of people. I mostly ride alone. But there are lots of great roads with little traffic and lots of good hills. Some great easy rides right out of town and some killer rides less than a half-hour away. Why, do you ride?"

"I was a bike cop for two years in Ann Arbor and did road rides most weekends. I haven't ridden at all since I got here though."

Anne and Beth discussed the finer points of frames and components for a while, and Beth promised to show Anne the River Road, a beautiful ride along the Piscataquis River Valley, with gently rolling hills, little if any traffic, and small family farms. Both were looking forward to testing the other's ability, and Anne realized she better get her CycleOps bike trainer out of the closet and start putting in some time or Beth would likely crush her come spring.

Still looking mildly competitive, Beth asked.

"How do you get along with Doug? Is he good to work with?"

"He's a good detective. I'm going to learn a lot from just watching him work, and he's a good colleague – low key, reserved, and solid. And he doesn't miss much."

"What does he think of you so far, do you think?"

Anne frowned.

"I'm not sure. He told the sheriff he thinks I'm going to be difficult."

Beth looked surprised, whispered "difficult," as she looked down at her lap, and asked.

"Are you interested in Doug?"

"Of course I am. He knows a lot and I am always have an interest in the people I work with."

Beth shook her head.

"You know what I mean. Are you interested in Doug?"

Anne sat silent for a moment, thinking about the question before responding.

"I'm not sure, are you?"

As Anne and Beth stepped out of Allie Oops into a heavy snowfall, neither noticed the man watching them from the alley between the fire station and the model railroad club building across Main Street.

That afternoon Doug and Anne entered the small dingy interview room in the county jail building, around the corner from the courthouse, and sat down across the table from Jake Yakholm. Jake was anchored to the floor by leg chains and had an elbow to fingertips cast on his right arm. He looked alert and hostile. Gazing directly at Doug, he blurted out.

"Bateman, you prick, did you break my arm?"

Doug returned his stare, and answered.

"You were so high you don't even remember do you? You attacked Detective Quinn here with a butcher knife, causing her to disarm you, so to speak." Doug seemed pleased with his turn of phrase.

Jake turned his attention to Anne.

"You bitch – wait till I get out of here. I'm going to enjoy using you as a punching bag."

Anne shook her head slowly.

"Jake, you're not getting out. Haven't you figured it out yet? You've been charged with attempted murder of a law enforcement officer. Under Title 17A of Maine's revised statutes that qualifies as aggravated attempted murder, which carries up to a life sentence. By the time you get out of prison, if you ever do, you won't be able to punch much of anything, particularly with that flipper of yours. But we're not here about that. We want to know where you were last Saturday – all day."

Jake didn't seem to understand what Anne had just said about the charges he faced. He laughed loudly, throwing his head back.

"You trying to pin something on me from last weekend? Good luck on that one, bitch. I got the best alibi in the world. I was in the Aroostook County Jail from Friday night through Sunday. I got a call Friday from somebody saying my ex-girlfriend Sharon wanted me to come up to Presque Isle and get her. They said she was in a jam. But when I got up there she called the cops on me, claimed I'd violated a restraining order. The cocksuckers, they locked me up. Go ahead, call em up." He laughed again.

A half hour later, after they had confirmed Jake's alibi, Doug and Anne had settled into a booth at Allie Oops at the end of a long day.

"It looks like Jake was set up, to get him out of town at least overnight Saturday night so his ice shack would be vacant. Another dead end," Anne concluded. Looking toward one of the TV screens over the bar, Doug casually asked.

"How was your lunch with Beth?"

"It was good. You were right – an excellent cheeseburger, and the fries were fresh cut." She paused just long enough to indicate she knew what he was asking, and continued.

"I asked Beth about the boyfriend story and she said she is just helping an old friend from college, Peter Fisher, who is looking for someplace to buy on the south shore up by Peaks-Kenny – a few innocent morning meetings at the Coffee House."

8.
THE THOMPSON FREE LIBRARY

Anne stopped by the Coffee House early the next morning on her the way to the courthouse and her morning strategy meeting with Doug, Sheriff McCormick, and Jim Torben. She had agreed to pick up coffee and a half dozen of the donuts she had heard so much about. Made at Elaine's Basket Café and Bakery in Milo, the next town east of Dover-Foxcroft, and delivered daily to several dozen restaurants within a 50-mile radius, the donuts were reputed to be the best in the state, or maybe, simply the best anywhere.

As she walked in the door Anne noticed Beth and Peter Fisher sitting across from each other at the table next to the front window, real estate ads spread out between them. For reasons she couldn't at first recognize Anne took an immediate dislike to Peter. Maybe it was the way he was dressed – a starched, bright white button-down shirt and bow tie, tweed jacket, crisply creased trousers, and brightly polished shoes. Or maybe she had instinctively reacted to his rather smug, self-important way of assessing her as she approached their table. Then it clicked – she realized he reminded her of the officious mid-level university administrators she had often encountered in the course of her job with the Ann Arbor Police. He could easily fill the role of an associate or assistant dean or a special counsel to the provost or vice-president for academic affairs – the types of positions usually filled by faculty who had been awarded tenure some years previously but were never going to be promoted to full professor rank. As they recognized they would never measure up as scholars they would escape into functionary administrative roles and days filled with meaningless meetings and petty struggles for recognition. Anne almost laughed out loud when she realized her reaction to Peter Fisher was not just because he reminded her of university apparatchiks, however, but also because he was so obviously not from here. He was from away, from Down East. She was starting to think like a local.

Anne's unease grew as she sat with Beth and Peter while Beth's barista, a quite attractive young white woman with massive dreadlocks, prepared the coffees and boxed up a variety of Elaine's donuts. As they talked about the various south shore camps that were on the market, Anne noticed that Peter's nails were manicured and were either highly buffed or had a coat of clear nail polish. His long and delicate fingers were constantly in motion – moving papers around or playing with his coffee cup. Peter's pasty face was unlined, suggesting a life spent indoors, and his perfectly shaped teeth were remarkably white – whitened, or maybe all caps, she thought. His immaculate hair was stylishly long but too uniformly dark to be natural. Peter, she thought, was altogether artificial. Although he assumed a relaxed posture as he and Beth casually bantered back and forth about the real estate ads, his gaze, when it strayed to Anne, was cold and hollow. Anne flinched when the barista plopped the box of donuts and the tray of coffees on the table in front of her, and she recognized her alert tenseness as a reflex response to perceived threat. Nothing Peter had said was remotely menacing but Anne still felt relieved as she made her escape from the Coffee House.

Doug had gotten into their office early, and along with photos of the victim and the articles of clothing associated with her, he had written a list of questions and loose ends on a white board for them to work through. He and Jim Torben were sitting at the small conference table, looking at the list. Anne joined them, placing the box of donuts in the middle of the table, and they started discussing the case. The first question on the list was "victim identity?" Brief notices of the case had appeared in the Portland and Bangor papers the day before, as well as in the local weekly, the Piscataquis Observer. The Bangor and Portland TV stations had also covered the case on the local news, including photos of the victim's hummingbird tattoo, but as yet no promising leads had come in.

Doug was reaching for a donut when he was interrupted by Tom Richard's barking dog ring tone on his cell phone. He answered, listened for several minutes, and responded.

"Thanks Tom. I will check my emails right now, and call me as soon as you hear anything on the DNA."

Turning to Tom and Anne, he summarized Tom's call. "Nothing new on the victim's identity, but they recovered DNA from both the wooden stocks and from the robe found in Jake's fishing shack – we should know if they get any hits from the data bases this afternoon. Tom also sent over an email detailing the results of the cross-referencing analysis of the Sebec Lake web site access history and web visits to the Spanish Inquisition web sites. There were multiple visits to the torture websites over the past three months from the same IP address that accessed the Sebec Lake web site three times after the daily archive coverage of the murder was posted – it's a computer at the library here in town."

Reaching for his coat, Doug looked at Jim Torben.

"I think I'll show Anne the town's library. Make sure the donuts are still here when we get back."

Built in the late 1880's by Elbridge A. Thompson in memory of his wife, and deeded over to the town, the Thompson Free Library was a sturdy red brick building that had served Dover and Foxcroft for more than a century. Located on East Main between the Dover-Foxcroft Police Department on one side and the Webber Ace Hardware on the other, it was a short walk from the courthouse. As they walked over to the library, Doug cautioned Anne.

"This may be difficult. Nancy Sullivan has been the librarian here for 30 years and she runs a tight ship. She is also Beth's mother, my mother-in-law, and I am not in her good graces right now. She blames me for Beth moving in with her sister, and you could say she is very forthright in expressing her views on the topic."

As they approached the front desk, an older woman in a floral pattern dress stood up and ignoring Anne, addressed Doug.

"Well, if it isn't Douglas Bateman. I've not seen you in quite a while. Have you spoken to your wife lately?"

Doug seemed ready to respond when Anne stepped forward and showed her badge to the librarian.

"I'm Inspector Anne Quinn, Mrs. Sullivan, with the county sheriff's office, and we're here on police business. We are investigating a suspicious death. A young woman found under the ice up west of the narrows. The death of this woman has been connected to one of the computers here in the library and I would like to ask you a few questions."

Stunned into silence, Nancy Sullivan glanced at Doug, and then led them back to her office. She retreated behind her desk and Anne and Doug sat in hard-backed library chairs facing it. Doug remained silent as Anne asked the questions.

"I can't go into specifics, but we have linked one of your public access computers here in the library to the case we are investigating. Do you keep a record of the individuals who use the computers? Do they have to identify themselves and sign a register of any kind?"

"I wouldn't give you access to records of what books our patrons have checked out, and I'm not sure I would be willing to provide formal records of who used our computers if we kept any. But if someone wants to use a computer all they need to do is sign their name and the time on the waiting list we keep by the computers – we limit usage to 30 minutes if someone is waiting."

"How long do you keep the waiting lists?"

"It's just a legal pad. When it's filled up we discard it and start a new one."

"May we see it?"

"Since they volunteer the information and they can put down any name they want, I don't see a problem with that."

She led them back toward the front door and then turned right into a large reading room. Two computers were on a table against one wall. Picking up an almost full yellow legal pad, the librarian leafed through the 20 or so pages filled with names and times, separated by headings indicating days of the week, and handed it to Anne.

"Here, you can keep it. It's almost full, and we can start a new one."

Anne thanked her and asked her next question.

"Are the computers used a lot?"

"Yes. There is almost always someone waiting, and we have to remind people of the 30-minute limit all too often. They are particularly busy on weekends and after school during the school year – less so in the summer months and earlier in the day during the work week."

"Do you have any closed-circuit cameras in the library that record people coming and going?"

Frowning and shaking her head, the librarian responded curtly.

"No, nothing like that. We also don't have a metal detector. It's a library."

Looking back toward the doorway to the reading room, Anne asked.

"I notice you can't see the computers from the front desk. Visitors interested in using them could enter the front door, turn left into the reading room, and would only be visible to anyone at the front desk for a short period of time."

"Yes, that's correct – what's your question?"

Anne looked at the email printout from Tom Richard.

"Well, the computer use we are interested in always occurred on weekday mornings, between 9 and 11 AM. Does that mean anything to you?

Mrs. Sullivan blanched, looked at Doug, and responded.

"That's when Betty fills in for me at the front desk while I catch up with the re-shelving. She is a wonderful help, but I am not sure how long she can continue."

"Why's that."

"Well, Betty is in her late 80s, and can't see too well any more. She is OK checking books out and simple tasks, but has to come and get me if someone wants a library card or has a complicated question."

Anne asked her final question.

"So do you think she would be able to identify anyone coming in the front door and turning into the reading room to use a computer?"

"No, at that distance from the front desk I don't think she would be able to see faces."

Anne reached out and shook hands with Mrs. Sullivan. "Thanks for your time. Please don't discuss this with anyone, and we will be back in touch if we have any more questions."

Anne began to turn away, and then added.

"I had coffee with Beth and Peter Fisher this morning – he seems very nice."

The librarian looked like she was going to respond, but then pressed her lips together in a frown, stood silently, and watched them leave.

"What was that all about, at the end?" Doug asked as they walked back to the courthouse.

"This Peter Fisher guy is creepy – really creepy. I just wanted to remind her that Beth is hanging around with a hollow man."

Abruptly changing the subject, Anne continued.

"Here's another clear indication that our killer knows this town. He scheduled his Internet access to when ancient Betty, who can't see much, was manning the desk. If it's OK with you, I would like to put Jim Torben on sorting out the library computer waiting list. I doubt it goes back far enough to pick up the inquisition web site visits, but it should include the Sebec Lake Webcam hits and we can compare them with the waiting list sign up times."

Doug was skeptical that it would yield anything worthwhile – the killer was not going to identify himself – but nodded agreement as they climbed the steps to the courthouse. As they entered the office, Doug and Anne both noticed that the box of donuts that had been sitting on their conference table had disappeared. Anne gave Jim the two lists and listened to his blank-faced denial of any knowledge regarding the whereabouts of the missing donuts. Jim was back to Anne and Doug in less than ten minutes with the results of his list comparison.

"That was easy – only one name showed up on all of the library waiting lists for the three mornings that the Sebec Lake Webcam was accessed – Sunday, Monday, and then again Wednesday, but not since then. It's a weird name – 'Thomas Torquemada,' and it's written in an ornate curly script. I didn't recognize it and couldn't find it in any county data bases or local phone directories. And here, look, after he signed in day before yesterday he wrote 'Did you enjoy the show?'"

"That's our killer," replied Doug. "He must have noticed we pulled the archive footage from the web site. He was in the library just a few days ago but I doubt he will be back again. And you won't find his name in the county records – he's been dead for 500 years. Tomás de Torquemada was the grand inquisitor of the Spanish Inquisition. Once again, the killer is thumbing his nose at us."

Anne spent the next hour bringing the computer case files up to date, and then followed up on two questions she had been thinking about since her morning chat with Peter and Beth over coffee. Her first on-line search was to track down one of the real estate listings that Peter and Beth had discussed that morning and that Peter had dismissed as being too run-down and too small. It was a new listing, which explained why it hadn't shown up on any of her earlier searches, and it was a good fit with what she had been hoping to find. Her lease on the Autumn Street rental house wouldn't be up until the summer, but she had been looking for a waterfront place to buy since she had arrived in Dover-Foxcroft. She wanted an older camp with character that was structurally sound and had a good location and a large wooded lot. Large lots were not that common on the older camps, which tended to be jammed together on postage stamp properties. But this camp, built in 1926, was on two acres. It also had propane heat, electricity, a well, and a septic field. It was a summer cottage and hadn't been winterized, but its foundation was set up on boulders and cinder blocks, so the floors could easily be insulated. The interior had beautifully aged original pine plank walls that could also be removed for insulation and then reinstalled. The cedar shake shingle exterior would need staining, but the house had a relatively new metal roof and a large screened porch. It was situated on a small point on the south shore, had a good view west down the lake, and was maybe 30 minutes out of town. It was small, a little over 1200 square feet, and since it was within the 100-foot lake-edge setback, couldn't be expanded. But it would work for her. And given the low asking price the listing seemed too good to be true. She called and agreed to meet the listing agent at the property in a few days.

Anne then accessed the Maine Criminal History Record Database and did a name search on Peter Fischer. Using an age bracket estimate of 30-40, she came up with two listings, neither of which seemed to match Beth's friend – the first was for armed robbery and the second for failure to pay child support. A second name search, this time with a different spelling for his last name – Fisher rather than Fischer, turned up a possible match. A protection from harassment order had been granted to a woman in Portland, Maine, against a Peter Fisher in 2013. Anne wrote down the name and contact information for the person who had filed for the protection order, planning to call her later in the day.

Doug and Anne walked down to Pat's Pizza for lunch, and after they had ordered – Anne went for the cheeseburger with fries again, just to confirm the consistency of their quality – her phone rang, showing a number she didn't recognize. She answered, talked for several minutes, and after hanging up, looked down at the table and turned to Doug with a quizzical expression.

"That was June Torben, Jim's wife, inviting me over for dinner tonight. It seems that their daughter plays on the varsity girls basketball team at Foxcroft Academy and they have a home game tonight against Caribou at 7. She suggested I could come for dinner and then go to the game with them. Do you know anything about this?"

"Well, I may have mentioned to Jim that you played college ball. I think their daughter Ashlee is a junior and a promising three-point shooter. Pretty sure she plays point guard."

"What have you gotten me into here?"

Doug gazed past her, folded his hands on the table, and then looked directly at her.

"As you have probably figured out, I am not exactly an expert on the way women's minds work, but I would guess several things are going on. June is a stay at home mom with two teenage daughters who are a handful, and has a loving but pretty traditional husband. He likes to spend time with the guys and go to karaoke on Thursday night at the Bears Den. He and June have had some ups and downs over the years but things seem to have pretty much settled down now. June, I am sure, wants to check out the new woman in town who works with her husband. She wants to find out who you are. Should she welcome you to town or be on her guard? At the same time I would also guess that she is hoping you just might be a good role model for her daughters. The account of how you disarmed Jake Yakholm is also making the rounds, and being embellished in the telling. You made your way in the big outside world, graduated from college, and have a career in a profession dominated by men. So the only thing you are getting into here is life in Dover-Foxcroft."

Anne was about to respond when Doug's phone started barking.

"Hey Doug, we caught a break. The DNA from the wooden stocks yielded a match in our sex offender registry – and the guy lives right there in Dover-Foxcroft. His name is Dwayne Benz. Does that ring a bell?"

"It doesn't offhand, but I'm sure that Jim or Berry will know him. Thanks Tom, we will check him out today."

Jim had worked the Dwayne Benz case and gave them a brief rundown when they got back from lunch.

"It was quite the scandal in town three years ago. Dwayne was 21 then and a part-time assistant track coach at Foxcroft Academy. He and his girlfriend Louise, the school's 17-year old star sprinter, were caught necking in the equipment room after practice one day. Given their respective ages and his employment by the school, what they were up to qualified as unlawful sexual contact under state law. They were in love, but her father, a prominent dentist in town, objected to their relationship and decided to press charges. It was a class E misdemeanor, so Dwayne faced a $1,000 fine and up to six months in jail, but he got six months' probation. Because of the conviction, however, he was added to the sex offender registry and of course he lost his job at the Academy. But when Louise turned 18 she told her father, the uptight dentist, where to stick it, and she and Dwayne got married. They seem to be doing OK. They have a toddler and Louise works at the hospital. Dwayne works at the Webber Ace Hardware here in town."

"Right next to the library," said Doug as they headed for the door.

Dover-Foxcroft supports two hardware stores; the True Value Hardware right downtown and the Webber Hardware farther out Main Street, just past the library. Both were housed in historic brick buildings, both had a loyal customer base, and which one you went to depended mostly on the specific items you were looking for.

Dwayne Benz's primary job at the Webber Hardware was the management of their lumber warehouse; a large sheet metal structure set behind the hardware store. It had large open entrances at both ends that allowed vehicles to drive right through it for easy loading of lumber, which was stacked two stories high on either side of the central passageway.

Dwayne had just finished cutting the last of a number of 2x6x16s into eight-foot lengths for an order to be picked up later that day. Glancing up, he noticed that a sheriff's SUV with its engine running had blocked the far entrance to the lumber warehouse. Jim Torben waved at him from behind the wheel and Dwayne gave a puzzled wave in return. Removing his hearing protection earmuffs, he heard approaching footsteps coming from the direction of the other end of the warehouse, and turned to greet Doug and Anne. They approached to within about eight feet, and Doug showed his state police badge.

"Dwayne, I'm Doug Bateman with the state police major crimes unit, and this is Anne Quinn from the county sheriff's office. We'd like you to accompany us back to the courthouse for a few questions."

"Sure thing," Dwayne responded. "Just let me tell Bruce that I will be gone for a while."

"That's OK, Dwayne. We let him know. He says you can take the rest of the day off."

Once they were seated around a table in a sterile cinderblock-walled waiting room in the courthouse, Dwayne broke his silence.

"Is it my father-in-law again? Is he ever going to leave us alone?"

Doug set a small tape recorder down on the table, stated the date, time, and location and that the interview of Dwayne Benz was being conducted by himself and Anne Quinn, Piscataquis County Sheriff investigator.

"Dwayne, first, let's be clear. You are not under arrest at this time. We are asking for your cooperation in a murder investigation, which is a serious matter, and you can have your lawyer present if you want."

"I don't need a lawyer sir, just tell me how I can help."

"Here's the problem we need to clear up Dwayne. Your DNA is on file in the state's sex offender registry, and it has just been matched to DNA from a 2x4 recovered from the scene of a murder. Can you explain how your DNA ended up there?"

Dwayne blanched, and his mouth dropped open.

"Dwayne, can you answer the question?"

"I think I need a lawyer."

Jim Torben, who had been sitting quietly by the door, spoke up.

"Excuse me Detective Bateman, can I ask Dwayne something?"

Doug nodded and Jim turned to Dwayne.

"Dwayne, didn't I see you and Louise at the Center Theatre last Saturday night for the children's winter pageant? Wasn't your little girl a snowflake?"

Dwayne nodded.

"Ayup. We got there early to help set up. Becky, that's our daughter, she fell asleep in her stroller soon after 6, but we stayed till the end."

"What time did you get to the theatre and what time did you leave?" Jim asked.

"We got there about 4, 4:30, and left about 7 I think. You could check with Louise or with the other parents who helped with the set up and take down."

Doug visibly relaxed.

"We will Dwayne. How do you think your blood and DNA turned up on the 2x4 found at the crime scene?"

"Blood. You should have said that right off. I handle lumber all day and I don't like wearing gloves. I can't get a good grip. I also occasionally get careless with the chop saw. My hands are always pretty torn up, and I get blood on the lumber sometimes."

Dwayne held up his hands, displaying an impressive crosshatched pattern of cuts and scratches, and a right index finger that was missing its tip.

"Dwayne, I think that's all we need for right now. I have just one final question. How many 2x4s do you think you have sold in the last year?" Doug asked.

"Well, it depends on the length and if they're pressure treated. I can give you exact counts if you want, but I'd guess in total it's got to be up above five or six thousand."

9.

A WITNESS

Even though it was a Saturday morning and the case seemed stalled, Anne decided to go into the office to bring the files up to date and to check a few more of Dwayne Benz's alibi witnesses for Saturday night. When she arrived at about 9 she saw a pink phone call slip taped to her computer screen. The message read, "Please call Charlotte Laughlin – she thinks she knows who the murder victim is." The call had come in an hour earlier from somewhere in Maine based on the 207 area code of the callback number.

Anne called the number and after several rings a man answered, "Northwoods Outfitters, how can I help you today?"

Northwoods Outfitters, Anne knew, was located about an hour away up in Greenville, on Moosehead Lake. She had gotten a great price on a carbon fiber kayak paddle there the previous fall. Anne asked for Charlotte Laughlin, heard the man call out, "Charlotte, phone for you," followed by the sound of the phone being set down. When Charlotte picked up Anne could tell from her rushed, nervous responses that she was both frightened and close to tears. She had first called the state police hotline number mentioned on the local TV news the night before, she explained, but got a recorded message to call back on Monday. She couldn't wait that long she said, so had called the general number for the Piscataquis County Sheriff's office.

Having already fielded a number of calls from people claiming to know the victim, Anne somewhat curtly got right to the point.

"Who do you think is the victim, and why?"

"It's my friend Angeline Bouchard, I just know it is," whispered Charlotte. "She's 23, blond, and has a hummingbird tattoo on her left arm, just like they said last night on the news. And she left Greenville over a week ago but never got home to Saint Georges." She quickly added. "I work till 6 tonight. Can you please come up and talk to me, please?"

Anne confirmed that Northwoods Outfitters was just across the street from the Shaw Public Library in Greenville, and assured Charlotte that they would be up to talk to her that morning. She called Doug, who said he would pick her up in half an hour in front of the courthouse, and asked her to email Tom the information. Tom in turn could contact the police in Saint Georges, a town in Quebec about a half hour north of the border with Maine, and see if Angeline Bouchard has been reported missing, and any information they could provide on her.

Construction on the bridge over the Piscataquis River in Guilford caused a backup, and then an overturned lumber truck between Abbot and Monson slowed their progress up Route 6 to Greenville. It was just after 11 when they crested the final hill at the Indian Hill Trading Post and the stunning view of Moosehead Lake opened up before them.

For the first half hour of the trip north Doug and Anne had gone over the case again to see if they had missed something. They agreed that the DNA match with Dwayne Benz was a false lead – they were victims of their advanced technology, and that the 2 by 4s used to construct the stocks, like the other materials recovered from the crime scene, wouldn't lead them back to the murderer. The cloth and paints and cordage and candle from the *auto de fé* ceremony were too easily purchased in too many places to be of any help. Tom had tried to track down the robe found in the ice fishing shack, and had established that five different customers in Maine had ordered it online from the maker, ARUS, in the last six months. But the buyers all turned out to still have their robes. The robe had also been offered for sale in one of the discount stores in Freeport earlier in the year, however, and the killer could have paid cash for it there, leaving no trail for them to follow. The bathrobe puzzle underscored for them the extent to which the killer had them running in circles and second-guessing themselves. They were piling up evidence, but none of it seemed to get them any closer to the killer. He was hiding in plain sight and deliberately taunting them with his knowledge of the community. He knew the Toad was the town crier of salacious slander. He knew how to get Jake Yakholm out of town long enough to use his ice shack. He knew where the beach cam was located and how it operated, and had left them a record of the crime if they were smart enough to find it. He was clever enough to access the Internet from the library computer when he was least likely to be remembered, and even left them a message when he realized they had discovered the beach cam footage. He bought his lumber at the local hardware. He knew how to operate a snowmobile, and knew his way around Sebec Lake. The killer was a local. He was organized and methodical. He thought he was smarter than his pursuers, and he enjoyed toying with them – demonstrating his superior intellect. He was playing a game with them and so far he was winning.

By the time they passed through the small town of Monson, Doug and Anne had settled into a comfortable silence. Monson sat astride the Appalachian Trail at the southern entrance to the 100-mile wilderness. In the summer months the town hosted a steady stream of seasoned hikers stocking up on 10 days of provisions before they continued on to the northern terminus of the trail at Baxter State Park and Mt. Katahdin. In the dead of winter, however, the streets were empty except for several pickups parked outside the Spring Creek Bar-B-Q restaurant, known for having the best barbeque in the state. Ordinarily Doug would have suggested they stop for lunch, but today he was anxious to talk to their witness and hopefully get some traction in the case.

Continuing north along Route 6 toward Greenville under a bright blue sky, with the deep green forest on either side, Doug returned to puzzling over why he and Beth had drifted apart. The death of their son Eric was certainly a big part of it. Doug had heard that the Toad was spreading the story that he had killed his son, and he still felt that maybe there was some truth in that. Eric had just turned 13 when he died. He had not yet hit puberty, and was small for his age. Beth had not wanted him hanging around on the bridge with the older teens, but Doug talked her into allowing it, as long as he was with his friends. It was a long-standing rite of passage on the north shore, Doug emphasized, and he had done it as a kid, starting at about Eric's age. Beth relented and Eric and several other boys from Bowerbank, including a few just up for the summer, started going down to the bridge on hot afternoons. After the drowning Beth had never pointed the finger at Doug, never mentioned her opposition to the bridge jumping, but Doug knew she blamed him. And he blamed himself. But Beth had been gradually withdrawing from their relationship for a long time before Eric died. Maybe their son was all that was holding them together, and when he was gone, she saw no reason for staying.

Beth and Doug had started out in high school as not just sweethearts, but as best friends. They were inseparable. It wasn't just the sex, although that was a big part of it. They were both into sports and rock music. He went to all of Beth's track meets and cheered her on. During his senior year, when he was pretty well ranked in the 195 weight class, Beth followed the Foxcroft Academy wrestling team all over the state as Doug compiled a long undefeated streak, finally losing on points in the second round of the state tournament. Beth had the lead in a few school plays and Doug worked on the sets. They studied together whenever they could, went to all the school's formal dances together, and Doug helped put together the homecoming parade float every year for Beth's Father's insurance business.

Doug wondered now if the trouble in their relationship couldn't be traced all the way back to their basic personalities and the different aspirations their parents held for them. Before he passed away a few years ago, Beth's dad Irwin Sullivan had been the State Farm Insurance agent in town, and he was very active in Rotary and Kiwanis. Her mother had been the librarian at the Thompson Free Library for as long as Doug could remember. They both wanted the best for Beth, who was the younger of two sisters. Beth's older sister Courtney had gone on to college and one of the best schools of veterinary medicine in the country at the University of Pennsylvania, and was now a partner in a very successful vet clinic over in Dexter. They wanted the same for Beth – a successful career, hopefully involving her relocation away from Dover-Foxcroft – down to Portland or Boston, or even beyond. They were thrilled when Beth was awarded a scholarship to Bowdoin, a small, highly ranked, elite college that attracted talented students from all over the country. They were sure she was on her way out of Piscataquis County.

Doug Bateman had initially seemed like a reasonable match for Beth based on their assumption that his interest in law and justice would lead him to pursue a law degree. Their assessment of him changed dramatically, however, when it became clear he wanted to go into law enforcement rather than become a lawyer, and they were quite relieved when Beth and Doug stopped seeing each other after she started college. They thought Peter Fisher, Beth's new boyfriend at Bowdoin, was a good match for her. He was from a well-off family outside of Boston, wanted to be an architect, dressed extremely well, and had a distinctive upper class bearing. Beth was invited down for long weekends at the Fisher's sprawling summer home on Isleboro Island off the coast of Maine, and given Beth's interest in business administration her parents were confident that she and Peter would make good partners in business and in life.

Doug's parents of course also wanted a good life for their children. But their concept of "success" was quite different from that of the Sullivans. Doug's fore bearers on both his mother and father's sides had first settled in Piscataquis County in the early 1800s, and they had a deep and strong family history in the area. For them, a fulfilling and worthwhile life was centered on family, community, heritage, and a connection to the land. Doug's interest in becoming a Maine State Trooper like his dad before him was encouraged from an early age. They thought Beth would be a good match for Doug, and hoped that she and Doug would marry, start a family, and build a life together in Piscataquis County. Doug's parents did not live to witness Beth and their son's marriage, however. In early January of Doug's senior year at the University of Maine a drunk driver hit their car head on, killing them both. They were buried in the Bateman plot of the Bowerbank Cemetery, alongside Doug's sister, who had died of AML, acute myelogenous leukemia, when he was five.

Along with being raised with a different idea of what made for a full and successful life, Doug was also, he had been surprised to learn, a classic introvert. He had always considered himself to just be shy. But Beth had talked him into taking a personality test one day on the Internet and he discovered that he had many of the characteristics of an introvert. He disliked crowds and the feeling of being hemmed in. He always preferred an isle seat close to an exit when he and Beth went to the movies. He didn't like small talk or meeting new people and would gravitate toward people he knew at social gatherings rather than make an effort to introduce himself to strangers. He much preferred getting together with a few close friends rather than attending large gatherings, and tended to feel alone in groups, even when he knew many of the people around him. He avoided answering his phone if he could, even when the calls were work related, preferring to call people back when he was ready to talk. His partner Tom had figured this out and routinely texted him now rather than wasting a phone call. Doug relished solitude and quiet surroundings and needed down time built into his days. He could lose himself in a solitary task he enjoyed, and would easily spend an entire afternoon applying a fresh coat of varnish to the Otter, his vintage Chris-Craft wooden boat, and be surprised that the time had passed so quickly. He was methodical in working through complex situations and had an excellent eye for detail. He was largely solitary in his investigative work, rather than relying on large group collaboration. Interacting with Tom and with Anne was a perfect work setting for Doug as he compiled evidence and analyzed possibilities and patterns. His isolated home on the north shore of Sebec Lake, and the small communities and large spaces of Piscataquis and Aroostook Counties were a comfortable cultural and natural landscape for him, and he couldn't imagine having to deal with the crowds and the noise of Portland or other big cities. He didn't understand Beth's longing to escape Dover-Foxcroft for a faster pace of life and a greater measure of success that she thought could be found by moving to Portland or Boston.

Beth, in turn, was frequently frustrated by her inability to get Doug to come out of his shell and expand his horizons. She enjoyed meeting new people and drew energy and enjoyment from the constant interactions she had on a daily basis in the Center Theatre Coffee House. But Dover-Foxcroft was not Portland and she knew she could do better, and would only truly be successful if she made it in the big city. She felt stuck in Dover-Foxcroft and dreamed of the full and rewarding life that was waiting down on the coast. Beth thought she still loved Doug but knew that if she stayed married to him she would never make it out of Piscataquis County.

Sitting next to Doug on their drive up to Greenville, Anne was thinking back over last night's dinner at the Torben's, and the Foxcroft Ponies girls' basketball game they went to afterward. Anne and June, Jim's wife, had hit it off right from the start, and Anne thought that they could become good friends. June was attractive, with shoulder-length brown hair, brown eyes, and a warm smile. For Anne, meeting June had made the prospect of settling in Dover-Foxcroft a lot brighter. Dinner at the Torben's was informal, bordering on chaotic, in ways that made Anne nostalgic for Manistee and her two older brothers. The Torben girls, Jacquie and Ashlee, sniped at each other constantly through dinner and June had to frequently intervene to bring them into line. Ashlee's raven ponytail was in constant movement as she peppered Anne with questions about her college career as a point guard. Dressed in her maroon and white basketball uniform, she vibrated with teenage energy as she passed the meat loaf, mashed potatoes, and canned peas around the kitchen table. Two years younger than Ashlee, and eager to get out from under her sister's shadow, Jacquie had a dazzling smile, a sharp wit, and an excellent ability to get under her sister's skin. Both girls were tall and athletic, and thriving under the watchful eye of their parents. Jim said little during dinner but gazed on his wife and daughters with obvious pride and love. It was a solid family and Anne felt relaxed and comfortable. She answered all of Ashlee's questions directly and in detail.

Anne had forgotten the excitement and energy that filled a gym during a hard-fought basketball game, and after dinner, as they took their seats in the bleachers, surrounded by the familiar crowd noise and the sound of basketballs hitting the backboard and sneakers squeaking on the polished wood floor, she felt like she was home. Jim had drifted off to talk to friends and Jacquie joined the student cheering section down front, leaving Anne and June to chat as they watched the game from higher up in the stands. The gym was not that crowded – not many fans had made the long trip down from Caribou, so June and Anne could talk freely.

With a refreshing frankness June thanked Anne for coming to dinner on such short notice and asked if she might consider giving Ashlee and the other girls on the Foxcroft team a few pointers on basketball. That sounded OK to Anne, as long as their coach was comfortable with the idea, and June suggested that she could email him and see what he thought. They only had a half dozen games left before the state tournament, but June said it would be great for them to interact with a former Big Ten college player.

June then asked Anne all about her upbringing and her college years, her job with the Ann Arbor Police, the two years trying to make things work with Kevin, and the lakefront house she was thinking about buying. June offered to go with her to check out the place, and they agreed to meet up at the Coffee House before going out to meet the realtor at the camp. June in turn told Anne about growing up in Dover-Foxcroft, about the remarkable history of Foxcroft Academy, and what life was like in a small town in central Maine. Anne was surprised to notice that the first half had ended. She had been so involved in her conversation with June she had hardly seen much of the game, but promised she would pay closer attention during the second half.

During the intermission June steered their conversation to Doug Bateman. Despite her subtle prodding Anne listened but offered little in the way of her own impression of Doug, other than to say that he was a good detective, easy to work with, and that she was learning a lot. June and most of her friends thought that Doug's wife Beth must be insane. Her desire to relocate away from her hometown, and her dream of finding success in the outside world, seemed ludicrous to June. June and Beth had been close friends until Beth had left for Bowdoin, but June thought Beth was never the same person when she returned from that "snooty" college. After Beth and Doug had married and moved into their Bowerbank home, Beth didn't seem to ever be completely content. It was as if she now viewed Dover-Foxcroft from a distance, as an outsider just visiting from the real world.

The consensus was that Beth had the perfect husband, and more than a few women in town were either thinking about or actively making an effort to snag him. Part of his appeal for them, of course, was that many of them had made attempts, going all the way back to high school, to peel him away from Beth, but hadn't had any success. Beth, Anne learned, was not the only girl to have followed Doug's high school wrestling career with great enthusiasm. In addition to being tall, broad shouldered, and quite good looking, with bright blue eyes and an easy smile, Doug was quite the athlete, June stated with a broad grin. A dozen or more girls would often flock to the home meets to cheer him on and to admire how impressively he filled out his wrestling singlet.

Doug was very popular in high school, June said, and had a small group of close friends. He had always been quiet, almost shy, and it took a while for him to warm up to people. Even though he was sort of a straight arrow, and a serious student at Foxcroft Academy, Doug wasn't considered a nerd. He smoked weed and drank beer with the guys and didn't shy away from shutting down showoffs and bullies. Nobody picked on freshmen or any of the foreign students at Foxcroft if Doug was around. June remembered the time a wrestler from a large high school down on the coast somewhere had trash talked Doug in front of the crowd just before he was to compete against him in the state tournament, and then had passed out when Doug audibly but "accidently" dislocated his shoulder in a takedown.

June also remembered like it was yesterday the cold winter afternoon when she was with a group of people that had gathered to watch a large stray dog that had fallen through the ice on the Sebec River over by Milo, east of Dover-Foxcroft. Doug was driving by and happened to see the people watching the dog struggling to keep its head above water, but making no move to try to save it. Grabbing a rope and blanket from the back seat of the Jeep, Doug pushed into the cluster of onlookers, looped one end of the rope under his arms and handed the other end to one of them, along with the blanket, before walking and sliding straight out on the ice. He broke through into the freezing river right next to the dog, gathered it in his arms, and yelled, "Pull us in." When Doug and the dog reached shore, the man with the blanket wrapped it around Doug's shoulders, and Doug promptly removed it and wrapped up the dog and carried it to his car without a backward glance. To June, that was Doug Bateman in a nutshell.

Anne's daydreaming was interrupted by their arrival in Greenville. As they parked in front of Northwoods Outfitters she noticed a young woman watching them through the window. She met them as they came through the front door, visibly trembling, eyes wide with fear.

"I'm really scared. Is he going to kill me? Can you protect me?"

Doug put his hand out, and as she shook it, he quietly replied.

"He's not after you Charlotte. You're safe. Don't worry. Go get your coat."

As Charlotte hurried toward the back of the store Doug turned to Anne.

"There are too many people in here – take her next door to the library and ask to use their classroom. It'll be quiet there. I'm going to talk to her boss, and then I will be right over. See if you can calm her down."

Anne watched Charlotte put her coat on and walked with her across the street to the Shaw Public Library. When Doug joined them a few minutes later Charlotte had calmed down considerably. She was in her early 20s, a full foot shorter than Anne and Doug, and wore Birkenstocks, red striped socks, black tights, and a "Moosehead Lake" t-shirt that showed off her full sleeve tat of an elaborate swirling dragon. Short cropped black hair tipped with purple highlights, dark iridescent eye shadow, and vivid red lipstick rounded out her presentation of self.

Doug introduced himself and let Charlotte know that her boss had given her the rest of the day off. He then showed her the morgue photo of their victim. Charlotte confirmed that it was her friend Angeline Bouchard and then rushed to tell them everything she knew. Doug and Anne just let her talk. Charlotte said that she had first met Angeline at the Whoopie Pie Festival the previous summer when they had admired each other's tats. Angelina was about her age and had driven down for the festival from her home in Saint Georges, where she worked as a waitress. The two had hung out all afternoon and then made the rounds of the bars in Dover-Foxcroft that evening, ending up at the Bear's Den.

Angeline had stayed over with Charlotte that night, and headed back over the border the next day. Charlotte had gone up for a day to Angeline's last fall, and then had invited her to come down the previous week to go snowmobiling. Charlotte had joined the Moosehead Riders, a popular snowmobile club in Greenville, as a way of meeting people after moving up to Moosehead from Dexter the previous Thanksgiving. Her uncle, who she was living with until she could afford a place of her own, loaned her his snowmobile whenever she wanted to ride with the club.

Charlotte and Angeline had gone on the club's B52 Commemorative Ride on Thursday, and they had a blast. The snow was deep and well packed, and they took turns driving the sled while the other held on behind. The club riders headed east out of Greenville and up the side of Elephant Mountain to the site where a B52 Stratofortress flying on a low-level training flight out of Westover Air Force Base had crashed in January of 1963. The wreckage had been left in place as a memorial to the airmen who had died that day, and was a popular tourist destination.

At the crash site Angeline had struck up a conversation with one of the other riders who Charlotte had not seen before. He was older, had a soft voice and dark, almost black eyes. On the way back down the mountain Angeline couldn't stop talking about him. He was from Quebec City, she said, worked in a law office, spoke excellent Quebecois, seemed really nice, and had invited her to meet him at the Bear's Den for Thursday night karaoke that evening. Back in town, he had ridden off without talking to them again, giving Angeline a brief wave goodbye. Charlotte was a little miffed that the invitation didn't include her, and that Angeline didn't appear to care at all that she was abandoning her to go off with a man she barely knew. When Angeline left that evening to drive down to Dover-Foxcroft she said she wasn't sure if she would be back to spend the night at Charlotte's or not – she might just drive straight back to Saint Georges. Charlotte never saw Angeline again, and her phone calls to her since last week had gone unanswered. With a growing sense of frustration, Doug asked. "Do you remember what this guy's name was?"

"Angeline told me. It was a funny name, French, I guess – Tom Torkma or something."

Anne asked.

"Tom Torquemada?"

"Maybe. Yeah, that could be it."

Doug asked the next question.

"What did he look like?"

"Well, like I said, he was regular sized, kinda athletic, with dark eyes."

"What else?"

"I couldn't see his face. It was like 5 degrees, and we all kept our face masks on."

"What did they talk about?"

"I have no idea. They spoke French, and I can't speak it. It was really rude if you ask me."

"Is there anything else you remember?" Anne asked. "What he was wearing? What kind of snowmobile he was riding? Anything?"

Charlotte paused, wrinkled her brow in thought, and replied.

"No, not really. It was an older snowmobile, white and red – I don't know the different makes very well. He was wearing a full snowmobile suit. I think it was Cabella's, black, and pretty new. And he had a funny smudge under one eye

– like the black stuff football players wear – not sure if it was a bruise or grease or something."

Doug and Anne asked Charlotte questions for another 20 minutes but weren't able to learn anything more of any value. They now knew the killer spoke Quebecois, said he was from Quebec City, wore a black snowmobile suit and rode a red and white snowmobile. Not much more to add to their profile.

10.

PHOEBE ISLAND

Following the interview of Charlotte Laughlin in late January, just a week after the murder of Angeline Bouchard, the Ice Maiden case stalled for a full two months. Angeline's car was found the day after the Laughlin interview at the back of the parking lot at the Bear's Den, but it didn't appear that she ever made it inside for karaoke night. No one remembered having seen her, either alone or with anyone, and not being a local, she would have stood out from the regular karaoke night customers. If the killer had abducted her from the Bear's Den parking lot on Thursday night, which seemed likely, then he had held her, and tortured her, someplace near Sebec Lake for 48 hours.

Almost a thousand lakefront cottages and permanent homes bordered Sebec Lake and any one of them might have provided his hiding place. Over the next several weeks Doug and Anne, with help from the Sheriff's Office and the Dover-Foxcroft Police, systematically checked every dwelling around the lake, and came up with nothing. Canvasing of surrounding areas and appeals to the public for information similarly came up empty. The killer had faded back into the shadows. Although his victim was an outsider and apparently had been selected at random, Anne and Doug suspected that the killer had a larger plan and that it had a specific local focus. They feared that Angeline Bouchard was just the opening move in the killer's still unfolding game of death.

The day after Charlotte Laughlin's interview Anne and June looked at the south shore Victorian cottage that was for sale, and while it needed a lot of work, the price was reasonable, particularly compared to Ann Arbor real estate. Anne's bid was quickly accepted, and June was helping her find local skilled tradesmen who were happy to find work in the middle of the winter installing new windows and redoing the kitchen and bathroom.

Her friendship with June continued to grow, and Anne had met several times with Ashlee and her teammates on the Foxcroft basketball team. She liked their coach, Steve Alexander, a history teacher about her own age, and they had talked about the possibility of starting a summer basketball program. Anne was spending a lot of time on the road, learning the county and meeting local law enforcement officers. She participated in a raid on a meth lab up near Beaver Cove on Moosehead Lake, investigated a string of burglaries around Guilford, and handled an increasing number of domestic disputes and assaults, mostly alcohol or drug-related.

Anne and Doug were pulled back into the Ice Maiden case in late March, following a house fire on Phoebe Island. One of the smallest islands in Sebec Lake, and situated only a hundred feet offshore, just up the road from Doug's Bowerbank home, Phoebe Island was essentially a rock about 50 feet in diameter that extended ten feet or so above the lake at high water. A two-story white cottage took up almost the entire surface of the island. Many of the neighbors considered it an eyesore.

Doug got the call from the Bowerbank Volunteer Fire Department a little before midnight, and as he reached for his cellphone on the bedside table he noticed a red glow out his bedroom window. By the time he had dressed and reached Dennis Olmstead's place on the shoreline nearest to Phoebe Island it was clear that they were too late to do much except watch the flames roar up into the dark night. There was a slight breeze that night and fortunately it was out of the northwest, blowing the debris and embers from the fire out across the lake rather than shoreward.

The water was quite shallow between the mainland and Phoebe Island, and looking out at the expanse of thin ice, which was well illuminated by the fire, Doug noticed a narrow ice-free corridor, about the width of a canoe, connecting the island and the shore. Unfortunately the cluster of onlookers drawn by the flames had trampled the shoreline sufficiently to erase any hope of finding footprints or other evidence of an arsonist's trail. There was little doubt that it was arson; that the fire had been set deliberately, and the assembled onlookers had already begun joking about whom among them was responsible. No one seemed particularly saddened by the fire. An outsider, Herbert Walker III, a New Jersey developer, owned the island and the cottage, along with some lots up on Bowerbank Road. He only visited for a week or two each summer, and didn't seem to have hit it off with his neighbors.

Investigators from the Sheriff's Office came out early the next morning and conducted a brief inspection of the charred and still smoldering debris pile – all that was left of the cottage, and declared the fire to be suspicious in nature. Before they could begin their full follow-up of the fire, however, Walker arrived from New Jersey and began arrangements to clear the island of the charred wreckage. Ignoring the pending investigation, he had decided to go ahead and rebuild on the existing footprint of the cottage, which was allowed under Maine's shoreline zoning law.

The following day Doug stopped in at the Sebec Country Store for a gallon of milk and some eggs, and noticed Junior Willis grabbing a six-pack of PBR out of the beer cooler. Junior had been in Doug's class at Foxcroft Academy, but dropped out to join the army. He now lived with his mother off the Old Stagecoach Road and got along day to day on veteran's benefits and by doing odd jobs around Sebec. Today Junior looked like a coal miner, with black overalls and black soot on his face and hands. The odor of burned wood filled the store. Doug asked why he was so dirty, and with a gap tooth smile, Junior replied that he and his cousin had been hired to haul the Phoebe Island cottage debris off to the dump. Surprised that the clearing of debris had already begun, Doug asked Junior to let him know if they found anything unusual. Laughing loudly, Junior reached into his pocket and proudly held up what he had found that morning on Phoebe Island, blurting out the punch line.

"OK Doug, I will be sure to keep an eye out for you."

In his hand Junior displayed a shiny glass eye with a bright green iris. Doug confiscated the eye and immediately drove out to Phoebe Island. A makeshift floating walkway had been extended out to the island from the front lawn of Dennis Olmstead's year-round home on the adjacent mainland. Olmstead and Herb Walker, the island's owner, were standing at the near end of the walkway and having a heated discussion about whether the debris from the burned cottage could be moved off the island across the floating walkway and then across Olmstead's property to the road. As Doug reached the two men, Walker turned his anger toward him.

"I'm tired of telling people to get off my property. You are trespassing, and I will have you arrested if you don't get your ass out of here."

Dennis Olmstead, who had been enjoying the argument with Walker, barely controlled his laughter at the man's angry outburst. He was paying close attention now so he could recount the unfolding drama in detail that evening over cocktails with his north shore neighbors. Walker didn't remember his previous encounter with Doug, four or five summers ago, when he had caught Doug's son Eric picking wild raspberries on his land and had marched him back to Doug's house to confront his parents with the boy's misdeed.

Doug smiled calmly at Walker, noting his beet red face and the pulsing veins in his neck, and stepped closer, invading his personal space. Hoping to provide Dennis with a good story to tell, he adopted his most officious and formal tone of voice.

"Mr. Walker, you're right. I am one of your neighbors. You may not remember, but we met several years ago when you caught my son picking raspberries on your property. I live right over there."

Doug pointed along the curving lakeshore to the rocky point where his home could be seen nestled back in the trees. Walker opened his mouth to continue his tirade, but Doug raised his hand to stop him, while producing his state police credentials with his other hand.

"But I'm not here as a neighbor today. I'm a detective with the major crimes unit of the Maine State Police, and am investigating a possible homicide. I should point out that we are not on your property. We're standing on Dennis' front lawn. So I am not trespassing on your land. I just checked, and the county sheriff's office suspects that the fire here was deliberately set, and their investigation is not yet complete. So any effort on your part to clear the debris will have to wait.

In addition, I am declaring Phoebe Island a possible homicide scene, and we will be coordinating our investigation with the county. The island is officially closed, and will be cordoned off. If you or any of your workers – Junior Willis or his cousin, or anyone else you employ, returns to the island, you will be arrested and charged. Do you understand?"

Herbert Walker III opened and closed his mouth several times and then abruptly turned and stalked off toward the road where his SUV was parked.

Doug turned to Dennis, shook his hand, and made a suggestion.

"Dennis, come to think of it, this puts Herb the third here in a difficult position. The investigation could easily drag on into the late summer or fall, delaying any possibility of rebuilding on the island. In addition, if we find a murder victim in that burned building, and I think we will, he is going to have a difficult time selling the island, once it's cleaned up, with or without a house on it. It would make a lot of sense for him to try to sell the island now, as is, and be done with it. Maybe you or someone else representing concerned neighbors could advise him, and make a generous offer to help him out of a difficult situation. It might also be worth looking into the tax advantages of granting a conservation easement to the state, or even an outright gift of the island to the state."

Dennis nodded enthusiastically.

"Doug, that's an excellent idea – I'll start making some calls."

Turning to gaze out over the lake, Doug thought he could see a large bird perched by the eagle nest on Pine Island. Judging from its size there was a good chance it was an eagle. Maybe there would be a nesting pair this summer.

Turning back to Dennis, he asked a favor.

"Dennis, I'm going to block off the walkway out to the island with some crime scene tape. If you can keep an eye on things to make sure nobody goes out there, it would be a big help. I hope to have people out here sometime tomorrow to start excavation of the debris pile. Is there any chance we could access the walkway across your property? It would save us a lot of time."

"Sure," Dennis replied. "No problem at all. Any way I can help, just ask."

After taping off the walkway Doug headed into town, making three calls along the way. The first was to Anne, who was over in Dexter looking into a burglary. He told her about the glass eye being found on the island and that he had a strong suspicion they would find another *auto de fe* victim beneath the remains of the burned cottage. Anne said she would meet him back at the courthouse as soon as she could.

His second call was to Melinda Blood at the University of Maine, asking if she might know of any archaeologists at the university who might be interested in helping with their investigation. She looked up the faculty listing for the Department of Anthropology and gave him several names and contact phone numbers. His first call immediately went to an answering machine, and the message indicated that Professor Sandweiss was conducting field research in Peru until the end of May. Doug's second call was answered on the first ring by Dr. George Miller, who was immediately enthusiastic about the possibility of excavating the burned debris and cooperating with the state police in their investigation. Miller sounded perfect for the job. He had just completed excavation of a thousand-year-old Native American village site in southeast Missouri that had been burned to the ground, and he was very familiar with the challenges and correct procedures for the excavation of burned timbers. Miller also thought he might be able to interest Jane Emery in taking part in the excavation. Emery was a visiting bioarchaeologist from the Smithsonian Institution, and she had considerable experience in studying human skeletal remains recovered from archaeological contexts, including the challenging analysis of the fragmentary remains of human cremations.

Miller said that from his end the timing was perfect in several respects. Spring break was starting in a few days so he could easily pull together a small crew of students for the project. His department, it turned out, was also under increasing pressure from the university administration to strengthen their profile of service to the broader community, so the opportunity for a highly publicized cooperative venture with the state police was of clear benefit to them.

Miller was as good as his word, arriving at Phoebe Island with three enthusiastic student volunteers the next morning. The skeletal expert, Dr. Emery, he indicated, would drive out from campus if and when they did in fact find any human remains. Doug had also asked Junior Willis and his cousin to come by to tell them what they had done to disturb the debris pile, and more importantly, exactly where Junior had found the glass eye. Doug had been puzzled by its near pristine condition. Junior showed them the area along the south side of the burned wreckage where they had just started to remove roofing material, and also was able to explain why the glass eye was in such good shape. He hadn't found it in the burned remains of the cottage. It had been placed in plain sight on top of a mooring post at the island's small dock, safely away from the fire. Junior speculated that somebody wanted it to be found.

Once Professor Miller confirmed that Doug was not concerned with documenting the burned structure in detail, but rather was interested in determining if there was a body in the debris, he said he was confident he could give them an answer within a day or two. The structure, he explained, had pancaked down, with the exterior walls and ceiling of the ground floor collapsing down, along with the roof, forming a layer cake of sorts. They would set up a TST, a total station theodolite, on an elevated stand at the edge of the island, and use it to record the piece by piece removal of the remaining identifiable structural elements of the cottage, starting with the uppermost roofing layer and working down. As the debris was removed they would pile it up around the edge of the island at the waterline. He thought the process would progress pretty quickly, and casually mentioned that the local media should be arriving soon. Doug looked at him in stunned silence as Miller hurriedly explained.

"Well, we need the media coverage to get the administration off our backs. That was the whole idea- to show our relevance to the community and our contribution to the efforts of the state police to fight crime."

Doug recognized the price to be paid for the professional help.

"O.K., here's how it's going to work. No media on the island, no statements to them by anyone on your team other than you. Your talking points are limited; you are assisting state and county law enforcement in the investigation of a possible crime, as part of the university's and Anthropology Department's mission. Period. That's it – nothing about searching for a body, nothing about the glass eye. The mystery will actually work for you – look serious and thoughtful, but explain that you can't comment. You should also get a University of Maine flag or something as a background for interviews – they love that sort of stuff. Be sure to mention your department chair and refer reporters to her. She can then talk about all the wonderful things the university does for taxpayers in the state."

Dr. Miller flashed a big smile, nodded his agreement, and started giving instructions to his crew, while also pulling his cell phone out to make some calls. Doug and Anne spent most of the day in Dennis' living room watching the work progress, and periodically going out to observe the excavation close up. It was hard, dirty work. Doug arranged for a stack of pizzas to be delivered for lunch and Dennis set up a 50-gallon barrel fire for the crew to warm themselves. Several of the local TV stations from Bangor showed up around noon and did short interviews with Miller in front of a University of Maine banner, scheduled to air on the evening news. Doug and Anne briefly appeared on camera, thanking Dr. Miller, his volunteers, and the university for their invaluable participation in their investigation. As agreed, the cameras were kept a reasonable distance from the island and were only able to capture the removal of burned building fragments. Doug was relieved with the coverage that night – it was presented as a feel good story about how much the university contributed to the well being of the citizens of Maine.

The next morning Miller's crew worked their way down through the pancaked building, and finding no body on the second floor, began to remove the ceiling of the ground floor. They started at the outside edge and continued in toward the center. Work went much more slowly now, and with greater care, as if they were approaching the central burial chamber of an ancient tomb. If there was a body buried in the rubble, this was where it was most likely to be found. As they progressed in toward the center of the ground floor Miller at first expressed optimism about the good possibility of preservation of any human remains they might find, since the collapsing plaster ceiling appeared to have smothered the fire in places. They were recovering fragments of burned but still recognizable carpet and furniture.

His enthusiasm drained away, however, as they neared the center of the room and the unmistakable smell of cooked meat began to seep up from beneath the last remaining section of plaster and lath. Just before noon, as Doug and Anne watched, Miller and his volunteers lined up along one edge of the remaining ceiling section, lifted in unison, and pushed it over, exposing the center of the room and its grisly occupant. Miller and his crew quickly backed away, and one of his crew stumbled waist deep into the ice-cold waters of Sebec Lake before throwing up. Doug had expected to find a human skeleton, or fragmentary skeletal remains, with perhaps some fragments of charred soft tissue, but not this.

The body of what appeared to be a woman lay face up in the center of the floor. Her skin was charred and her hair had mostly burned away. Lengths of wire were coiled around her neck and waist, binding her tightly to a charred wooden post. A pile of charcoal and ash at the victim's feet marked where a fire had burned at the base of the stake that had held her upright before the ceiling had collapsed, knocking it and her to the floor. A falling beam had sliced into her now bloated abdomen, allowing her intestines to protrude out like blackened balloons. Her arms and legs had contracted into the classic pugilistic posture of fire victims, like a boxer in the ring. Her legs were bent at the knees, her arms were raised and flexed in a defensive position, and her fists were clenched. It wasn't clear whether she had been burned alive or if she was already dead when the flames first burst up around her. Her face had been burned away, leaving a charred black skull, and her eye sockets appeared to contain the heat-shattered remnants of bright green glass eyes.

After first borrowing a bed sheet from Dennis to cover the charred body, Doug called his partner Tom Richard to alert him to the discovery of a second victim. Tom called back within a few minutes to confirm that Peter Martell and the evidence response team were available and could drive up from Augusta mid-afternoon to begin to process the scene. The university crew was huddled in shocked silence, and Doug joined them. He first thanked them for all their excellent work and then let Dr. Miller know that the skeletal expert from the Smithsonian wouldn't be needed, as the forensic crime scene people were on their way. Dr. Miller assured him that they had not taken any photographs of the victim and indicated they were ready to pack up their equipment and head back to Orono. Doug thanked Dr. Miller and his crew again, shook their hands, and reminded them to not discuss what they had found sealed under the plaster layer with anyone. Any inquiries from news organizations should be referred to Tom Richard with the state police in Orono. Looking at the fresh-faced students with a stern expression, Dr. Miller repeated Doug's admonition. Doug was skeptical that the crew would keep quiet for very long, and hoped that all they saw was a burned human body and not the evidence that the victim had been burned at the stake.

As the university van pulled away from the crime scene and headed up Fire Road 3 to the Bowerbank Road, Anne noticed a small momentary flash of sunlight reflecting off something across the lake on the south shore, and thought she saw movement in the trees. She watched for a while longer without seeing anything more before mentioning it to Doug. By the time he had turned to look, the man watching them from the south shore had lowered his binoculars and faded back into the darkness of the forest.

11.
THE WATCHER

The evidence response team made good time up from Augusta, pulling into Dennis Olmstead's driveway on the north shore of Sebec Lake a little after 2:30. The afternoon sun was bright in a cloudless sky and it was already well up into the 40s, offering good conditions for processing the crime scene. After taking a quick look at the charred corpse, Peter Martell, leader of the ERT, dropped the sheet covering her back into place and turned to Anne.

"You can call the funeral home and ask them to get transport out here as soon as possible. We handle bodies from suspicious house fires several times a year and have a good system worked out, so this won't take long. First we'll slide a tarp under the body and the charred post it's attached to as a single unit, and then wrap it and strap it onto a plywood panel. The panel and wrapped tarp then go into an oversized body bag for the trip down to Augusta. That way we can keep the attached wires intact, and not run the risk of any separation of extremities. Hands and feet tend to fall off of crispy critters if you're careless."

Smiling broadly, he added.

"The chief medical examiner is going to love this one."

Across the lake on the south shore, the man Anne had glimpsed watching them that morning was back and had settled in for an afternoon's entertainment. Seated in a folding lawn chair hidden behind a clump of blueberry bushes, he had an expensive digital camera with telephoto lens slung over his shoulder within easy reach. Observing the arrival of the ERT on Phoebe Island, he set his binoculars down and typed rapidly on the keyboard of his laptop computer. Once assured that the right program was open and running, he picked up a small white remote controller box, and powered up his newest gadget, a DJI Phantom Quadcopter Drone, and watched it glide smoothly north across the ice. Guiding it to a good altitude, where the HD video camera could record the ERT team and hopefully would not be noticed or heard on Phoebe Island, he locked the drone into stationary position above the island, focused the camera, and checked to ensure that the video stream was recording on his laptop. Reception and resolution were excellent and he was eagerly anticipating the moment when the sheet covering the body would be removed, allowing him to zoom in for a close-up.

Suddenly the video feed from the drone went dark, and a second later the sound of a loud gunshot rolled across the lake. Looking up to where the drone had been hovering he could only see empty sky. Close behind him, he heard someone say in a clear voice.

"Nice shot Dennis – just like shooting skeet, but easier." Turning in his chair, the watcher saw Doug Bateman return his cellphone to his left hand coat pocket. In his right hand, held down at his side, Doug held his Glock 9mm semiautomatic pistol.

In a relaxed, not unfriendly voice, Doug addressed the watcher.

"You don't need to get up just yet. Close up your laptop please, and fold your hands on top of it where I can see them."

The seated man complied, and as Doug moved around to his side, still about 10 feet away, he was surprised to hear the dark eyed man address him by name.

"Good afternoon Detective Bateman. There's no need for the weapon. I am not armed and there is no gun in my vehicle."

Doug holstered his weapon and replied.

"Am I correct in assuming that you are David Abernathy and the shiny new Range Rover in the driveway is yours?"

"Nicely done. I guess you ran the plate number?"

"Your vehicle registration lists a Portland address. What brings you up here Mr. Abernathy?"

"I have a place on the south shore down between South Cove and Tim's Cove. I spend a fair amount of time up here detective."

"And what's your interest in our investigation?"

Abernathy paused, frowned, and replied in a condescending tone.

"I don't have to answer any more of your questions. I have not broken any laws and might have to make a claim for the drone you just destroyed."

Standing up and folding his laptop and lawn chair, he continued.

"But I will tell you, I have an interest in serial killers, and the leisure time to pursue that interest. I find your case quite fascinating, based on what I have been able to learn so far. Tell me, does the victim on the island over there have green eyes by any chance?"

Getting no response, Abernathy turned and walked toward his car. Doug called after him.

"I will probably have more questions for you in the next few days, Mr. Abernathy. I'll be in touch."

Doug pulled into Dennis Olmstead's driveway at the Phoebe Island crime scene a half hour later. Anne watched him arrive and walked up to the driver's side window.

"Not much has happened since you left. The forensics team hasn't found much other than the victim and stake. Looks like the fire pretty much destroyed any other evidence. There was a burned gas can close to the base of the stake, so the killer used an accelerant to start the blaze. The Lary Funeral Home is sending a hearse out in a few hours to transport the victim down to Augusta for the autopsy. It should be day after tomorrow. Good thing Dennis warned us before he shot down the drone. We didn't even know it was up there. What was that all about?"

They sat on a bench in the bright afternoon sun, sheltered from the wind by Dennis' boathouse, and Doug filled her in.

"It looks like we have a murder groupie. It was his drone. His name is David Abernathy, with a permanent address in Portland and a home here up toward Tim's Cove. I don't know him but I think I know the house – a hideous lakeside Masshole McMansion in the middle of a big lawn. They must have cut down hundreds of trees, which isn't allowed under shoreline protection laws, but he got around them somehow. Judging from his Range Rover and address in Portland he's got some money as well as time on his hands. He said he has an interest in serial killers and he finds our case fascinating. He's a definite squirrel but hopefully will keep his distance. He asked if our victim had green eyes so he has probably been talking to Junior Willis. He has also somehow concluded that the Phoebe Island body and the Greeley's Landing murder are connected, so he might have other sources too. As soon as we are finished here we can see what the Internet has on Mr. Abernathy and also check with MCU-South to see what they know about him."

Wikipedia had a long entry on David Abernathy. He was sixty-four years old, born in Boston, dropped out of Harvard his freshman year and got a job working at a crab shack on Route 1 just north of Portland. He borrowed some money from his father, bought the crab shack, and within ten years had another half dozen seafood restaurants along the Maine coast.

His net worth grew steadily as his chain of restaurants expanded and then took an exponential jump when he married Judith Aronson, an heiress he met while on a cruise along the Dalmatian Coast. She was older than Abernathy by a good ten years and it caused quite a society stir when she married a much younger man who ran restaurants for a living. But they seemed to be happy, by all accounts, and were married for almost ten years before she died tragically in a boating accident off Bar Harbor. Abernathy sold his restaurants soon after the death of his wife and had since lived a life of leisure. He had a variety of interests including big game hunting, often on private hunting reserves in Texas, and adding to his collection of vintage wooden boats – mostly pre-war Chris-Craft, Hacker-Craft, and Gar Wood gentleman racers and runabouts. He owned homes in Portland and Dover-Foxcroft in Maine, as well as a place in Santa Fe, New Mexico, and a large lakefront estate on Lake Winnipesaukee over in New Hampshire, where he kept his collection of trailer queen woodies.

Doug checked a few more online sources for information on Abernathy, including a story in Forbes Magazine that mentioned his estimated worth in the neighborhood of 200 million dollars. He also found a number of newspaper articles from the Portland Press Herald, including several covering his wife's death, and learned that he was a friend of Governor Paul LePage and had made substantial donations to his election campaigns.

Doug then called a longtime friend, a detective who worked in MCU-South, which covered Cumberland County and the greater Portland area. From him Doug got a much more candid, and concerning, profile of the man he had found watching the Phoebe Island crime scene from the south shore. Abernathy had no criminal record but he had a long history of encounters with law enforcement agencies in Maine, none of which had ever resulted in formal charges being filed. He had been a person of interest in his wife's death but the investigation never went anywhere. Abernathy had been the only witness to her falling overboard when he made a sharp turn in their vintage 25' Gar Wood triple cockpit runabout, and her body was never recovered. A formal inquest had been held and her death had been ruled accidental. A number of 911 domestic abuse calls had been received from a series of women over the years since his wife's death, but all the callers declined to press charges. He had also been drunk in public and involved in public altercations along the coast on a fairly regular basis, but never charged.

Of even more concern to Doug was Abernathy's increasing fascination over the past decade with murder cases coast to coast in which the victims were young women. He had repeatedly been cautioned for becoming too involved in ongoing investigations and had been suspected on numerous occasions of attempting to acquire case reports and information from witnesses and other individuals involved in the cases. His efforts to gain information were thought to include bribing law enforcement personnel and employing computer hackers and private investigators. So far, however, nothing had ever been proven.

Doug thought about Abernathy's interest in their current case for a few minutes, absently doodling on a blank page in his notebook, before calling Tom Richard.

"Hey Rocket, what's up in the big city?"

Doug listened to Tom bitch for several minutes about their new commanding officer at MCU–North, whom Tom had started to refer to as "Lieutenant Dud", both because Tom thought he was a dud, and as a shorthand reference to Dudley Do-Right, a clueless Canadian Mountie cartoon character.

"Well, I'm glad I am not over there in Orono while you break him in Tom. I'm calling because we need to take all our Sebec Lake case files off the secure server over there. Anne and I will keep them encrypted and on an external hard drive that will be kept in the safe over here when we aren't working on them, and we'll access them using a laptop that's not connected to the Internet. I know it sounds paranoid, but we learned this morning that the case has attracted the interest of a nut-case homicide groupie from Portland who has a place on Sebec. His name is David Abernathy and he has a lot of money and appears to have a history of hiring experts to hack into law enforcement computer systems. I'd like to head that off before he tries, if he hasn't already done so. Also, can you find out all you can on Abernathy – particularly real estate and businesses he owns or has an interest in up here in Piscataquis County, as well as his friends and family and business associates? Does he have any places other than his lakeshore house up here – maybe a hunting cabin or something? He has a new Range Rover, but what about other vehicles – a pickup truck, ATVs, snowmobiles, or boats? I'm hoping he is just a Sherlock Holmes wannabe and that he will limit himself to nibbling around the edges, but it won't hurt to find out as much as we can about him now in case he develops into a person of interest."

A short time later Doug and Anne walked down to Allie–Oops, the sports bar at Pat's Pizza, taking the corner table at the back which had a good view of both the front door and the side hallway over to the restaurant. Anne ordered a Sauvignon Blanc, and Doug an Allagash beer. They talked over the case and their next steps. Anne agreed that they should keep the case files well protected from the possibility of Internet hacking, while also finding out as much as they could about Abernathy. His home up by Tim's Cove was only 15 minutes by snowmobile across the lake from where the first body had been found. If he owned another, smaller place off the lake, they should take a look at it. And if he owned a white snowmobile, he would become even more interesting. Anne said she would check at the library and at the Ace Hardware to see if anyone recognized him, ask Beth if he ever came in to the Coffee House, and see if the Toad remembered him or his Range Rover. The Toad had a good memory for people and their vehicles.

June and Jim Torben walked in the front door of Allie-Oops, brushing off the snow that had begun to fall, and Doug waved them over. As they reached the table, June glanced at Anne first, then Doug.

"The girls are staying late at school for play practice – they're doing 'Our Town' this year and Ashlee has the role of Emily. We figured we would sneak out for dinner by ourselves for once. Date night."

Doug glanced across the table to Anne, and replied. "Maybe we could all have dinner. I haven't had their cheeseburger in a while."

Anne nodded, pretending not to notice June's smile, and Jim and June pulled up chairs from a nearby table. Jim asked Doug if he had read the recent Department of Inland Fisheries and Wildlife status report on how Maine's moose population had fared over the winter. Maine had the largest moose population in the lower 48, estimated to be in the range of 60,000 – 70,000 animals, and the large ungainly animals were both a big tourist draw and the top target for Maine hunters. Each year thousands of hopeful Mainers entered the moose lottery, vying for one of the limited number of moose hunting permits that were issued.

There was widespread concern over a continuing decline in the Maine moose population, particularly in the last two years, apparently due to unusually warm fall weather and a resultant explosion in winter tick populations. As a result of the decline in Maine's moose herds, the IFW had reduced the number of moose permits from 4,000 down to less than 2,800 the previous year, and Jim and other avid moose hunters were worried about another potential reduction. Jim had not won a coveted permit in the lottery for the last five years and was hoping for better luck this year. The IFW was two years into a five-year initiative to try to figure out what was causing the moose decline and had radio-collared more than a hundred animals to monitor their health through the winter seasons. So far they had not come up with much, other than documenting very high tick infestation rates.

Anne ordered another glass of wine when her fish and chips arrived, and laughed at the good-natured ribbing the others gave here about not having a cheeseburger, her usual choice for lunch and dinner.

"Well, you know," she said, "It's always a good idea to try new things and expand your horizons."

Again, Anne ignored June's wide smile and upturned eyebrows, and resisted the urge to tell her to shut up. Conversation flowed easily across the table during dinner, from the building resentment in central Maine communities to the proposed East-West Corridor, to how long it would be until ice-out.

The threat of an East-West Corridor had been looming over the region for a number of years. The proposed project would involve using private funds to cut a five-hundred-meter-wide corridor across the state to allow trucks, and a suspected pipeline, to carry oil and other commodities from Canada across Maine to ports on the coast. Several of the proposed routes, which were still only described in vague terms, would impact Dover-Foxcroft and other nearby towns, and change the peaceful landscape of vast forests and small farms forever. Signs opposing the corridor were common along the roadsides and many communities had passed local ordinances designed to keep it away from them. Suspicions were running high regarding the possibility that the current state government would allow eminent domain to be used to seize the land needed for the corridor, and promises that it would bring a boom in tourism and thousands of local jobs were roundly jeered.

Speculation surrounding ice-out was a springtime tradition across New England, as it was a major date on local calendars, marking the waning of winter and the promise of warmer weather. For people with camps on Sebec, or an interest in the lake, there was an annual contest to see who could predict the day and time that the ice on the lake would break up, allowing free passage or "open navigation" by a boat all the way from Willimantic at the western end of the lake to the dam at Sebec Village at the eastern end. Everyone's predictions were listed on the Sebec Lake website, along with ice-out dates going back to 1879, and the winner was announced the day after ice-out occurred, usually sometime from mid-April to the first week in May. Neither Anne nor Doug had placed their bets yet, and both were cagey about what date they would pick.

As they were chipping in to pay the bill, Doug mentioned that he thought the eagles might be back and nesting on Pine Island. As he voiced his hopes for the eagles return he realized that Anne, June, and Jim were the first people he had told. He hadn't said anything as yet to Beth, and wasn't sure that he would.

12.

A POPE'S PEAR

Anne was in the kitchen of her small rental house on Autumn Street in Dover-Foxcroft early the next morning, packing up her kitchen utensils in anticipation of the move to her south shore cottage that was now only a week away. WMEH, the NPR station out of Bangor was on the radio and Charles, her large white tomcat, was entertaining her by hiding in the cardboard boxes scattered around the room and rushing out to attack her ankles at regular intervals.

Over the winter, as the cottage renovations were going forward, she and June had talked a lot about how to upgrade the cottage and make it a year-round home while still retaining its original character. Now their plans were taking shape. The replacement wooden sash windows were a close match to the originals, and the recently installed energy efficient baseboard heating system was unobtrusive. Anne had also bought a used Jøtul wood stove from a lobsterman in Phippsburg, down on the coast, to replace the cottage's cracked cast-iron antique. She kept the kitchen cabinets and original two-basin enamel cast iron sink, but added soapstone counter-tops along with a new stove and refrigerator.

There was still a lot of work to do on the place but it was livable, and she was anxious to get started on a few indoor projects. The floors and most interior walls of the cottage were 80-year old pine that had aged to a beautiful dark golden color, and would be pretty much left alone. She planned on cleaning and resealing the floors, washing the pine walls, then starting in on painting the new window frames and kitchen cabinets a dark forest green.

Once warmer weather arrived Anne could start the major outdoor projects, with her main goal for the summer being power washing and staining the cedar shake shingle exterior of the cottage a dark brown, with forest green trim, to blend in with the surrounding forest. Doug had a paint sprayer he said he would lend her, and the "Paint Queen" over at the Ace Hardware had helped her pick out the exterior colors. Once the exterior painting of the cottage was finished she had plans to rebuild the small boathouse on her property, and if zoning allowed, to turn the upper storage area into a sleeping loft for guests.

Anne's packing was interrupted by a call from Doug asking if she could pick him up at the Sebec Country Store in about an hour – the autopsy for the Phoebe Island victim had been moved up to late morning, and they could make it if they left soon. Anne said she would stop at the Center Theatre Coffee House for coffee and donuts on the way to pick him up. Doug responded.

"Just coffee. No donuts. We're going to make a quick stop at the mother ship." He hung up before Anne could ask what the mother ship was.

The Coffee House was busy when Anne got there, and Beth seemed uncharacteristically out of sorts. She ordered two large lattes, and when Beth turned to the espresso machine, Anne thought she moved awkwardly. As Beth steamed the milk she unconsciously pulled up her left sleeve, revealing a string of bruises from her wrist up to her elbow. Quickly pulling her sleeve down, Beth turned to look at Anne and realized that she had seen her arm. Anne's inquiring gaze as she paid for the coffee was met with stony silence.

Doug was waiting by his Cherokee when Anne pulled up, and he told her to continue east on Route 6 rather than turning south on the Old Stagecoach Road.

"Isn't this way longer?" Anne asked.

"In terms of distance, Yes, definitely. But it takes about the same time to get down to Augusta this way since we pick up I 95 sooner, and can make better time. Plus, we need to go through Milo."

Anne decided not to ask why. When they reached Milo about 15 minutes later and crossed over the Sebec River into downtown, Doug asked her to park. When she asked why, he pointed out the driver's side window to the other side of the street, where a small sign announced "Elaine's Café and Bakery." Reaching for the door handle, Doug said.

"Your first visit to the mother ship."

Ten minutes later, having been introduced to the bakery ladies, the café staff, and a few of the customers, Anne walked back to the Land Cruiser with Doug, carrying a white pastry box holding a dozen donuts. She had been contemplating one of the more elaborate varieties but Doug had insisted on the basic plain donut for her first visit. As they drove east out of Milo he opened the box and held it out for her. Anne reached in, grabbed a warm donut, and took a bite.

As the donut hit her taste buds a number of impressions flooded over her. She was 11 again, and tasting something new and delicious that she had never experienced before, with the wonder of a young innocent. She also wondered if they should turn back – a dozen was not nearly enough. How many was Doug going to want to eat? And on a deeper, spiritual level, Anne experienced an epiphany: this donut was life. It was simple, unadorned, and straightforward. It was pure, yet carnal. And above all, it was fleeting. This was the crack cocaine of donuts.

A few miles east of Milo they crossed over the Pleasant River and Doug pointed out the Sharrow site, where the ancestors of Maine Native American groups had been coming to fish in the nearby rapids for almost 10,000 years. They made good time down to Augusta once they hit I 95, and as they pulled into the parking lot of the office of the chief medical examiner on Hospital Street, Doug asked if it was OK if they gave Mike Bowman, the Chief Medical Officer, the four donuts that survived their trip down from Dover-Foxcroft. Anne hesitated and then agreed, realizing that after viewing the autopsy she most likely would not be interested in any food on the return trip. Bowman met them at the door, and looking at the white paper box Doug was carrying, asked.

"Is that what I think it is?"

Doug nodded, and after taking the box from him, Bowman turned, and with a hurried, over the shoulder, "I'll be right back," disappeared into his office. He soon rejoined them, without the box, after closing and locking his office door.

"Can't be too careful around here," Bowman explained. "Elaine's donuts have a way of disappearing. Before we go in, I suggest you seriously consider watching from the observation room rather than up-close. The smell won't reach you in there. Otherwise, you may lose any enjoyment you take in barbequed meats for quite a while."

Doug and Anne both declined Bowman's advice, and once they had put on facemasks, gloves, and protective clothing, they entered the autopsy room. Even though the victim of the Phoebe Island fire was on a stainless steel examining table at the far side of the room, the smell enveloped them in a thick toxic fog as soon as they stepped through the swinging doors. Before Bowman could turn to observe their reaction, Doug handed Anne a small, almost invisible, swimmers nose clip, which she slipped over her nose. It seemed to help a bit, but the smell of burned and rotting meat was still overpowering. Fighting back a gag reflex,

Anne focused on taking measured normal breaths, while resisting a strong urge to turn around and make a rapid escape.

Seemingly disappointed in their lack of a visible response, Bowman led the two detectives over to the body, and deeper into the thick, putrid, and somewhat cloying fog that rose from the charred mass of human flesh.

"We already have answers to several basic questions. First, I think it's safe to connect this victim to the other Sebec murder. When the body was separated from the stake that it was wired to, we recovered a small unburned remnant of yellow cloth – likely part of a tabard like that worn by the first victim. We also found several partially burned strands from a rope that will, I am confident, match the noose recovered from the other murder victim. When added to the glass eye found at the Phoebe Island scene and the shattered glass eye fragments still retained in the victim's orbits, there is compelling physical evidence connecting the cases.

Second, analysis of a blood sample drawn from the victim showed a quite elevated blood carboxyhemoglobin saturation level – well above 50%, indicating that the victim was alive and breathing in the smoke and fumes generated by the fire. We will of course look for the presence of soot in the airways below the level of the vocal cords – that will support the CO-Hb finding that the victim was alive when the fire started. Death likely occurred within 5 minutes or so and cause of death was almost certainly from asphyxiation due to smoke inhalation. It's a homicide – no question."

Bowman paused briefly, appeared to collect his thoughts, and continued.

"So here is the likely scenario. The victim was still alive when wired to the stake in the center of the ground floor room of the Phoebe Island cottage, and probably unconscious. I certainly hope so. A considerable amount of wood was piled up at the base of the stake, gasoline or some other accelerant was pored over the faggots, and they were ignited. The wood fire would have quickly reached 1500 degrees Fahrenheit, igniting the victim and sucking up all the oxygen in the room, leading to death by asphyxiation. Within ten minutes or so at that temperature the victim's thicker dermal layer of skin started to shrink, allowing the underlying fat to leak out and burn."

Bowman paused and pointed to several places on the body where the charred skin had cracked and yellow fatty deposits had oozed out.

"Things get interesting at this point. Body fat is a good fuel source and given the right circumstances a body can sustain its own fire for up to seven hours before its soft tissue is mostly consumed, leaving just a skeleton coated in the greasy residue of burned flesh. That didn't happen here, however. The initial fire was so intense that it caused the plaster and lathing on the ceiling to collapse, probably within 15 minutes or so, covering the corpse and sealing it off from the fire. Part of the falling ceiling also sliced into her abdomen and opened her intestines in several places – that's the source of the strong fecal perfume. There does not appear to be much bleeding associated with the abdominal wound, which indicates death occurred prior to the collapse of the ceiling."

Warming to his topic, Bowman became more animated. "Above the victim, now sealed below the ceiling plaster and protected from direct contact with the flames, the fire continued to burn unchecked through the night. This slowly cooked the corpse at a lower temperature, resulting in what we have before us. It's roughly comparable to a weekend barbeque cook having a few beers and putting the bratwurst on a charcoal grill too soon, when the fire is still too hot. The skin of the brats quickly turns black, and they split, allowing fat to stream out from inside, feeding the flames. The cook rushes over, pulls them off the grill, and pronounces them done. But even though they are charred black on the outside they may be hardly cooked in the middle."

Smiling broadly now, Bowman turned to Anne and Doug and brightly asked.

"Shall we begin?"

Taking their silence as assent, he reached over and flicked the switch on the wall that activated the video and audio recording systems. Turning back to the table, he began.

"The victim is female, about five feet six inches, weighing 110 pounds, with a live weight of about 125 pounds if water loss during burning is factored in. Her body was found wired to a wooden stake under debris resulting from a house fire. Blood analysis indicates death was likely due to smoke inhalation. The victim's hair has burned off and the skin is extensively charred, with abundant heat induced shrinkage and splitting, exposing the underlying fat layer. A large laceration extends across the abdominal cavity, exposing and penetrating the large and small intestine, with resultant leakage of contents. This occurred post-mortem. Legs and arms are contracted and expressed in typical pugilist positions. Notable external evidence of premortem damage to the victim includes the removal of both eyes and the implanting of glass eyes, which subsequently shattered during the fire, leaving glass fragments *in situ* within the orbits. The glass eye fragments, cloth fragment, noose fibers, and wire that attached her to the stake have all been sent across the street to the crime lab for analysis and comparison to specimens recovered from the first murder. In addition, there is evidence of bi-lateral blunt trauma crushing injuries to the distal humerus-proximal radius/ulna, and distal femur-proximal tibia/fibula articulations- the elbow and knee joints, likely caused by a sledgehammer or other similar implement. All of the victim's teeth were also extracted premortem."

Bowman reached over and turned off the recording devices before continuing.

"The logical conclusion one might draw here is that the murderer extracted the victim's teeth in order to make it more difficult for us to ascertain her identity through dental records, but I don't think so. I think that the killer assumed that the first victim's soft tissue, and the evidence of torture it carried, including skin stripping and foot burning, would be well preserved in the cold waters of Sebec Lake. But he expected the soft parts of his second victim would be completely consumed by fire, so he made sure to leave damage that would survive the flames – shattered glass eye fragments in the orbits, extracted teeth, and crushed joints. He also left one other mark of his handiwork that did have to do with damage to soft tissue."

Bowman walked over to a computer on the counter and with a few keystrokes, brought up an x-ray image on the screen. Motioning Doug and Anne over, he pointed at a dark pineapple-shaped image on the screen.

"When we x-rayed the victim to document the joint trauma, we saw this. At first we thought it might be a grenade."

Bowman chuckled and continued.

"So we cleared the autopsy room and called the Bombs/Explosives Unit. They brought in a bomb-sniffing dog, a Lab named Baxter, but he wouldn't go anywhere near the body and strained at the leash to get out of here. His handlers were also pretty anxious to get away from the smell. They looked at the x-ray and decided it wasn't an explosive device. Any guesses what it is, detectives?"

Doug and Anne both shook their heads and Bowman, looking pleased, continued.

"I didn't have a clue either, but given the medieval torture angle on the killings, I did an Internet search on torture devices and came up with a likely answer. Shall we see if I'm right?"

Turning the recording equipment back on, Bowman stepped over to the charred human body and forced his gloved hand and arm between the victim's legs, releasing a new wave of stench that forced Doug and Anne to involuntarily take a step back. With a look of concentration he explored deeper into the groin area of the corpse and then appeared to be rotating his wrist, as if unscrewing something. After a dozen or so wrist rotations he paused, turned to look at them, and with a flourish, extracted his hand, while at the same time exclaiming, "Et viola."

Nestled in his hand was a pear-shaped metal object with a central screw mechanism at one end. Carrying it over to the sink, Bowman washed it off and then carried it back into camera range before displaying it for the detectives.

"It's called a 'Pope's Pear,' or a 'Pear of Anguish' and was supposedly used as a torture device as early as the 1600s, if not earlier. There were different versions, for different orifices – oral, anal, and vaginal, and this appears to be a vaginal pear. It was used to extract confessions from, and to purify, women who were suspected of fornicating with the devil or his familiars, or generally being of poor moral character. It has four spoon shaped leaves having sharpened tips and edges, and when screwed closed, as it is now, it resembles a small, elongated pear. It would be inserted in the closed position into the vagina of the accused and then opened far enough that the sharpened tips would encompass the cervix when fully extended into the vaginal cavity. Then the screw would be turned and the pear would close, slicing off the end of the cervix. I went back and looked at the autopsy notes and records for the first victim, and the cervix had been mutilated, likely with a Pope's Pear."

Setting the instrument of torture down on the counter, Bowman headed toward the doors of the autopsy room.

"I need a break before going any further with this. I don't see any point in you sticking around for the internal examination. We know it was homicide and we have good evidence to link it to the other victim. Once I look at the trachea I can confirm smoke inhalation as the cause of death. She is not going to tell us much about her identity, however – no fingerprints, no dental record for matching. A large section of skin was excised from her lower back, so she may have had a 'tramp stamp' tattoo. Given the burning I don't expect much likelihood of DNA preservation. You two will have to find out who she was some other way. Me, I'm going to have a cup of coffee and several donuts."

13.
THE OTTER

Driving back north on I 95, Doug and Anne had just passed the Waterville Exit when Anne checked her rear-view mirror and asked.

"Did you notice that white pickup three cars back?"

Doug checked the side mirror.

"With the camper on the back? Is he still back there? I think he picked us up way back at Elaine's in Milo."

"That's him – he pulled out of Elaine's parking lot just as we left."

Doug thought for a moment, and replied.

"I bet it's David Abernathy, our wealthy Sherlock Holmes with a drone. Maybe we can rattle his cage a bit."

Picking up his cell phone, Doug called Tom Richard, explained their situation, and asked if he could arrange for one of the state police cars from Troop E to be waiting for them on one of the northbound entrance ramps to I 95 somewhere around the Newport interchange – Pittsfield, Palmyra, Newport or Plymouth would work.

Anne looked at Doug with a puzzled expression, and Doug asked her to take the next exit – Fairfield, and if the pickup followed them, to pull over on the shoulder at the top of the ramp. Anne took the exit, and by the time she pulled over on the left shoulder the pickup was halfway up the ramp. It slowed momentarily and then pulled up beside them. Doug rolled down his window.

"Afternoon Mr. Abernathy. Any particular reason you've been following us all day?"

Abernathy smiled smugly.

"Oh, just curious as to how the autopsy went. Anything new to report?"

Doug smiled back.

"The analysis of recovered evidence isn't complete yet, but we should be issuing a statement to the press in a few days. Watch your paper for further developments."

As Doug began to roll up his window, Abernathy called out. "You can't keep the lid on this much longer Bateman – I can guarantee you that."

Anne had just merged back onto I 95 when Doug's cell phone barked.

"Hey Doug, the trooper is in position at the Pittsfield entrance – what's the plan?"

"We should be there in about 15 minutes. Tell him to watch for us. We are in a dark green Toyota Land Cruiser. Once we pass he should fall in a few cars back of the white pickup with a camper that will be following us. As soon as we get a few miles north of Pittsfield we will be increasing our speed gradually to 90 or so. If the pickup tries to keep up, let's see if the patrol can catch him going 15 over the limit – might even warrant a reckless driving citation."

Tom said he would relay the message and ended the call. Glancing out the side window as they passed the Pittsfield entrance, Doug saw the patrol car rolling down the ramp, slipping into traffic several cars behind the pickup. Anne increased her speed, and as they topped 90, with the pickup keeping pace, they both saw the bright flashing blue lights of the state police patrol car as he closed in on the white pickup.

Anne reduced her speed back down to the speed limit.

"Is this Abernathy going to be a problem?" she asked.

"Oh he's a problem alright. Might be a big problem. He has a lot of money, a lot of connections, and a history of violence against women. I think there is a good chance he killed his wife and got away with it. And his current fixation with serial killings of young women would certainly get the attention of profilers at Quantico. I'm not sure my efforts to shut him down and irritate him are the right approach, but I can't think of how else to handle it. Playing Lestrade to his Sherlock and sharing information with him is definitely the wrong thing to do, and he is not going to go away. For now, I think pushing him back with jabs when we can, in ways he can't easily counter, might keep him at arm's length. But we can count on him causing mischief. He is definitely a possibility as our killer, and we don't want to underestimate him. There is a definite threat there."

Doug's phone barked again, and he listened as Tom gave him an update.

"Hey Doug. As you might expect, Mr. Abernathy owns a lot of stuff. In addition to his Sebec Lake home and the white pickup that you already know about, he has a boat and trailer, two snowmobiles, and an ATV registered under his name at the Sebec address. More interesting, however, is his other property up there, which isn't registered to him directly, but under a real estate company that he owns. I tried finding it on Google Earth but apparently the address doesn't exist. It's just listed as a number on a fire road."

Doug wrote down the address and replied.

"OK Tom. Great work. I know about where that is – up between Bucks Cove and Bear Pond, on the north shore of Sebec Lake west of the narrows. Not much up there but logging roads, and not easy to get to. We'll check it out right after lunch."

Ending the call, Doug turned to Anne.

"Sherlock has an isolated camp up north of Sebec Lake. The only way to get there is over on Bowerbank Road and then up a logging road at the fire station and town hall. My place is on the way and I need to pick up a few things before we try to find it. How about lunch at my place? We can also pick up that paint sprayer I was going to loan you."

They changed vehicles at the Sebec Country Store and as they pulled into Doug's long driveway on the north shore Anne noticed a two-story tree house nestled in the trees and wondered how many other reminders there were of his son Eric. Parking by the large three bay garage, they walked 50 yards or so to the main lakefront cottage, passing a guest cabin and a small building that looked to be a tool shed converted into an office. It was still too cold to sit on the screened porch that stretched across the front of the cottage, so they ate their sandwiches at the ancient kitchen table, warmed by the bright afternoon sun. Anne had lots of questions about Doug's improvements to the camp over the years and was filing his answers away for possible application to her south shore place.

The paint sprayer and other items Doug wanted to pick up were stored in his workshop. As they stepped through the side door of the garage and Doug turned on the lights, he heard a sharp intake of breath from Anne, followed by silence, as she stood frozen in place just inside the door.

"Are you OK?" he asked.

Still speechless, Anne walked over and pulled the light dustcover from the bow of Doug's vintage Chris-Craft. Running her hand along the chine and pulling the dustcover back farther, uncovering the front seat and engine box, she replied.

"They didn't start making this version of the Sportsman until 1952, and changed to the Plexiglas windscreen in 1955, so I am guessing it's 1952 or 1953. The front seat pass-through is not original, and the seat upholstery of

103

course is new."

Anne paused at the back corner of the boat, glanced under the dust cover, read the name on the transom – "OTTER," and continued.

"Given the twin exhausts it's not the original engine, but otherwise the Otter looks to be all original, including the bottom, and it's in great condition. They made some beautiful boats at the Cadillac Plant. How long have you had it?"

"Five years. I bought from a guy down at Lake Winnipesaukee. It had been garage stored for three years and the bottom was dried out. Its engine, a Chrysler Crown, was shot, and anyway was not the original. Hi-Gloss Boat Restoration in Linconia brought her back to life and installed the new engine – a GMC Vortec. It's a good reliable small-block V-6 but I had a bitch of a time getting it running right. And you're close on your guesses. I tracked down the hull card for the boat at the Chris-Craft Archives in Newport News and it came off the assembly line at the Algonac Plant in July of 1952, just before they shifted production of the 17-foot utilities over to the Cadillac factory. So how do you know so much about woodies?"

"My dad loved wooden boats, especially Chris-Craft, since they were made in Michigan, and we had a 1951 22-foot Sportsman – a 'Golden Pond' boat, when I was a kid. I spent lots of summer days cruising in it and being pulled behind it on tubes and water skis. When my dad died my brother Jonathan inherited the boat. He takes good care of it and uses it every summer up in Manistee. He's a vet and his dogs love to go for rides as much as his kids. But it's a user boat, not a trailer queen like this one."

Doug straightened up.

"Oh, the Otter is no trailer queen. She's in the water from mid-May until mid-October and I take her out as often as I can. I wish she didn't attract so much attention, but so far she is the only woodie on the lake. Tim Merrill up at Greeley's Landing has an early 50s Century but he rarely puts it in the water. I have been waiting for some other people to join in with bringing back wooden boats to Sebec –there were maybe a dozen back just after the war, but they faded away. Now the Otter is the only one."

Doug's comment was clearly a challenge, and Anne smiled. "Hey, I'm still paying for a new house but a couple of years down the road, who knows? Maybe a few rides in the Otter this summer will help inspire me."

Doug pulled the paint sprayer off a shelf, along with two small camouflage boxes with straps hanging off the backs. As they drove west on Bowerbank

Road, he outlined his plan.

"I thought we could set these camera traps up on the road leading into Abernathy's hide-away camp between Bear Pond and Bucks Cove. Since there is only one way in by road, we can check every few days to see if they catch the white pickup going by. In the winter he could cross the lake on a snowmobile from his south shore place, but it's too late in the year to try that now. We have a few snowmobiles going through the ice every winter and this time of year it's pretty unpredictable. He could also come up around the west end of the lake but that would involve driving all the way to Guilford, up Route 150 toward Packard's Landing, and then to the end of Green Point Road. Then he would have to cut through the woods for several miles on an ATV. That's at least an hour of driving and he would have to trailer an ATV. Way too much trouble for him, I think, and he would attract too much attention. My guess is that this is the only way in till next January."

Anne noticed a few abandoned farmhouses and little else until they reached the Bowerbank Town Hall and Fire Station. As they turned right onto a rutted gravel road she couldn't help but agree with the proud motto on the sign of the Bowerbank Volunteer Fire Department: "Living on the edge of the wilderness." There was no signal on her cell phone, it had started to snow hard, and the Cherokee bounced roughly as they navigated the deeply rutted road. Every few minutes they would pass large debris piles of tree limbs marking where freshly harvested timber had been loaded onto the lumber trucks that were a common sight on the roads of central and northern Maine. It was a desolate and ravaged landscape, far different from the world of Dover-Foxcroft and the south shore.

Doug seemed to read her mind, and like many Bowerbank residents, enjoyed contrasting the north shore with citified life south of the lake.

"We're not in Kansas any more. It's easy to get lost up here on the logging roads and there are still quite a few bears and other predators around. In high school we would drive up here to drink beer and smoke weed and watch the bears at the dump. The logging trucks have the right of way, and we'll have to pull off if one comes by. They drive fast and loose and sometimes enjoy forcing other vehicles off into the ditch. It's good they have been using this road recently, though. Abernathy won't be able to sort our tire tracks out from theirs. The road over to Bear Pond will be the third left, and we should hit it in about 10 minutes. If I'm right there should be smaller tire tracks from his pickup turning off. We'll put the cameras there at the fork to catch his truck coming and going. This fresh snow is good – it will cover my footprints when I mount the cameras on trees back a bit from the road, where they won't be noticed."

Anne asked.

"We're not getting any closer than this? Shouldn't we check the place out?"

"Not yet. Abernathy has money and judging from his drone he's into surveillance gadgets. There's a good chance he has this Bear Pond place, whatever it is, covered by cameras, and maybe motion sensors. I thought I would see if Tom Richard might want to get away from the office and recon the place for us. He used to do this sort of thing in the military, although he won't talk about it much – some sort of secret seal team oath of silence. I'll call him tomorrow and see if he's up for getting his ghillie suit out of storage and crawling around in the woods."

It was almost 4 in the afternoon by the time they got back to the Sebec Country Store, and before opening the door to step out into the heavy snowfall, Anne thought again about mentioning the bruises on Beth's arm to Doug, but decided against it.

"Beth called me yesterday and invited me to dinner tonight at Allie Oops. She said it was important. Any idea what it's about?"

Doug shook his head.

"Nope, not a clue. You should skip the Sauvignon Blanc for once. It's a south shore drink. Try a good Allagash beer, Anne. The Black would go well with a cheeseburger."

In spite of the continuing heavy snowfall, which was not all that unusual for late March, there was a good crowd in Allie-Oops when Anne arrived. Beth was sitting at the left end of the bar, by the window, and waved Anne over. Remembering Doug's suggestion, she was thinking of trying an Allagash Black when Katie, the redheaded waitress, materialized with a generously filled glass of Sauvignon Blanc and set it down in front of her. Always full of energy and high spirits, Katie smiled brightly at Anne as she set another menu down on the bar.

"Hi Anne. The fish and chips are good tonight and there is still some meat loaf left. Just let me know when you're ready to order."

Frowning slightly, Beth watched Katie walk down to the other end of the bar before taking a sip of her red wine and turning to face Anne.

"Thanks for coming Anne. How are you? How is the case going? Any ID on the Phoebe Island victim yet?"

"Not yet. The autopsy was just this morning. Still early," Anne replied. She had managed to get in a hard hour of riding on her CycleOps bike trainer before joining Beth for dinner and was eagerly anticipating getting out on the roads around Dover-Foxcroft as soon as it got warm enough.

"How soon till we can ride the River Road?"

Beth laughed, relaxing into the evening.

"Probably not for another month or so – black ice can be scary right into May."

Anne replied.

"Oh good, my bike is still in storage. That means I can put off any roller work for another two or three weeks or so."

Beth's bright smile indicated she wasn't taken in at all, and was probably planning on now upping her own mileage in preparation for their upcoming "friendly" rides.

Katie came and took their orders, and their conversation wandered comfortably for a half hour or so: Governor LePage's latest antics, their predictions for ice-out this year, Beth's new haircut – she highly recommended the Modern Image Salon across from Bob's Farm, Home, and Garden Store to Anne.

They shared a good laugh over Vern Rodger's recent string of "accidents." Apparently Doug's response to Vern's unpopular gossip had caught on, and Vern had been punched out several more times in the last week. He was finding lots of excuses now not to work the pumps and his uncle Lem was not at all happy about having to find someone to fill in for him.

Anne finally addressed the reason she thought Beth had invited her to dinner.

"How's your arm doing, Beth?"

Beth frowned again.

"It's fine. Peter and I are working through some things, and he's under a lot of pressure at work. He's trying to break into the high-end custom designed home market down on the coast, and it isn't going well. He invested a huge amount of time on plans for a home to be built down on Roques Bluff, and they just backed out of the project. He gets very emotional."

"Is that why you broke up at Bowdoin?"

"Yes, but he has changed. He felt very bad about my arm. And he has been a big help identifying places I might be interested in investing in down on the coast."

"So you have decided to leave Dover-Foxcroft?"

"Pretty much, but it might take a while to find the right opportunity."

Anne paused before asking.

"When are you going to tell Doug?"

Beth avoided her gaze as she replied.

"No point bringing it up until I know for sure, don't you think?"

Anne shrugged and was about to respond when Beth continued.

"Anyway, that's not what I wanted to talk about. I don't know you all that well, but can I ask you something personal?"

Anne looked back at Beth and nodded, expecting her to ask again if Anne's relationship with Doug was purely professional. She was surprised by Beth's question.

"Are you a lesbian?"

Shaking her head, Anne responded.

"No Beth, I'm not. Why?"

"I figured you weren't but wanted to make sure. The Toad has been spreading the rumor that you are, and it's starting to take hold in town."

"Why would people believe the Toad?"

Beth smiled indulgently.

"Oh, let's see. You work in a masculine profession dominated by men. You carry a semi-automatic weapon and have demonstrated your prowess with your 'baton.' You are a jock. You have short hair, don't wear makeup, never wear heels, skirts or dresses, just work boots, jeans and sweaters. Nobody has ever seen you with a man except in work situations. You're strong and independent and don't seem concerned about how you come across. Not the feminine archetype, I would suggest. The ladies at the Modern Image Hair Salon asked if I knew which team you were on. I said I would check. And I'm also worried about Katie"

Surprised, Anne looked down the bar and watched Katie as she chatted with an older man she had seen several times in the Coffee House.

"Katie? What are you talking about?"

Beth shook her head in frustration.

"Katie likes you Anne. Haven't you noticed?"

"Well I like her too – she has great energy."

Beth rolled her eyes.

"No, she *likes* you Anne. She has a crush on you, and she is hoping the Toad might be right. Katie is a nice person, and just got out of a long-term relationship. She worked for several years as a paralegal at a law firm in Bangor and got involved with one of the partners – an older woman. The woman dumped her a few months back and Katie retreated up here to live with her cousin, who runs the bar. She's pretty fragile now, behind the bubbly exterior. So it would be good if you could somehow clarify your sexual leanings for people in general and Katie in particular. Maybe you could occasionally show your feminine side to the rest of town – wear a skirt now and then, or go out on a date? Most people in town don't care which way you lean. It's the uncertainty. People just would like to know which team you play for. It's like the stock market – people get uncomfortable with uncertainty."

Lying in bed that night, with Charlie purring contently on the pillow above her head, Anne tried to think of a way to let Katie down easy, but couldn't come up with anything. She needn't have worried, as the problem would solve itself the following day.

14.

ONAWA

It was Doug's turn to bring the donuts and coffee in to work the next morning, and as he and Anne sat at the conference table in their courthouse office, an open box of Elaine's donuts between them, Anne asked if he had heard the Toad's gossip about her being a lesbian. Doug tried to look surprised as he suppressed a smile and responded.

"Welcome to Dover-Foxcroft – you're part of the community if the Toad starts spreading gossip about you."

Doug was too slow in raising his hand and the blueberry donut hit him square in the face. Smiling broadly now, he carefully collected donut fragments from the front of his shirt, placed them on his napkin, and then slowly and methodically popped them, one by one, into his mouth.

"This counts as one of your donuts Anne, and I think it's your last one."

Doug's phone barked. His partner Tom Richard had mostly good news.

"Count me in on doing the recon you requested; all unofficial of course. Dudley Do-Right won't miss me for a few days. I should be up there by noon, and am bringing Lou Binford along. Lou is fresh out of the military and is our resident drone expert, with thousands of hours guiding them over in Iraq and Syria. Not the big predator drones that blow people up – the small surveillance ones. They are not your cheesy hobbyist items, either. These are quiet, can stay up in the air for up to an hour, and have amazing optics. Lou wants to field test one of the new drones we just got, and can scope out the recon target this afternoon, see what kind of camera coverage it has, and then I will go in tonight.

Also, you got pretty close to joining me here as a desk jockey, partner. This Abernathy character apparently went ballistic when he got pulled over on I 95 yesterday. He was screaming at the trooper about entrapment and calling him all kinds of names one wouldn't use in polite society. Put up quite a fuss – ended up being cuffed and charged with resisting arrest in addition to reckless driving, along with an expired driver's license. He spent the night in jail. Some high-up politico called early this morning and got him released. He will probably end up with just a fine and suspended sentence, but you managed to piss off a lot of well-placed people in Augusta. And this Abernathy guy is still livid.

On a more positive note, we finally turned up a promising lead on the glass eyes. It turns out they're vintage, made in Germany, and some of them had serial numbers on them. Since they're vintage we figured maybe they were bought off eBay or another online auction site, and were able to get a serial number match. The eyes are part of a group of a dozen bought last fall off eBay. The buyer paid by money order so that's a dead end. But we do have a delivery address – it's in someplace called Onawa, up around where you are. Maybe we could check it out this afternoon."

"This is great, Tom. Excellent news," Doug replied. "Onawa is north of Sebec, not that far from Abernathy's hideaway, so Lou can check his place out with the drone this afternoon while we follow up on the eyes. How about Anne and I meeting you and Lou at Allie-Oops about noon for lunch?"

Just after 12, Tom and Lou walked through the front door at Allie-Oops. Nobody paid much attention to Tom, but the lunchtime crowd stared openly at Lou Binford. Doug had just assumed that Lou was a man, but it was obvious now that Lou was short for Louise.

"Oh great," Doug thought, "Tom's got a new woman. What happened to the professor from the Sorbonne?"

Slender, moving with an animal grace, and just short of six feet, Lou looked to be about 30. She was dressed in all black: black combat boots, bloused black fatigue trousers, and a black down jacket over a black polypropylene jersey. Her shoulder-length raven black hair, streaked with purple, was pulled back into a ponytail. Devoid of makeup except for bright red lipstick, Louise was a stunner. Ignoring the stares of the lunchtime crowd, she followed Tom over to the table and displayed an easy charm and bright blue eyes as introductions were made. Katie brought over menus and told them the lunch specials.

After they ordered their meals Lou reached into her messenger bag and extracted the computer tablet controller for the unmanned aerial system she would be deploying that afternoon. Pulling up a satellite map of the Sebec Lake region on the tablet's screen, she asked Doug to locate the general area between

Bear Pond and Bucks Cove where Abernathy's hideaway was located and keyed its GPS coordinates into the tablet. Discussion then shifted to where she should establish her base station. The state police quadrotor drone she would be piloting, a Lockheed Martin Quad Indago, had a maximum range of 2000 meters, about a mile and a quarter. They could have approached that close to the target by way of the lake at other times of the year, but the ice was too thin now to support a snowmobile and any attempt to try it by boat through the ice would attract too much attention. They finally decided on a long unused and overgrown logging road that was just barely visible on the satellite map, but came within a mile or so of the target area. Anne called Jim Torben, who agreed to guide Lou to the spot where she could set up, using Doug's Cherokee for the off-road approach.

Conversation then shifted to the other lead they would be pursuing that afternoon. How would they approach the glass eye delivery location on Owana Road along the south shore of Lake Onawa? Since their planning didn't involve her, Lou excused herself and walked over to sit down at the bar where Katie was standing. Katie and Lou were soon leaning in across the bar and talking quietly.

Doug turned to Tom.

"So Tom, are you and Louise an item?"

"Unfortunately, Doug, Louise is not much interested in men. It's a real loss. But she and the redhead definitely seem to have hit it off."

Anne and Doug both glanced over to where Lou and Katie were talking, and Doug raised his eyebrows and smiled.

"Looks like your problem may be solved, Anne."

Lake Onawa is an isolated mountain valley gem about 10 miles north of Sebec Lake. Shaped like a backward J and 4 miles long, north to south, it is nestled just east of Borestone Mountain, which casts its shadow across the lake in the late afternoon. Popular with kayakers and canoeists, Onawa has only a few cottages scattered along its shores and is thankfully devoid of jet skiers. Its southern end provides a great view of the massive Onawa railroad trestle, the longest and highest in New England. To reach Lake Onawa, Anne, Doug and Tom drove west to Guilford, then north up to Willimantic where they picked up Mountain Road, finally going east on a well-maintained gravel road over to Onawa. There, they turned on a side road just before the boat ramp, and pulled up to the address where UPS had delivered the glass eyes the previous fall.

Next to a narrow driveway that curved off into the dense woods, a mailbox was mounted on a small platform that also held a large hinged metal box the size of a footlocker. On the front of the box was a hand printed sign that read, "Please put packages in here." After they had walked a short distance up the drive a large white clapboard house came into view, and partially hidden behind it, a low barnlike outbuilding. Gingerbread detail across the front porch suggested the house dated to the late 1800s. An old porcelain bathtub had been turned on end and buried halfway into the front lawn, providing shelter for a statue of the Virgin Mary. It drew Doug's interest; as such bathtub shrines were more common up along the St. John's River Valley, and relatively rare in central Maine. The front porch steps were newly shoveled clear of snow, and sparkling clean windows and a brightly polished front door knocker suggested a well cared for home. There was no need to use the brass knocker to announce their arrival, however, as a black Labrador Retriever looked at them through one of the front door's sidelight windows and began to wag his tail and bark with anticipation.

A middle-aged man with short salt and pepper hair, dark eyes, and a neatly trimmed van dyke beard answered the door. He wore sharply creased dark slacks and his starched white shirt, frayed at the collar and cuffs, was buttoned all the way up. His warm greeting carried a slightly puzzled tone.

"Welcome, welcome. I'm Francis Grollig. Please come in. Let me take your coats."

After introductions Grollig hung their coats on a hall tree next to the front door and led them into the living room, his expensive looking hand-stitched moccasins gliding soundlessly across the polished pine plank floor. The lab padded after them, sniffed each of the visitors in turn, and settled down in front of the fire. Above the fireplace mantle hung the only wall decoration in the room, a large ornate crucifix depicting Christ with a crown of thorns and bleeding from multiple wounds. Grollig urged his visitors to sit, and leaning forward in his chair, asked.

"What do the state police and county sheriff want from me? Please tell me this isn't another CITES inspection."

Tom responded.

"CITES – as in the Convention On International Trade in Endangered Species?"

"Yes. Usually it's the Feds, the US Fish and Wildlife Service, that conduct spot checks of my specimens, not local law enforcement."

Doug replied.

"We're not here about endangered species, Mr. Grollig. We're investigating several recent homicides down at Sebec Lake. You have probably heard about them on the news."

Grollig pursed his lips.

"I don't have a radio or television in the house – too distracting. I get all my news on the Internet. It makes it easier to selectively filter out all the trash that does not interest me. And I don't know anything about any murders. What do they have to do with me?"

Doug responded.

"Mr. Grollig, we're interested in the shipment of glass eyes you received last fall."

"Glass eyes? Well, you'll have to be more specific, Detective. I order a variety of different glass eyes, depending on what I'm working on."

Noting their puzzled expression, Grollig stood and took a few steps over to a set of pocket doors, slid them open, and waved them through. The large room they entered had an entire wall of floor to ceiling windows that provided a stunning view north the full length of Lake Onawa. Along both sidewalls were wooden shelving units holding a variety of mid-sized to large taxidermy mounts.

Grollig spread his arms wide.

"I bring God's creatures back to life. People from all over the world send me their dead and I resurrect them. I specialize in predators: carnivores, raptors, all the weasels and cats, wolves, and lots of others. Each animal is a challenge, a puzzle. Getting their posture and expression just right involves seeing the species in life, watching videos. How do they move? How do they approach their prey? How do they crouch and attack? Once I decide on posture and expression, as well as mounting medium, I defrost the specimen, skin it, and position the pliable body in the position I want. Then I make casts, which in turn are used as molds to produce an exact polyurethane copy of the living animal's body, which I match up with the skull and lower legs of the animal. This is not your average garage animal stuffing. This is art."

Stepping over to a wooden cabinet with numerous wide shallow drawers, Grollig opened the top drawer and stood aside so they could view its contents. The drawer had several dozen small compartments, each containing glass eyes of different sizes, colors, and iris configurations.

"If you can tell me the species, or delivery date, I can look it up." Grollig said, moving to a large central table holding a partially finished wolverine mount and a laptop computer at one end.

"It was a shipment of a dozen vintage human eyes, purchased on eBay," Doug responded.

Grollig turned, indignant.

"Human? Oh I never use human eyes – even for bears or other large predators – they just don't look right – and that would be blasphemous – putting human eyes in one of God's creatures."

Tom handed Grollig the eBay order and UPS delivery record, and Grollig opened an excel file on his laptop, scrolled through it, and shook his head.

"See for yourself. I have no record of this order or the delivery. I guess it's possible someone had it delivered here and then retrieved it from the box out by the mailbox before I got to it. It would be easy enough to do if they were tracking the package delivery. George, the UPS deliveryman who usually does this route, doesn't like coming up the drive. He can't turn around once he gets up to the house, so he has to either back all the way in or all the way out. So I put the box out there for him to pop the deliveries in."

Anne asked.

"How often do you check the box?"

Not too pleased by a woman interrupting a conversation between men, Grollig kept his gaze on Tom as he answered the question.

"It depends. If I am in the middle of a particularly challenging or engrossing mount – a hyena for example, I may not go outside for days at a time. But if a shipment I am expecting is overdue, I may check several times a day, particularly in the summer. My specimen deliveries are shipped frozen and I don't like them to arrive soft."

Doug picked up the questioning.

"Who knows about the delivery box routine? Friends? Neighbors? People who attend the same church as you do?"

"I can't think of many who would know. George the UPS man of course, but I don't get many visitors. And I don't deal with my neighbors. They are all slack jaw white trash. And there aren't any churches around here worth attending – Sunday church services have become entertainment now – light shows and trying to relate to our decaying culture. It's disgusting. Occasionally I have informal Sunday gatherings here and our prayer group discusses the word of God. Lem and Vern often attend, and a dozen or so other people from the area."

Doug asked.

"Is that Lem and Vern Rodgers from Dover-Foxcroft?"

"Yes, of course – they are very good men. Devout. I met them last summer at a revival over at Dexter, and we keep in touch."

At Doug's request Grollig printed out a list of the dozen Sunday prayer service attendees, along with a copy of his most recent email newsletter. As Doug pocketed the documents, Anne asked the next question.

"Where do you store the frozen specimens?"

Grollig looked toward the ceiling and sighed dramatically.

"I have several freezers out in the garage for the incoming specimens," he responded, glaring at Anne as he gestured toward the partially mounted wolverine on the worktable.

"Are we done here? I am on a tight schedule."

Smiling now, Anne shifted topics.

"Are women welcome at your Sunday meetings? I'm interested in learning more."

Standing ramrod straight, fists tightly clenched at his sides, Grollig responded.

"Women of good Christian values are always welcome here if they are accompanied by a male relative or their husbands."

Anne's smile widened.

"You don't like women, do you?"

Sneering, Grollig hissed in response.

"There are two kinds of women. Good Christian women who respect their husbands, procreate, and make a home, and those who have fallen from grace and lost their way. Whores. Sluts. And I have no doubts about which category you belong to."

Enjoying herself, Anne asked.

"And what should be done with the whores and sluts, Mr. Grollig?"

As if speaking from the pulpit, Grollig swept his arms out wide.

"Every effort should be made to bring them back into the fold; to save them from eternal damnation. Save them from the fires of hell. They must first repent, of course. Admit their transgressions and ask Jesus for forgiveness. Then they can be welcomed back into God's arms and rejoin the community of Christ."

Her smile vanished as Anne asked her next question.

"And how do you deal with the whores and sluts that cannot be redeemed?"

In response, Grollig pressed his hands together in prayer, gazed heavenward, and quietly, with a condescending tone, whispered.

"I pray for them, my child."

Anne was about to respond when Tom broke in.

"Thank you for your time Mr. Grollig. We won't keep you from your work any longer, and we can show ourselves out."

Grollig shook hands with Tom and Doug but ignored Anne's outstretched hand as he turned to work on his wolverine mount.

When they reached the bottom of the front porch steps Tom made a quick left and walked back toward the low barn behind the house. He opened one of the large swinging doors and disappeared inside, reappearing less than a minute later. Rejoining Doug and Anne, he reported seeing two freezers, both locked, and a large interior room with a locked door. The barn also contained a white snowmobile, a late model Ford pickup with a canoe on top, and an ATV. All three looked to have been used recently, suggesting that Grollig might not be quite the reclusive homebody he professed to be.

From an upstairs bedroom window Grollig held a cell phone to his ear as he watched Tom emerge from the barn and rejoin the other two detectives.

"They just left. You're right Lem, the woman is a whore, a daughter of Lucifer, a fornicator." Grollig listened intently, nodding his head, and they continued talking for a good while.

On the way back to Dover-Foxcroft, Tom, Doug and Anne discussed what to make of the glass eye delivery and their strange encounter with the self-proclaimed genius taxidermist. Could he be the killer or was he another false lead? Grollig's explanation of someone else ordering and intercepting the eyes was certainly plausible. The killer may well have anticipated that they would trace the eyes through the serial numbers they found on them, and had deliberately led them to Grollig; someone who would certainly attract their interest as a potential suspect in the murders. Grollig, after all, was a close match with the predicted profile of a serial killer of young women. He was a single white male, between 30 and 45 years old, lived alone, and was socially isolated. He was an archetypal misogynist and a rigid, self-righteous religious zealot, with plenty of free-floating hostility. His statements regarding the need for atonement and admission of sins by fallen women also fit the killer's elaborate acting out of the *auto de fé*.

Tom thought Grollig could well be psychopathic given his grandiose sense of self worth and shallow emotions, while also being "on the spectrum" of autism disorders, judging from his intense fascination with, and remarkable ability in, a chosen area of expertise- in this case dead animals and taxidermy. If his outburst in response to Anne's questions could be believed Grollig was also a textbook example of a psychopath with the Madonna-whore complex. He

117

categorized women into two groups: women he could admire and women he found sexually attractive. Reaching back to his undergraduate days and an abnormal Psych class he had taken, Tom pointed out that Freud believed the complex could develop in men whose mothers were cold and emotionally distant on the one hand, while also overprotective, resulting in severe emotional damage to the child. As adults, the boy-turned-man who had suffered through such a childhood would seek to avenge his mistreatment through sadistic attacks on women who were stand-ins for mother.

Playing devil's advocate, Anne argued that maybe Grollig was the killer, and not just another red herring deliberately designed for them to track down. Perhaps he was enjoying the game, toying with them, displaying his superior intellect and challenging them to catch him. Didn't he seem to have been expecting their visit? His physical description generally matched the man that Angeline Bouchard, the first victim, had met on the snowmobile outing and later met at the Bear's Den before disappearing, and the snowmobile in the barn was the same color as the one the killer had ridden. Grollig also had a canoe on the top of his truck, which was unusual in the winter, and could have been used to access Phoebe Island with the second victim. His connection to Lem and Vern Rodgers would provide him with both a source of information on what was going on in Dover-Foxcroft and a conduit for leaking information into the community. And what about his fascination with death and dead animals, and his daily handling of skinning tools and dismemberment?

They rode in silence for a while, and then Doug chimed in just south of Willimantic.

"It's hard to tell at this point if Grollig is a false lead or if he's our killer. The guy is definitely not normal. Even if it ends up being a waste of time we're going to have to follow up and get more information before he can be ruled out as a suspect. Tom can start with some background checks on him tomorrow when he gets back to Bangor. I sure wish we could get a handle on what goes on at those Sunday prayer meetings."

With a dead serious expression, Tom replied.

"We could infiltrate it. How about getting Louise Binford and her new girlfriend Katie the redhead to attend their next meeting?"

Anne laughed appreciatively.

"Great idea. I am sure they would welcome with open arms two assertive, self-confident, and beautiful young women who are in a lesbian relationship. No threat there. Grollig's head would probably explode."

Doug reached into his coat pocket and unfolded the congregation list for the Sunday prayer meetings that Grollig had given him.

"We might not have to send Lou and Katie up to Onawa just yet. The third name on this list looks familiar: Steve Alexander. Anne, isn't he the basketball coach over at the Academy?"

"Well that's a surprise," replied Anne. "I wouldn't have picked him as the serious religious type. He's quiet, soft-spoken, sort of a wallflower, but seems like a nice enough guy. I need to call him anyway about trying to get the Lady Ponies together for an informal basketball clinic over the summer. If I invite him out for coffee a few times I can also work on improving my heterosexual profile in the community."

Doug smiled and Tom looked puzzled. Anne explained.

"Beth, Doug's wife, let me know that the word around town was that I'm a lesbian, and that Katie from Allie-Oops had developed a crush on me. She suggested I might set things straight by using the best information network in town by getting my hair cut at the Modern Image Salon. I could talk about how my boyfriend of several years walked out on me last year and I am still a little gun-shy. Now that Lou and Katie seem to have hit it off, that solves part of the perception problem, but having coffee with an eligible bachelor and wearing a skirt and a little makeup wouldn't hurt. And once I have Steve spellbound I can use my feminine wiles to find out about the Onawa prayer meetings."

15.
THE FRIENDSHIP BRACELET

When Tom, Doug, and Anne arrived back at their courthouse office in Dover-Foxcroft, Lou had the drone tablet connected to the TV monitor and was ready to run the digital file from the afternoon's fly-over of Abernathy's hideaway.

"It was a good flight. Here we are following the lumber road. You can see the tire tracks of Abernathy's truck. Here is the turn-in to the cabin. It's a square single story building, maybe 40 feet on a side. No indication of any surveillance devices – cameras or otherwise, out away from the target building. And the building itself only has four cameras – one at each corner. The drone does a quick circuit of the building here, so you can see the cameras. I had to navigate around a lot of trees, that's why it's a little jerky. The drone stays above the sight lines of the cameras, so they can't pick it up. This is a close-up of one of the cameras. They are pretty standard off-the-shelf units – Amazon has them for a thousand dollars or so. The good thing is that they're infrared. When the light level drops at dusk they switch over to sensing a heat signal. Should be easy for Tom to approach tonight with his thermal evasion ghillie suit. There is also a keypad by the door and a weight-sensitive welcome mat – a pretty basic domestic suburban homeowner type setup."

Tom looked at the close-up image of the cameras captured by the drone.

"Should be a cakewalk. No moon tonight, and a good breeze through the trees to provide some ambient background noise. I'll do a full slow-silent approach, just for fun, and shoot some balloons to make sure none of the cameras have motion sensors with lights."

Seeing the look of puzzlement on Anne's face, Tom explained.

"It's my own invention, although it has been copied a lot. It's totally low-tech. I use a wrist-rocket slingshot and shoot small water balloons past the cameras. If they have motion sensor capacity the lights go on, but there is nothing for them to see or hear – the balloons are past the cameras, and they burst when they hit something, leaving small bits of material. I pick the correct colors for the balloons – tonight it will be brown and black so they blend in with the background after bursting. They have been field tested against much tighter targets than this place, and work well."

Anne headed home a few minutes later, wishing them luck on the night recon and agreeing to call Steve Alexander the next day and set up a meeting over coffee. She thought she would wait until their second 'date' before working the conversation around to religion and hopefully the Sunday prayer services up at Onawa. Lou packed up her drone tablet, shook hands all around, and let Tom know she was heading back to Bangor in a few hours and wouldn't be going back with him in the morning

"Katie, from the restaurant, is giving me a ride back tonight," Lou explained. "She hasn't been to that new Japanese restaurant in Bangor yet and we thought we'd try it out. You two bromancers have fun practicing your night moves out there in the woods."

After a leisurely dinner at Allie-Oops, Tom and Doug drove back up through Sebec Village and west on Bowerbank Road toward Abernathy's Bear Pond hideaway. Just before they reached the Ram Island Road turnoff for Doug's place Tom suddenly pointed out the driver's side window into the gloom.

"What the hell was that, just there by the fence? It was as big as a moose but looked like a fucking yak."

Doug laughed.

"That's Haggis – he's a bull, and a mean bastard. There used to be a whole herd of them in that pasture – Scottish Highland cattle well adapted to the harsh winters here. It's just Haggis and a small calf now – the two are inseparable. The rest of the herd was moved down to a pasture off Route 15 on the way into town. They kept breaking through the fence and getting out on Bowerbank Road. There's a framed photo of them running down the road in the Bowerbank town clerk's office – it's labeled 'The running of the bulls.' People had enough of it, so they had to be moved."

Tom smiled and replied.

"I wouldn't want to run into him some dark night."

They parked a few hundred yards from the target building. Tom stepped into the thermal evasion ghillie suit, picked up his backpack, and started down the lumber road. After a few steps he faded silently into the darkness. Doug must have dozed off, and was startled awake when Tom rapped on his window a little over an hour later. He rolled down the window and Tom filled him in as he took off the camouflage outfit.

"No problems. No motion sensors, no lights, and once I gained entry, there were no indications of any alarms going off."

"Gained entry? What the fuck Tom – you could have alerted him and shot the whole operation. We don't have a search warrant."

"Relax Doug. I gained entry but didn't go inside. I drilled a small hole through the wall with a hand drill up under the eaves and installed a fiber optic pinhole camera and microphone. It's wired into the power feed to one of the cameras and should allow us to see and hear what's going on whenever Mr. Abernathy shows up. As an added bonus, he's pretty careless with his Internet security, and doesn't have any password protection. He probably figures he doesn't need it out in the middle of nowhere. So we can use his Wi-Fi to get our feed out. We will get an alert on my tablet whenever someone enters the hideaway, and it has encryption so nothing can be traced back to us. Worst-case scenario is he finds the camera and knows someone is watching, but I doubt he will. And when we need to it can be pulled without leaving a trace."

The next morning Anne stopped by the Center Theatre Coffee House to pick up coffee. She also wanted to tell Beth both about Katie's new girlfriend and her plan for strengthening her own heterosexual persona in town. She had called Steve Alexander and June Torben the night before and set up a lunch meeting in a few days to talk about organizing a summer basketball camp for the Foxcroft girls' basketball team. Anne had also worked a few questions about Steve into her conversation with June – enough, she was sure, to suggest to June that she had an interest in him. It would probably be all over town by nightfall.

David Abernathy was just coming out as Anne opened the front door to the Coffee House. He glared at her as he brushed past, and snarled.

"Don't worry, bitch, your turn is coming."

The same teenage barista, tall and Nordic looking with blond dreadlocks and several tattoos, was standing behind the counter texting on her phone. Anne asked if Beth was around and the barista indicated that she had gone to the storeroom and would be right back. Anne thought the distinctive interlocking triangles tattoo on her forearm looked familiar, and asked about it.

"This is the Valknut, or Viking knot of the slain," replied the young woman with a broad smile and obvious pride. "My parents are from Denmark and we are descendants of Vikings. The Valknut symbolizes birth, pregnancy, and cycles of reincarnation."

Anne was about to ask more about the tattoo when Beth walked in the side door that connected the coffee house with the lobby of the movie theatre carrying several boxes of napkins and coffee cups. She sported a black eye, which Anne judged to be a few days old, based on its yellowing tinge, and a split lip.

Before Anne could say anything, Beth glared at her.

"So I ran into a door, OK? No big deal."

Anne looked at the barista and tilted her head toward the door Beth had just come through. Taking the hint, the teenage barista moved toward the door.

"Hey Beth, I'm going for a cigarette, be back in a few minutes."

Anne followed Beth behind the counter and spoke to her back as she shelved the supplies.

"Beth, you need to press charges against this guy. He's not going to change."

Turning around, Beth replied.

"I figured that out a few night ago, Anne. Right after he punched me in the face. He's gone, and not coming back. I also realized Portland is not far enough away from this dead-end shit-hole. I am thinking something on the west coast maybe. Anyway, it's none of your business. Leave me alone."

Obviously Beth was in no mood to talk, and it was not a good time for Anne to tell her about Katie and Lou and her 'date' with Steve. Turning for the door she told Beth she would call her later – maybe they could meet for dinner later in the week.

Walking up the steps to the courthouse, Anne met Doug and Tom coming out the front door.

"They want all three of us to come in to Orono right now." Doug explained. "There's been a break in the case. We don't know what, exactly – they said they'd tell us when we got there."

When they reached the Orono state police barracks, rather than going back to the major crimes unit offices, Doug, Tom, and Anne were asked to wait in the small conference room off the lobby. Their puzzlement grew when a few minutes later the door opened and Stanley Shelter, the commanding officer of MCU-North, aka Dudley Do-Right, entered the room. Close on his heels were Robert Ivey from the state police office of professional standards, and Herb Snow, a detective from the MCU-South unit. As the three took seats across the table, Doug thought. "What an odd group. This doesn't look good."

Shelter was a small, deceptively meek looking man with a constant Casper Milquetoast expression. His recent appointment as CO of MCU-North came as a surprise to the unit, as he did not have any previous experience in major crimes. For almost a decade he had been a mid-level administrator in the Augusta-based executive protection unit, which was charged with protection of the governor and his family, as well as visiting dignitaries. The rumor was that his promotion to command MCU-North was linked to his continued discretion in regard to questionable activities of the governor or members of his family. Shelter had a reputation as a devious political climber known for his remarkable kiss-up and kick-down personality. He was always ready to please whomever had authority over him, while having very little regard for people working under him. In the short time he had been at MCU-North, Shelter had established a reputation as a stickler for bureaucratic details who would not hesitate to throw his detectives under the bus.

Seated next to Shelter, Herbert Snow was physically striking. As the result of an autoimmune disease, alopecia universalis, he was completely hairless, from his bald head to his hairless toes. His eyebrows were tattooed on. His nickname in MCU was 'Harry.' When he smiled, Snow had a disturbing resemblance to Jared Loughner, the loner who had killed six people and wounded former congresswoman Gabrielle Giffords in Arizona. Despite his odd appearance and his loud, abrasive personality, 'Harry' was well connected to a range of businessmen and politicians in the state, and Doug had long suspected that he was often a source of inside information regarding ongoing police investigations. Snow and Doug had a longstanding mutual dislike for each other, and Herbert's crazed looking Loughner-like glare from across the table suggested he was looking forward to this meeting, and anticipated things not going well for Bateman.

The third individual taking a seat across from them was almost as odd looking as 'Harry.' Robert Ivey was a tall, stooped, beanpole of a man in his early 60s, with a thin greasy gray comb-over, a prominent Adams apple, and a perpetual sour expression. His job was investigating charges of unprofessional conduct against Maine State Police officers, and he seemed to derive great enjoyment from pursuing even the most minor of offences of detectives and troopers. Ivey had been in charge of the investigations into Tom's recent difficulties that led to his current desk assignment, and Tom despised him as a result. Squinting through thick coke-bottle glasses, Ivey had an irritating habit of constantly sucking his teeth, which became more pronounced when he got excited. Judging from the almost non-stop sound of tooth-sucking coming from across the table, Ivey too smelled blood in the water.

Anne looked at Doug and Tom with a puzzled, "What the fuck?" expression, as Shelter began the meeting.

"I've called this meeting, which for now is off the record, to see if several aspects of the investigation ongoing up at Sebec can be clarified before anything official is initiated. I have asked detectives Snow and Ivey to sit in on the meeting, and I thought it would also be appropriate to have Investigator Quinn join us, since she has been part of the investigation from the beginning."

Opening a folder on the table in front of him and glancing down at it, Shelter asked, without looking up.

"Detective Bateman, can you provide more background for why, exactly, you decided to deviate from established best practices by removing all of the case files from our secure computer system and server? How and where are the files now stored, and how are they protected?"

Even before Shelter was finished asking his question, Tom pushed back his chair from the table and stood up. Moving toward the door, he indicated he would be right back.

"I have some files at my desk that relate to this, I'll just go and get them."

A silence of several minutes lasted until Tom returned to the conference room, broken only by the sound of Ivey sucking his teeth. When Tom sat down again, Doug responded to the question, adopting the bureaucratese favored by Shelter.

"The nature of the case is such that I concluded that it was both possible and prudent to forego the convenience of the shared secure server, and to implement a more secure protocol. This was on the one hand possible because of the limited number of individuals involved in active investigation of the crimes, and on the other hand, I thought it was prudent because it would preclude the possibility of highly sensitive information being compromised through unauthorized access to our secure server."

Looking directly at Doug now, Shelter asked.

"And what led you to think that our server might be vulnerable to being hacked?"

"Early in our investigation, just prior to the recovery of the second victim from the Phoebe Island house fire, we learned that an individual named David Abernathy had taken an interest in the case. He is quite wealthy and his hobby is infiltrating serial murder investigations, particularly when the victims are young women. He has a long history of interfering in and compromising such cases. We looked into his history in this regard and contacted other departments who had dealt with him in the past. We learned that he employs sophisticated hackers in attempts to gain access from outside, and also often looks for insiders who are willing to provide him with information from official law enforcement case files. As I said, he has substantial financial resources to put toward such efforts."

Doug paused, and looked pointedly toward Snow as he continued.

"Our concerns were subsequently borne out. In a conversation that Abernathy had with Investigator Quinn and myself, he mentioned elements of the case that could only have come from our official files before they were removed from the server. We believe that there is a high probability that someone inside MCU accessed our case files and passed the information on to Abernathy."

As the sound of Ivey's tooth sucking increased in intensity, Snow lowered his gaze to his hands, which were tightly clenched in his lap. Before Shelter could ask another question, Tom slid the file he had earlier retrieved from his desk across the table to him, explaining what it contained.

"When Doug alerted me to the possibility of an internal breach of our case files, I ran a few programs recently developed by the FBI to track access histories on high security computer systems. The file you have includes a full list of all of the MCU personnel who accessed our case files prior to them being removed from the secure server."

As Shelter opened the file, Snow reached into his pocket and glanced at his phone. Standing abruptly, he moved toward the door.

"Please excuse me Lieutenant Shelter, I have another urgent meeting I must attend."

Surprised by Snow's sudden departure, Shelter stared at the file Tom had given him, flashed a brief tight-lipped smile, and passed it to Ivey. Looking across the table, he addressed Doug, Anne, and Tom.

"Thank you Detective Richard, for sharing this information. It looks as if MCU-South has a problem. I am sure that Detective Ivey will get to the bottom of this."

Pausing briefly, he somewhat reluctantly concluded.

"It appears, after review, that you made the right decision in removing the case files from the secure server."

Ivey opened the file, scanned down the list of names, and with a whispered apology to Shelter, followed Snow out of the conference room.

Folding his hands on the table, Shelter continued.

"There is one other aspect of the case that we need to discuss. Detective Bateman, were you personally acquainted with the first victim, Angeline Bouchard?"

Surprised by the question, Doug replied.

"Not at all. We interviewed her friend Charlotte Laughlin, and spoke with her parents and the local authorities in her home town, but I never met the young woman."

"Did you have any physical contact with the body during its recovery?"

"No. None. I observed it through the optical feed while it was still under the ice, but did not examine it after it was removed from the lake and bagged."

"We have a puzzle then, Detective Bateman. The results of the DNA analysis of all of the materials recovered with Bouchard are now in. No usable DNA was recovered from any of the clothing she was wearing, but they were able to recover DNA from the woven friendship bracelet that was found on her wrist during the autopsy. It was a solid match with your DNA. If you were not acquainted with Angeline Bouchard, and in fact had never met her, can you explain why she was wearing your friendship bracelet?"

A long silence filled the conference room as Doug sat stunned in his seat and stared expressionless into the middle distance. He could hear cars passing in the street outside, and the ticking of Anne's wristwatch. Taking a long deep breath, he looked at Anne and Tom, and then answered Shelter's question.

"I'll offer an answer to your question, and will expect an apology from you for the implication that I was in some way involved in the death of Angeline Bouchard. You don't appear to be aware of the fact that she was not wearing the friendship bracelet. The killer had surgically implanted it under her skin. DNA recovered from the bracelet can well be a solid match to mine, at the level of comparison that was carried out. But it's not my DNA. I suspect that a fuller analysis will demonstrate that the DNA is not mine, but that of my son Eric."

The quiet in the conference room deepened as Anne, Tom and Shelter absorbed Doug's statement. Finally, Shelter broke the silence.

"That's an interesting theory Detective Bateman. We can easily test it by further DNA analysis of the bracelet. But if it turns out to be your son's DNA, his death will be reopened as a possible homicide, and linked with the other murders. I will have no choice but to immediately remove you from the case and shift it out of MCU-North. Detective Richard will also be reassigned, and the Piscataquis County Sheriff will have to decide what to do about Investigator Quinn here. This will be a major blow to the investigation, and heads will roll. Given Mr. Abernathy's animosity toward you, and his political connections, I would predict that you would be reassigned out of major crimes, perhaps to a field troop or to the training academy. Once that happens it could be a long time till you are considered for a transfer back. It will also be a major embarrassment to MCU-North, and I wouldn't be surprised if it blew up into a major media firestorm, with Abernathy feeding the flames."

Shelter let his comments sink in, and then continued.

"On the other hand, it would be easy enough, for now, to hold off on the additional DNA analysis and to assume that the bracelet was somehow contaminated with your DNA at some point after the first victim was discovered. That's what I would propose. The case could then move forward, keeping the current investigating team in place. You three would be aware, unofficially, of the possibility that Eric's death is linked to the other murders, and would reconfigure your investigation accordingly. Right now only the four of us know about this, and it can stay that way. No written indications of this development, no reference to it by phone or in emails, and nobody else told. What do you think, Detective Bateman?"

Anne and Tom both looked to Doug, as he slowly nodded his head.

16.

CALIFICACION

Doug and Anne drove in silence for most of the trip back to Dover-Foxcroft. For Doug, learning that it was Eric's friendship bracelet on Angeline Bouchard's wrist was like losing his son for a second time – knowing that someone had likely murdered Eric, a gentle boy just starting out in life. It was of course possible that the killer acquired one of Eric's friendship bracelets in any number of different ways. But it seemed likely that he took the one Eric was wearing that day at the dam as he bludgeoned him and dropped him to his death in the deep pool below. They would go back and check to see if he was still wearing one when his body was recovered. Doug was convinced that embedding the bracelet under the skin of Angeline Bouchard's wrist had been a personal message to him from the killer. While other investigators could easily miss the significance of the bracelet, the killer had expected that Doug would eventually figure it out.

The DNA results also provided support for Anne's suggestion early on that the killings were not random but part of a carefully orchestrated plan with a specific target. It now appeared that the target was either Beth or Doug Bateman, or perhaps both. Eric's death obviously did not fit with the female victims, who had been selected based on some sick criteria, and their torture and murder had a sadistic religious foundation. Both Angeline Bouchard and the as yet unidentified second victim had been subjected to *auto de fé*, which suggested they had had been raised Catholic and had abandoned the faith. Angeline had been a party girl and her free-living lifestyle had been a great disappointment to her family. It would not be surprising, they thought, if the second victim also turned out to be a good Catholic girl who had fallen from grace.

Confirmation of their suspicions was waiting for them in a plain brown manila envelope resting on the conference table in their courthouse office. Doug's name and the courthouse address were printed in block capitals on the front of the envelope, but it was the return address that froze Doug as he reached to open it. In the upper left corner was an elaborate calligraphy signature: *Thomás de Torquemada* – the first grand inquisitor of the Spanish Inquisition, and the same signature they had found on the computer sign in sheet at the Thompson Free Library. There was no postage on the envelope, and after slipping it into a plastic evidence sleeve, Doug called down to the front desk. The envelope had been hand delivered by a postal clerk that morning, he learned, who had recovered it from the mailbox outside the Dover-Foxcroft Post Office, a few blocks away, and thought it might be important.

Carefully cutting open one end of the envelope, Doug used tweezers to extract a single piece of paper. It contained a lengthy message written in the same calligraphy as the signature on the envelope:

CALIFICACIÓN
I am the Redeemer, the Grand Inquisitor.
I look for lambs lost in the darkness, waiting to be found.
I lead them back into the shining embrace of God.

They are cunts. Whores who have left the true faith.
They have fornicated with the children of Lucifer.
They come onto me and I absolve them.

They were blind, so I took their sight.
With new eyes, clean green eyes, they can see the true faith.
Apostates, sluts, they confessed their sins of the flesh.
Questioned, they confess their transgressions.
Accepting their penance, they are washed clean by Sebec.

Angeline, the Québécois slut, baptized and lost.
She floats beneath the ice of Sebec, joined now with God.
Candace, the Bangor whore, diseased and sour.
Purified by fire, cleansed now, free from worry.

They join the innocent one, the first to die.
He was pure, no sins to confess, he sleeps in Sebec.
The next to be called is a heathen, a pagan cunt.
She too will join God in the sacred depths of Sebec.

Doug slipped the message into another evidence sleeve and called to Anne to come and look at it. She read it quickly and looked up as Doug started talking.

"He's impatient with our progress – we're taking too long," he suggested. "And he's goading us again. Dropping his *calificación*, his report, in the post office mailbox last night to let us know he's still hiding in plain sight, here in Dover-Foxcroft or close by. He wants us to get on with the game, offering the identity of his two *auto de fé* victims and acknowledging that he murdered my son, even though he doesn't name him. This sick monster is getting more confident every day now, even offering some insight into his bizarre faith-based justification for how and why he selected his last two victims, and promising to kill again. But why Eric? How does he fit into his game?"

"Eric's the key, I think," Anne said. "You or Beth are the target and he is exacting revenge for some part that you played in his past life. Something you did, or he thinks you did. And it is wrapped up, in his twisted worldview, with women falling from grace and his desire to save them, to make things right. Maybe there was a woman who was close to him that you or Beth somehow wronged. Or maybe he sees Beth as a fallen woman who needs to be saved; to be cleansed by the *auto de fé*. Maybe he is leading up to her punishment and offering foreshadowing of what's to come – and in the process showing what a fool you are. He's unfolding an elaborate game of punishment and revenge that is targeting you. First he kills your son, maybe so you and Beth suffer a loss equal to the one he has suffered. Then he challenges you to a game of 'catch me if you can.' He plans on humiliating you and demonstrating that he is the superior intellect, and in his own mind, the superior moral authority. He's working through his plan, and you or Beth or both of you are his final targets. So what do we do with this?"

Doug's response is immediate.

"I need to talk to Beth and warn her she might be in danger. That's not going to be easy. I doubt she will listen. I don't want to tell her yet, if I can help it, that Eric was quite likely murdered, since we are not supposed to know that. We also need to try to stop him before he kills again, but I'm not ready to put out a general warning to all pagan women that they might be in danger. He's laughing now, since if we put out such a warning we look like fools – 'Pagan women watch out.' But if we do nothing, and he claims another victim, then we look guilty of letting it happen. Maybe there are informal local groups of druids or other sects that we can locate, but even then, what kind of warning can we provide? We also need to see what we can find out about the Phoebe Island victim – Candace, the Bangor whore. Tom can track that down. Was she Catholic? Was she actually a prostitute, or is that just the killer's term for fallen women in general? Who knows her? When was she last seen? And then we need to get this message from the killer to the lab to see what they can tell us – prints, trace evidence, DNA?"

Doug picked up his cell phone and called Beth's number, but it jumped immediately to voice mail.

"Beth, call me as soon as you get this – it's important."

As he ended the call, Anne put her hand on his arm.

"Doug, when you call Tom, ask him also to take a closer look at that architect, Peter Fisher, the one Beth is friends with."

Doug gave her a questioning glance, and she looked away from him before explaining.

"He's been beating up on her recently. We need to rule him out – check his alibis for the killings."

Doug gave Anne a hard stare, keyed Tom's number on his phone, and left a message when it went to voice mail.

"Tom, we got a message from the killer. I will text you a photo of it. See what you can find on a Bangor woman named Candace who went missing in the time frame for the Phoebe Island victim. She's mentioned in a message from the killer I am texting to you. She might be a prostitute. Also, have a chat with that pretty boy Peter Fisher, the architect based in Portland– see what his story is. Apparently he has been beating up on Beth. Give me a call."

Beth returned his call a few minutes later with a crisp question.

"What's so important Doug?"

"I need to talk to you – something's come up in the investigation and you may be in danger."

Immediately assuming that Anne has told him about her bruised face and split lip, Beth tersely responds.

"It's none of your business Doug – Peter is working through some things, and he gets emotional. And besides, I've told him to stay away from me."

"Beth, it involves more than Peter – but Tom will be talking to him in the next few days."

"Tom? You turned Tom Richard loose on Peter? Tom, 'the hammer?' You know his white knight history of dealing with domestic abusers. He's violent Doug – he hurts people. And anyway, I was going to call you. My friend Helen invited me out to Santa Fe and I am flying out there by the end of the week. I will be out there for a week or so, so you don't need to worry about me."

"Beth, we need to talk, and not over the phone. It involves Eric."

Beth responded angrily and ended the call.

"Eric is dead Doug. The past is the past. I'll let you know when I'm back from New Mexico."

The rest of the afternoon passed quickly. Tom called back to let them know that he had started a search for Candace, and was trying to set up an interview with Peter Fisher. The letter and envelope from the killer was sent down to Augusta for analysis, and Anne and Doug began to try to identify pagan groups in central Maine, without much luck. Anne felt somewhat ashamed over the elation she felt on hearing of Beth's trip to Santa Fe. The River Road was dry now, and warmer weather was forecast for the coming week. With any luck she would be able to get in a lot of road miles on her Trek Madone WSD before Beth returned, and be ready to crush her on their first ride together.

The next morning, early, Anne put on her winter cycling tights, a heavy long-sleeved jersey and windbreaker, and parked the Toyota by the cemetery just outside of town. She rode slowly east on the River Road, out past the Baron Harry Oakes Mausoleum, and as she passed it, wondered if they would ever exhume his body to settle the mystery of his violent death in the Caribbean seven decades earlier – was he beaten to death or shot multiple times behind the left ear?

Anne warmed up on the long gradual downhill and then picked up the pace past the beautiful River Run Farm, with goats grazing on the left and long vistas down to the Piscataquis River on the right. The sun was bright, she had a sweet breeze at her back, and her legs felt strong. She was in the zone – riding smoothly with a high cadence and breathing easily. Redwing blackbirds were perched on cattail stands along the road, she could smell the freshly turned earth, and she passed several hawks watching the fields from telephone poles. The River Road surface was smooth, with just a few potholes and frost heaves, and the only traffic was an occasional tractor or farm truck. As she passed Eagle View Ranch she whistled to Jake and Jim, their two enormous draft horses, and noticed the recent progress on the new cattle barn going up.

It was an easy ride, with gently rolling hills, and Anne reached the turnaround at the Old Stagecoach Road in less than a half hour. Rather than returning back on the River Road she turned south on the Stagecoach Road, crossed over the Piscataquis River Bridge, and rode the long uphill up out of the river valley into Atkinson. Her legs started to burn, and she was up out of the saddle for the last hundred yards, pushing hard but pleased with her leg strength and breathing. Turning right at the crossroads onto Range Road, she headed back west toward Dover-Foxcroft, paralleling the river valley. Passing the famous Northwoods Canoe workshop on the right, Anne started to tire a bit on a series of five steeply rolling hills before turning right, re-crossing the river, and rejoining the River Road. The long gradual uphill back to the cemetery was a good cool down, and Anne was pleased with her first ride of the season as she loaded the bike into the back of the Toyota.

A quick stop for a post-ride chocolate milk, back home for a shower, and Anne arrived at the courthouse a little after Doug. They were able to confirm that David Abernathy and Francis Grollig, the deranged taxidermist from Lake Onawa, were both in town, and either one could have dropped the calificación in the mailbox night before last. Unfortunately, there was no CCTV coverage of that end of Main Street.

A little before noon, Anne headed out for her lunch meeting with June Torben and Steve Alexander to discuss the possibility of some informal summer basketball sessions for the Foxcroft Lady Ponies. She turned left off Main Street at the True Value hardware onto the Dexter Road, drove past Pat's Dairyland, and then right on the Sangerville Road. The Charles Chase Memorial Field Airport came up on her left. There was a nice new painted sign, but it was still just a grass strip with a tattered windsock and an explicit sign on the weather-beaten wooden airport building. "Don't even think about blocking this drive, asshole."

After another few miles toward Sangerville, Anne turned into the small parking lot for Stutzman's Farm Stand and Bakery. The Farm Stand building was on a ridge with a view out over the farm's sprawling fields and gardens, and Anne paused to take in the view. She could hear chickens in their nearby enclosure and an occasional goat bleat in the distance. Stutzman's had a long history as a farm stand and they had just recently added a bakery and café.

The entrance was on the farm stand side of the building, and a quick glance around the room showed that so far, strawberries, rhubarb, beets and beet greens, and kale were in, along with the headliners everyone had been waiting for – peas and new potatoes. Freshly shelled peas, new potatoes, and fresh-caught landlocked salmon from Sebec Lake made up a traditional late spring dinner in the region. There was a short line of customers waiting to pay at the register, and more were milling about, particularly in front of the pie case in the corner. There were only a couple of rhubarb and strawberry pies left for sale, and they wouldn't last long.

Anne walked through a doorway into the small café part of the building. It was packed, as usual, but June and Steve had managed to grab a table in the corner. Seeing her enter, they joined her at the counter, grabbed plates, and selected pizza slices from four different options displayed on the counter. There were also soup and salad selections in the buffet line, but Anne always went for the pizza. The dome shaped wood fueled oven was just behind the counter, and the pizzas were always fresh and varied and delicious.

Anne had been apprehensive about the lunch meeting – Steve Alexander had been very reticent and seemed rather dull the few times she had met him at Foxcroft Academy basketball games. But today he was a different person. He and June gossiped and giggled about other teachers at the school, and June was openly flirting with him – touching his arm frequently and smiling at him as they sat next to each other across the table from Anne. Anne noticed too that Steve was not at all bad looking when he was animated – short cut blond hair, dark eyes and broad shoulders. He was an athlete of some sort, self confident, with a warm and open manner.

Anne asked him how long he had been at the Foxcroft Academy, and Steve replied that he had joined the FA staff as a history teacher five years ago and had also taken over as head coach of the Lady Ponies. He played basketball a lot as a kid, he explained, and had even made the varsity team as a walk-on at Assumption College, a small Catholic liberal arts school in Massachusetts where he had gotten his teaching degree. After graduation Steve had moved back to his home town, Fort Kent, about three and a half hours north of Dover-Foxcroft, and right on the Canadian border, where he taught at Fort Kent Community High for five years before moving to Dover-Foxcroft.

Anne's opinion of Steve became even more positive as he talked about the summer basketball sessions.

"I think we need to keep it low key and fun. I can't be involved, and we shouldn't have it at the school – it gets too complicated if it gets too closely linked to Foxcroft Academy. In order to satisfy state guidelines on high school athletics we would have to advertise it and open it up to anyone who was interested. There's a half-court by the tennis courts across the road from school we could use, but it would be better to use the municipal court over by the Mill. It's kind of run down, but off the street, secluded, and rarely used. My preference would be no drills, no instruction, and maybe start with June's daughter and three or four others. It would be just informal games with Anne joining in, giving a few tips, and lots of encouragement. Not many of the girls will ever go on to play college ball, and the idea is to build their self-confidence and give them an enjoyment of physical accomplishment and the simple joy of playing. And also to get them used to each other's style of play in a relaxed, informal setting. Anne could be a great mentor and role model for them, not only in terms of her skills on the court but also her career and contribution to the community. There are lots of pitfalls, wrong turns in life that these girls will have to contend with."

Nodding her head in agreement, Anne looked at June, who had a Cheshire Cat grin on her face. Glancing at the women putting out fresh pizzas, Anne noticed that they were stealing glances at her table and smiling as they exchanged whispered comments. Anne figured her heterosexual credentials had just skyrocketed, and that the news about the budding romance between the basketball coach and the lady cop would spread quickly.

Returning to her reason for setting up the lunch, Anne approached the topic of the Sunday services at Onawa obliquely.

"A lot of the girls have jobs, so along with playing late in the afternoon on weekdays when we can work them in, weekends would be good days for the games. Would playing on Sundays be OK, do you think?"

June shrugged and nodded, clearly having no problem with playing on Sundays. Steve looked at her directly, smiling slightly, and then laughed before responding.

"I'm interested in religions, but not actually all that religious myself. So Sundays are fine with me. I got interested in fringe religious sects in college, like the Warren Jeffs sect, and Jonestown, when I took a course on deviant Christianity, and am working on a book with my old professor now. There's a really interesting, really weird sect that meets near here on Sundays, but they creeped me out, so I stopped going. So that won't interfere with Sunday basketball. And anyway, I don't need to be at your practices. I was hoping Anne and I could meet occasionally to talk about the players and how they work together, but otherwise it would be hands off."

Anne was disappointed at this. It sounded like Steve was pretty much a dead end in learning more about Francis Grollig and the Sunday services at Onawa. But she figured another lunch wouldn't hurt, and not only to learn about Grollig. The informal basketball games did sound like fun, and she also wanted to get to know Steve better – he seemed interesting. Anne and Steve lingered over desert after June had left to pick up her daughter Ashlee from a doctor's appointment, and as they passed the counter on the way out of the café, Anne overheard Nancy, the ebullient dark-haired woman pulling pizza out of the oven, comment *sotto voce* to the woman standing next to her.

"I wonder if they're going to compare batons in the parking lot?"

Tom called mid-afternoon with a probable identification on the Phoebe Island victim – Candace Gray – a prostitute with a long list of arrests in Bangor over the past five years for panhandling, solicitation, shoplifting, drug possession, and simple assault. She had not been reported missing by anyone, but when asked, people who knew her from the street said they hadn't seen her around for the last month or so. Nobody had thought much about her disappearance – people came and went with little notice all the time, and there didn't appear to be any leads regarding her abduction, and nowhere to go on following it up.

Candy had been sour and unattractive, always whining to whoever would listen about the raw deal life had dealt her. Years of methamphetamine addiction had ruined her teeth, which she tried to pass off with a Cockney accent, but in recent years she had even had difficulty attracting Johns for quick blowjobs in the dark doorways of downtown Bangor. Tom had been able to talk to her daughter down in Washington DC, who told him that her mother was a devote Catholic and had worked for the federal government for a number of years until she had gotten hooked on pain killers and then switched to heroin and other drugs.

After considerable calling around, Tom had also been able to locate and interview Beth's architect boyfriend, Peter Fisher, tracking him down to a hospital bed where he was recovering from being robbed and badly beaten the night before. Peter had arrived home from work and just turned off his home security system when he was attacked from behind and badly beaten. His jaw and several ribs had been broken, both eyes were swollen shut, and he had a mild concussion. His attacker had taken his watch and wallet.

He said he didn't remember much about the attack, couldn't recount anything his assailant might have said to him, and couldn't provide any description. He seemed anxious to conclude the interview and any investigation of the crime, saying he just wanted to get on with his life. Tom was able to confirm with his parents that he had been at their family estate on Isleboro during the weekend that Angeline Bouchard had been abducted and killed, so he could be ruled out as a suspect in the murders.

Doug let the silence grow after Tom finished his report until Tom responded to the unasked question.

"Look Doug, I was nowhere near the guy. I was home watching TV, and can prove it."

17.

HAGGIS

Lea Walker, one of the volunteers at the Center Theatre, called about ten the next morning, asking to speak to Doug. She had been a year ahead of him in high school, but he hadn't seen her in years. He remembered her as a quiet, nervous girl with a shuffling walk and buckteeth. Lea said she was concerned about Astrid Ragnarson, who had been working for Beth at the Coffee House the last month or so. Beth was hoping that Astrid would take over while she was out in Santa Fe and had asked the teenage barista to start opening up in the mornings to see how she did.

Clearly alarmed, Lea said that Astrid usually was very dependable but that she hadn't appeared yet this morning. Beth wasn't picking up her cell phone, so Lea decided she should call Doug. What didn't make sense, Lea said, was that Astrid's motorcycle was parked in the lot next to the theatre. That was weird, Lea continued, because Astrid loved that bike – a vintage mid-sixties Triumph Tiger Cub, and she always brought it inside to the theatre lobby when she worked. And to make it even stranger, several people had been waiting at the Main Street entrance of the Coffee House for it to open when Astrid rode up Main Street and around the corner out of sight into the lot. They heard her turn the engine off and patiently waited for her to enter the employee's side entrance from the lot and open up for business, but she didn't appear. After a few minutes they walked around the corner into the lot but she wasn't there.

Doug got Astrid's contact information from Lea and called her cell number, which went to voice mail. He tried the other number that Lea had given him and reached Astrid's mother, who confirmed that her daughter had left for work at the usual time, and that she had not heard from her since she left that morning. With growing concern, Doug asked if Astrid was religious. Her mother paused before responding.

"That's a strange question. I guess you could say she is, but not in the way you might think. She just graduated from FA and will be starting at Wellesley in the fall, and for her senior honors thesis she researched her ancestry in Denmark. The Internet was a big help, and she traced her great grandparents back to their hometown near Viborg in Midtjylland. While working on her thesis Astrid became fascinated by her Viking heritage. She saved up and got several Viking tattoos, and she took up Odinism – the religion of the Norse gods. It's attracting new adherents all the time now. So I guess you could call her a pagan."

Doug and Anne spent an hour interviewing Astrid's mother, but found out nothing of any use. Astrid had not received any threats – most people found her Odinism amusing – the passing fancy of a bright young woman on her way out of town, destined for bigger things. Astrid worshiped Beth, they learned. Beth had encouraged her independence and freethinking, and urged her to find a life beyond the confines of Piscataquis County. There had been no spurned boyfriend, no disturbing phone calls, nobody following her – nothing to raise the suspicions of Astrid or her parents.

Beth had gone to Bangor that morning to talk with several suppliers, but rushed back to town when Doug contacted her with the news of Astrid's disappearance. She was visibly shaken and couldn't add anything to what they already knew. Downtown Dover-Foxcroft was canvassed and nobody had seen a thing that morning. Even the Toad, who seemed to miss nothing that happened on Main Street from his gas station vantage point had not witnessed her sudden disappearance. The CCTV footage from the Center Theatre showed Astrid making the turn into the parking lot on her motorcycle, wearing a helmet with Viking horns, but then she passed out of the view of the camera and vanished into thin air. There was little doubt that Astrid Ragnarson, the young Viking barista, was the pagan victim they had been warned about, and that the killer had managed to snatch her off the street in downtown Dover-Foxcroft on a bright sunny morning in early summer.

Inquiries from the media began to come in the next day about Astrid's disappearance and if there was any link to the two Sebec killings. Doug was glad that Tom Richard was handling them. He was fending them off pretty well so far. Technically it wouldn't become a true serial killing case until there were three victims, and Eric's death had not yet been officially linked to the other two. So far, Astrid was missing, but not dead.

A week flew by with no breaks in the case. Beth had decided to cancel her

Santa Fe trip but Doug convinced her there was nothing she could do by staying in Dover-Foxcroft, and that Lea and other volunteers who had worked in the coffee house previous summers could take over in her absence. Doug and Anne were coming under increased pressure from the sheriff and Lieutenant Shelter for some results.

Sitting at a back table at Allie Oops they were going over their lack of progress. No one had come forward with information on Astrid, and questioning of her friends, fellow Odinists, parents and other relatives had yielded neither leads nor any potential persons of interest. Tom's continued investigation of Candy Gray's disappearance had similarly turned into a dead end, with no solid information regarding where or even approximately when she had been abducted, and there had been little apparent interest in her killing after the initial newspaper stories about her identification and possible link to the earlier Sebec slaying had appeared.

Katie, the redheaded waitress, brought their lunch orders over and lingered to tell them her good news – she had just been offered a well-paying job with the largest law firm in Bangor, and was moving back, and moving in with Lou Binford. She was just beaming with happiness, and when Anne said how much she hoped it would work out with Lou, Katie's response was immediate and delivered to both of them with a huge smile.

"Well, ya never know how things will turn out, but you have to follow your heart and be able to recognize when something just feels right. As my dad the golfer used to advise on putting – 'never up, never in.'"

As Katie moved back to the bar, flashing an impish grin at Anne over her shoulder, a middle-aged man with graying temples and a rumpled look approached them and offered his hand.

"Investigator Quinn, Detective Bateman, I'm Wesley Cohn from the Boston Globe. OK if I ask you a few questions for a project I'm working on?"

Doug looked to Anne, and when she nodded, he motioned to Cohn to take one of the empty seats at the table. As he sat down, Cohn continued.

"Please, go ahead and eat. I can give you my pitch and see what you think."

Anne and Doug picked up their burgers, and the reporter continued.

"I'm working on a longer piece for the Boston Globe magazine, which I am hoping to turn into a book, and wanted to get your perspectives on it, if you would be willing – either on deep background or with attributable quotes, and everything in between."

Doug started to speak, and Cohn rapidly continued.

"I've already talked to Tom Richard over in Orono and he suggested I also drive over and talk to you two. Please check with him if you want. My story does touch on the case you are working on, but it's peripheral to what I'm interested in. The focus of the story is David Abernathy, the self-styled modern Sherlock Holmes, and his involvement in law enforcement's serial killer investigations over the years, specifically the killings of young women. As you probably know, he is quite a controversial figure- very wealthy, very well connected, and very eccentric, with a history of skirting close to the edge of what's legal. He was even a person of interest in the death of his wife, but charges were never filed. I have been building up a chronology of the cases he has inserted himself into and have traveled around the country for the past year, on and off, talking to law enforcement people and others involved in the investigations, from Seattle and southern California to Santa Fe and through the Midwest to Florida and Connecticut. During all of this Abernathy has been surprisingly open with me and I have interviewed him a number of times to get his perspective on the cases and his involvement. You won't be surprised to hear that he considers law enforcement efforts to solve these cases totally incompetent and the people involved to be morons.

I have now worked my way up to the present-day and to the Sebec killings, and wanted to get your reactions, in whatever form you might be willing to give them, to his characterization of what has been going on. I know the case is ongoing, and I can assure you that nothing will appear in print until the case is closed, or alternatively, until you have reviewed any material relating to the case. So, what do you think?"

Working her way through her fries, which were excellent, as always, Anne replied first.

"Detective Bateman is the lead on the case, so I'll defer to him on this."

Doug nodded, and gave Cohn a thin smile.

"I've been burned a lot by reporters over the years, but you seem straight, so start with your questions, and for now, everything is deep background from unnamed individuals familiar with the investigation. Notes are OK, but no recorder. OK?"

Cohn nodded and pulled a small notebook out of his pocket.

"What kind of direct interaction have you had with David Abernathy?"

"Our first interaction with him was when he was encountered attempting an unauthorized low-level drone flyover of the second murder scene on Phoebe Island."

"Abernathy told me that his drone was shot out of the sky, and that you accosted him with a drawn firearm."

Doug paused, collecting his thoughts, before answering.

"He's puffing himself up. The property owner adjacent to Phoebe Island shot down the drone when he considered it a possible danger to himself, his property, and the crime scene investigators. He's an avid skeet shooter, had no idea if the drone was friendly or not, and it was coming close to his home. Abernathy was offered the opportunity to make a complaint after it was shot down and demurred."

"What about the drawn weapon?"

"We happened to observe an unidentified individual on the south shore of Sebec Lake, directly across from Phoebe Island, prior to the drone flyover, and I drove around the lake to check it out. The individual in question, who turned out to be Abernathy, had trespassed on private property without permission of the property owner, and had hidden himself behind bushes. He was observing an ongoing investigation at a crime scene with binoculars and a camera with telephoto lenses, as well as the drone. Killers have been known to enjoy watching crime scene investigations of their handiwork, so following standard procedure, I approached Mr. Abernathy with my weapon drawn but held down at my side. I stopped a reasonable distance away – about 20 feet, identified myself as a police officer, and as soon as his hands were in plain sight I holstered my sidearm, we had a brief conversation, and he left.

The only other direct interaction we have had with Mr. Abernathy was when we drove from here down to Augusta for the autopsy of the first victim, Angelina Bouchard. Abernathy started trailing us in Milo, just east of here, followed us all the way to the autopsy, and then picked us up again on the return trip. We pulled off I 95 to ask why he was following us, had a brief conversation, and continued on our way. Mr. Abernathy apparently was subsequently pulled over for speeding and reckless driving, and spent a night in jail."

Cohn continued writing briefly after Doug finished before asking his next question.

"Abernathy of course has a quite different, quite fanciful characterization of those interchanges, none of which stands up according to other's accounts of what happened, including yours. Do you suspect Abernathy of interfering in your investigation in other ways?"

"We can't prove it yet, but we suspect that based on confidential information he mentioned to us he may have been behind efforts to hack into our computer case files – that's under internal investigation now."

"He may still be at it," responded Cohn. "He indicated to me that the killer has sent you a message that identifies three victims and a planned fourth. He also told me that you had linked the killings to a string of still unsolved murders that occurred five to six years ago in the northern Minnesota Boundary Waters Region. The so-called 'Boundary Waters murders.' Any reaction?"

Looking at Doug, who nodded, Anne answered.

"I can respond to the Boundary Waters reference. I was marginally involved in that investigation – one of the six victims was an undergraduate student at the University of Michigan when I was with the Ann Arbor police. We have made no connection between those murders and the two confirmed and linked victims we have here in Piscataquis County. The two sets of killings are quite different in terms of both victim profile and how the crimes were carried out – the only resemblance I can see is that lakes provided a background of sorts in both cases. The Minnesota victims were three couples, a middle-aged male and female, two males in their 30's, and an older retired couple. The two confirmed victims here are both females, and killed separately, with a considerable time interval between the murders. The Minnesota couples were all killed on the same night, as they slept in their tents at campsites within a mile of each other. The case was also pretty much solved – the authorities are confident they know who did it, but the suspected killer committed suicide before any charges were brought. I can give you a good contact person with the Forest Service in Ely Minnesota who can provide details on the case. There are a lot of other discrepancies between the Minnesota killings and the ones we are investigating, which we can't go into for obvious reasons. So Abernathy is just spinning you a tale, trying to impress you with his inside knowledge, which has no basis in fact."

Looking impressed, Cohn asked the question Doug had been expecting.

"Do you consider him a person of interest in these murders?"

Doug paused, choosing his words with care.

"We are certainly interested in Abernathy because of the difficulties he poses to the investigation. But we are pursuing a number of leads and he is not yet a person of interest. And how about your opinion? You've been tracking his past involvement in similar investigations – should we be taking a closer look at him?"

Closing his notebook, Cohn rose and shook their hands.

144

"I wouldn't take him lightly – he has a lot of resources, a lot of free time, and a lot of free-floating hostility. You've managed to get under his skin and I expect he will keep coming at you. If you're lucky he'll get drawn off to some other case soon – he has a short attention span. He's impulsive and unpredictable, so you can't be sure what he might try next. But he'll try something. You can count on it. Thanks for talking to me, and let's keep in touch."

As the reporter walked away from the table, Doug turned to Anne.

"What was that all about – it sounds like Abernathy has some knowledge of the message we received from the killer. Is 'Harry' Snow still passing on information from our case files?"

Doug picked up his phone, called Tom Richard and left a long message asking him to see if he could track down the source of the leak to Abernathy. He got a text from Tom an hour later, saying he was in a meeting and would call back as soon as he knew something. When Tom called back in the early evening, apologizing for not having called sooner, Doug was down on the dock at his north shore camp, looking west across the lake toward Pine Island through his binoculars, searching for any sign of a nesting pair of eagles. Tom was confident that Abernathy had not found out about the calificacion from the case files, and suspected that he must have a source in the state crime lab, where it had been sent for analysis. They were discussing how they might try to figure out who the leak was in Augusta when Woody, the next-door neighbor's dog, began barking excitedly.

Doug automatically turned toward the sound and raised his binoculars. Seeing a metallic reflection in the trees at the end of his driveway, he focused in on it and saw David Abernathy crouching behind a large fern, wearing earphones, and pointing some sort of dish-shaped object toward him. It looked familiar, and Doug recognized it from watching NFL games – Abernathy was eavesdropping on him with a parabolic microphone. Doug paused, and then spoke in a loud voice into the phone.

"Gotta go Tom. Abernathy just stopped by for a visit."

Doug turned and started jogging toward Abernathy, who looked startled as Doug's comment came through his earphones. Abandoning his parabolic mike he turned and ran back into the woods. Doug heard an ATV start up and roar off down a path that cut through the woods over to Ostrum Road. Once Abernathy reached Bowerbank Road by going up Ostrum, Doug knew he would have to turn either west toward his Bear Pond hideaway or east toward

Sebec Village. There were numerous dirt tracks leading off into the woods from Bowerbank that he could use to try to escape, at least for a time. But those tracks didn't lead anywhere, and Abernathy could easily get lost in the dark once he got off the main road.

Doug guessed that there was likely a vehicle and trailer for the ATV parked somewhere along Ostrum or the Bowerbank Road that Abernathy was racing to reach. Climbing into his Jeep, Doug thought there was a good chance he could catch him by driving up Ram Island Road, which ran into Bowerbank quite a ways west of Ostrum, and then heading east.

It was a good plan but Abernathy also realized he would be trapped if he continued up Ostrum, so he took an overgrown path that he had noticed earlier that day on Google Earth. It split off from Ostrum, which meandered along the lakeshore, and went straight up to Bowerbank Road, cutting the distance he would have to travel almost in half. He made good time, ducking occasionally to dodge overhanging branches, and slowing to push through a single wire marking a property line. He sped up as he emerged out of the woods into a meadow, and as he came up over a rise, was surprised to see a small calf with long shaggy hair right in front of him.

The calf bellowed in fright and Abernathy swerved to try to avoid it, striking it a glancing blow in the hindquarters. The calf continued bellowing as it ran off and Abernathy, swearing, slowed to get around a large stump. Seeing a blur out of the corner of his eye, he turned his head in surprise as Haggis, the Scottish Highland bull, closed on him. Enraged and moving with surprising speed, Haggis lowered his head and rammed the right side of the ATV just behind the handlebars, tipping it sideways and crushing Abernathy's right leg from the ankle up to the knee. The bull's head continued to slide up the side of his body, and the tip of his right horn entered Abernathy's throat just above the windpipe. Instinctively, Haggis lifted and twisted his head, driving his horn up and completely through Abernathy's skull, lifting him off the ATV. Haggis carried Abernathy's now lifeless body for ten feet or so before shaking him off and going over to console the calf.

After finding his truck and ATV trailer parked along Bowerbank Road, Doug and Anne, along with Piscataquis County Sheriff's personnel and volunteers, searched for Abernathy through the night. Well aware of Haggis's aggressive nature, they avoided the pasture until full daylight the next day, when the overturned ATV was spotted through the trees bordering Bowerbank Road. Abernathy's body was removed to Augusta for a quick autopsy, and his death was eventually declared an "accidental death by misadventure." Everyone knew that Haggis was dangerous; the reasoning went, yet Abernathy had knowingly trespassed into the pasture, knocking down the electrified boundary wire in the process. He apparently then had deliberately and knowingly rammed the calf, resulting in the attack by Haggis. Given Abernathy's local reputation as a rich and obnoxious outsider from away, the possibility of euthanizing Haggis was not even considered. He became a local celebrity of sorts and suffered through a steady stream of admiring visitors for several months. Abernathy's death warranted only a brief article on page 3 of the Piscataquis Observer the following week, next to a piece on the new lending library in Sebec Village. It carried the headline "Portland man dies in ATV mishap."

18.
BUCKS COVE

Bucks Cove is easy to miss. Located at the northwest corner of Sebec Lake, it can only be accessed by two small channels. In the late 1800s it was home to a fish hatchery and served as a collecting area for rafts of logs floated down Ship Pond Stream on their way to sawmills at Sebec Village. Now, however, the fish hatchery and the log booms were a distant memory. As Sarah and John Paisley guided their 14 foot outboard through the east channel into Bucks Cove, with Jordan Island on their left and Perch Rock on the Bowerbank shore to their right, they entered a secluded and seemingly pristine expanse of quiet water, rock lined shores, and deep forest broken by only a few remote camps.

Sarah and John lived in Greenville, South Carolina during the school year. He was a poet and taught at a nearby university, and Sarah wrote novels and ran a creative writing program at a high school for the Arts. Every spring they would bundle their two daughters and three cats into the station wagon and make the long journey up to the south shore Sebec camp that had been in the Paisley family since the 1920s. Their place was just a half-mile down from the large McMansion that David Abernathy had built after clearing several acres of beautiful birch and tamarack forest, gaining the enmity of his neighbors. They had read about Abernathy's ATV accident and death in the previous week's Piscataquis Observer, and wondered what would become of the "mistake on the lake" – the name locals had given to his pretentious summer home.

In the mornings Sarah and John would usually write, and lazy summer afternoons would often be spent with their girls seeking out shoreline adventures and good fishing spots in Sebec's many coves. They discovered loon nests in Turtle Cove, watched the otter family in Seymour Cove, had picnics on the beach in South Cove, and joined the other boats that gathered off Greeley's Landing to watch the fireworks on homecoming weekend.

The girls had gone off to spend the day with friends in Dover-Foxcroft, leaving Sarah and John free to explore on their own, and after years of talking about doing it, they were finally going to search for the Marion. Forty-five feet in length, the Marion had pulled log booms and ferried freight, mail and passengers around Sebec Lake for almost fifty years before, in 1932, she was piloted one last time into Bucks Cove and scuttled in 30 feet of water. Rediscovered in 1975, the wreck of the Marion had become a popular dive site for scuba enthusiasts, and Sarah and John planned to explore it with their snorkel gear and fins.

The red buoy that marked the location of the Marion was missing however, probably taken away by winter ice and not yet replaced. John remembered its general location, and they anchored the boat close to where he thought they would find the wreck. Climbing down into the cold water, they swam slowly in expanding circles around the boat, looking down toward the log-strewn bottom of the cove. Sarah saw a dim shape off to her left. It wasn't on the bottom, however, but floating, suspended, about halfway up toward the surface. Puzzled, she swam toward it. Realizing suddenly that it was a human body, Sarah cried out into her snorkel, choked on a mouthful of water, and bolted to the surface and started back to the boat. Snorkeling on the surface some distance away, John heard Sarah coughing and shouting to him and turned in the direction she was pointing to investigate what she claimed to have seen. He swam around the suspended corpse several times before returning to the boat. After tying a float to their anchor rope to mark the location, they headed over to call for help at one of the camps clustered along the west shore of Bucks Cove.

John's 911 call to the Piscataquis County Sheriff's Office was patched through to Anne Quinn. She and Doug Bateman, Tom Richard, and the state police evidence response team were just finishing up their search and documentation of David Abernathy's hideaway cabin at Bear Pond, less than a mile east of Bucks Cove. Tom had arrived a half hour earlier than the rest of the team and removed his surveillance camera. Considerable evidence indicating Abernathy's interest in the case had been recovered. His computers provided numerous surveillance photos of Anne, Beth, and even Astrid, as well as the identity of the crime lab source that had leaked the information about the 'calificación' communication from the killer. His hard disk also contained a long and career-ending email stream that documented Herbert Snow's role in providing Abernathy with case files and other confidential information. They found considerable evidence of his employment of hackers and bribing officials involved in other serial murder cases across the country, and documentation of his fixation on the torture and killing of young women. The cabin also yielded a treasure trove of computer links to child pornography networks, and the FBI would be eager to get access to the files they had recovered. Abernathy appeared to have used the cabin primarily to play violent video games, pursue his interest in the serial killings of young women, and communicate with his sick community of child sexual predators.

There was still a lot of work to do, and Abernathy was not yet ruled out as a suspect, but there was nothing in the cabin to directly link him to the killings. Wesley Cohn, the Boston Globe reporter, would soon file requests to review the materials they recovered as well as the accident reports of the circumstances surrounding Abernathy's death, and these materials provided a compelling conclusion to what would become a best-selling book the following year.

Answering the forwarded 911 call from John Paisley, Anne listened to his account of the suspended body in Bucks Cove, and asked them to return to their camp – saying she would send Jim Torben around that afternoon to take a statement from them. She pulled Doug aside and told him about the discovery.

"It sounds like the body of Astrid Ragnarson has been found over in Bucks Cove. What's the best way to get up there with a boat?"

Doug thought for a moment, then turned to Peter Martell, the evidence team leader.

"Peter, do you have a body bag in the van?"

Peter nodded.

"Are you OK with recovering and transporting a body down to Augusta today? It's just been discovered very near here."

Peter paused, then reluctantly nodded again.

Doug tuned to Anne.

"Let's do this – You and Peter and I and one of his team can walk over to Bucks Cove with a body bag from here – it's 10 minutes or so. We'll send the evidence response team van around to Greeley's Landing, which should take them about an hour. They can wait there for the body, and in the meantime I can call Hayden and Tim Merrill at the marina and see if they can send a patio boat and someone with a mask and snorkel up to Bucks Cove to pick us up. From there, we can recover the body and transport it back to Greeley's Landing for the trip down to Augusta."

Anne and Peter agreed, and Doug arranged for the patio boat and diver to meet them. It arrived in under an hour and ferried them out from shore to the marker buoy John Paisley had placed earlier in the day. Carrying an underwater digital camera, the diver lowered himself into the water and swam toward the buoy.

Astrid was tethered to several cinder blocks on the bottom of Bucks Cove by an almost invisible 80-pound monofilament line tied around her ankles. Even in death she was beautiful. Magically suspended halfway between the bottom and the water's surface, her body was clothed in a white nightgown and glowed alabaster in the shimmering underwater light. Blood had settled into her lower legs, giving her the appearance of wearing pink socks, and indicating that she had been lowered into the water before or soon after death. Her arms were extended almost horizontally out from her sides, making graceful movements as they moved with the currents, seeming to beckon one to come closer. Astrid's long blond hair was loose, and floated gently around her head. Her green eyes were open but clouded in death. She had a peaceful, slightly bemused expression.

When viewed from the front, Astrid showed no clear evidence of torture, but what appeared to be the tops of a pair of slate gray wings could be seen just above her shoulders. The "wings" were in fact her lungs. Twin incisions had been made on either side of her spine, entirely freeing her rib cage, and her lungs had been pulled out and now fluttered against her upper back. Just visible inside her chest cavity were two tubular white objects that had been inserted where her lungs had been. They appeared to provide the buoyancy that was keeping her suspended above the bottom of Bucks Cove.

The line securing Astrid to her cinderblock anchor was cut, her body brought aboard the patio boat, and the long journey back across Sebec Lake to Greeley's landing began. The water was calm and they made good progress across the lake, through the narrows, and south to Merrill's Marina and the adjacent boat ramp where the evidence response team's van was waiting. As they approached the marina they could see that a small, solemn crowd had gathered. Astrid's parents were there, as were other close relatives and several dozen townspeople. Doug took her parents aside and confirmed their worst fears, as the other mourners watched in somber silence as the gurney with her shrouded body traveled the short, grim distance from the patio boat to the van.

Just before noon the next day Anne and Doug stood under the cold harsh lights of the autopsy room, fully gowned and masked, and gazed down at the gaping wounds in Astrid Ragnarson's back. The body had been transported face down in order to preserve the incisions and protruding lungs, and Mike

Bowman, the chief medical examiner, suggested that he give them an unofficial assessment before he started the video and audio taping of the formal autopsy. He looked at the severed ribs with interest.

"The individual ribs on both sides are all cleanly severed close to the spine, with consistent slight angles outward away from the midline toward the shoulders. I would guess that some sort of branch lopper was used to cut each rib, one by one, up both sides of the spinal column. A large blade was then employed for the lateral cuts above and below the rib cage that allowed the ribs to be pulled sideways far enough for the lungs to be pulled out of the chest cavity. The lungs themselves, surprisingly, are in quite good condition, considering. This was a careful and competent mutilation.

The body is also in pretty good shape. I would estimate it was in the water for a week or so. The skin here on the fingertips and palms is wrinkled, but not close yet to sloughing off or degloving, and there is not a lot of blotching, pimpling, or discoloration of the epidermis. The livor mortis in the lower extremities – the pink coloration of the lower legs, indicates that she was in a standing position at death or soon after death – with her blood pooling to the lowest parts of her body.

I think massive blood loss combined with the damage to her lungs was the cause of death. She was likely placed in the water very soon after she was mutilated. Hard to say if she was still alive when she went into the water, but I doubt it. I also don't see any ligature marks – no evidence of restraints, and no clear defensive wounds – so she likely wasn't conscious. The other two victims both had high levels of ketamine in their system, and I would expect that he used it here too. It's a dissociative psychedelic, widely used as an anesthetic. It causes a trance-like state and provides pain relief and sedation. It's also sometimes used for non-medical purposes – for its visual and auditory hallucinations and dissociative effects. It's fast acting, so his victims would be sedated and pain-free soon after it was administered, but only for a short period of time – a few hours perhaps, and then with the right dosage, they would be confused and hallucinatory as they regained consciousness. So I don't think she was aware of what was happening, or that she felt any pain. I sure hope not."

Reaching over to his set of instruments, Bowman selected a large pair of forceps and slipped them into the large wound on the left side of Astrid's back.

"Now, let's see what the killer placed in the chest cavity after he pulled her lungs out."

Moving the forceps around inside the chest cavity, he gained a grip on the object that had been inserted, and with a gurgling sound, extracted it and placed it on a surgical tray in the sink. Once out of the body it was easily identified as a boat fender – a foot-long white vinyl sausage-shaped float used to protect moored boats from hitting the dock. He extracted a second similar fender from the right side of her chest cavity. They were intended to keep the corpse suspended in the water column and they had functioned well in that capacity. They also each carried a message – a black felt tip marker had been used to write inscriptions on both fenders. They were not in any easily recognized language however, but Doug thought that they would be linked to the brutal and bizarre method that had been used to murder Astrid Ragnarson.

After taking pictures of the inscriptions and thanking Bowman, who said the formal autopsy report would be emailed over by the end of the day, Anne and Doug walked out into the fresh air. It was a beautiful cloudless day and a sweet breeze drifted across the parking lot. Doug opened his phone and called Beth in Santa Fe to let her know they had found Astrid's body. Beth broke into sobs and cut the connection, calling back several minutes later to say she would call Astrid's parents and would catch the first available flight back. Doug then called up to Orono to see if Dr. Melinda Blood might be available that afternoon to discuss the inscriptions on the bumpers and the method of death. She answered on the second ring, indicated she was in the office, and could certainly see them. Doug texted over photos of the boat fender inscriptions and they started up I 95 to the University of Maine campus.

Professor Melinda Blood was seated at the large worktable in her office with several large leather bound volumes open in front of her. She smiled and stood to greet Anne and Doug as they came through the door. Her large dog Jack was stretched out on the bare wood floor in a patch of sunlight coming in through an open window, snoring softly. The voices of summer school students playing frisbee drifted in from the quadrangle.

Dr. Blood looked at each of them in turn as they sat down before looking at Doug and asking.

"How's Beth doing?"

Doug answered in a matter-of fact voice.

"She's taken Astrid's death hard. Right now she's visiting a friend in Santa Fe, but has been talking about investing in a business out west somewhere and moving out there. Looks like we're splitting up."

Leaning forward, Blood responded.

"Doug, I'm really sorry for you. But it's not your fault. Beth has always struggled with her parent's expectations for her success in life, which meant leaving Dover-Foxcroft for the big world out there. She wouldn't ever have been happy here."

Doug raised his hand to stop her from saying anything more, and asked.

"So based on the photos of the writing on the boat fenders and the description of the mutilation I texted over, what can you tell us about the murder of Astrid Ragnarson?"

"Did you say her name was Ragnarson?" Blood asked, stunned.

"Yes, why?"

"Because the inscriptions on the floats recovered from her body are written in Old Norse and date to the Viking Age – roughly AD 800-1100. One of them comes from a skaldic saga entitled *Ragnarssona þáttr,* or the tale of Ragnar's sons."

Pointing to the page she was reading, Blood continued.

"Roughly translated into English, the relevant *Ragnarssona þáttr* passage reads:

'They caused the bloody eagle to be carved on the back of Ælla, and they cut away all of the ribs from the spine, and then they ripped out his lungs.'

Reaching for the other volume in front of her, Blood ran her finger down the page.

"Here's the Old Norse inscription that was written on the second float:

'Ok Ellu bak, At lét hinn's sat, Ívarr, ara, Iorví, skorit.'

It's from a skaldic verse written by Sigvatr Þórðarson between A.D. 1020 and 1038. Translated, it reads:

'And Ívarr, the one who dwelt at York, had Ella's back cut with an eagle.'

Both of these passages refer to a form of Viking execution called the 'Blood Eagle,' in which the intended victim would be held face down on a platform and the outline of an eagle with outstretched wings would be carved into their back. The victim's ribs would then be hacked from their spine with an ax, forced outward, and their exposed lungs would be pulled out of the chest cavity to form a pair of 'wings' that would flutter as they drew their last breaths."

Pointing to an illustration in one of the volumes, Blood continued.

"Here's a likely depiction of a blood eagle execution, from the Stora Hammars I stone from Gotland, Sweden. You can see the victim lying prone on a platform, with another man using a weapon on his back. Hovering above him are two eagles."

Anne pointed at a set of interlocking triangles depicted just above the victim's head in the illustration.

"Astrid had that symbol tattooed on her right forearm."

Professor Blood nodded.

"That's a 'Valknut', a Viking symbol – clearly she was interested in her Viking heritage."

Doug showed Dr. Blood a photo of the Valknut tattoo on Astrid's forearm.

"Her parents indicated she was involved in a revival of Viking religion – she practiced Odinism."

After a long silence, broken only by Jack's gentle snoring, Blood spoke in a low voice.

"Your killer is matching his method of killing to the victim's belief system, or rather his perception of what constitutes an appropriate form of execution. Catholic women who have become harlots face the punishment of the inquisition. An Odinist pagan girl earns a Viking execution."

They talked a few more minutes and then Anne and Doug stood and moved toward the door. Doug had stepped out into the hallway when Professor Blood touched Anne gently on the arm and spoke softly, so only she could hear.

"You two are good together, and Beth is a fool. But you need to give Doug a clear indication of your intentions – something small but intimate, something physical. You'll know when."

Anne stopped and turned to respond, but Blood was already halfway across the office, and waved casually over her shoulder without breaking stride.

19.
THE ONAWA TRESTLE

Beth's flight into Bangor was delayed, and it was almost 11 PM by the time her bag showed up on the luggage carousel. She had texted her sister to let her know she would be home in about an hour, and then texted Doug to let him know she was back and asked if they could get together after Astrid's memorial service the following day.

Stepping out of the front door of the Bangor International Airport, Beth breathed in the sweet night air, looked up at the full moon, and walked toward her car in the poorly lit daily parking lot. She put her suitcase in the trunk, and trying to reach the driver's door, squeezed between her car and a dark van that was parked too close. As she put her hand on the door handle she heard a sliding sound behind her and then a low snarl as a cloth hood was jammed down over her head and she was pulled backward into the van.

Doug got the call from Beth's sister a little after 2 AM, asking if Beth was with him, or if he had heard from her. She had texted when she landed to say she would be there in about an hour, her sister said, but hadn't shown up yet. And she wasn't answering calls or text messages. Doug said he would follow up, and tried calling and texting Beth, with no response. He called the Orono barracks of the state police, who put out an alert to watch for Beth's car, and called to ask Tom to check on the whereabouts of Peter Fisher. Tom reported an hour later that he had reached Fisher, who was attending a conference in Atlanta, and that he had vehemently denied having had any contact with Beth since his mugging.

Astrid's memorial service was held the next afternoon on the south shore beach at the Peaks-Kenny State Park, which was one of her favorite places growing up. It was a cloudless day, with a light breeze off the water, and across the shimmering blue surface of Sebec Lake, Borestone Mountain rose dramatically from the seemingly endless forest that stretched away on the north shore.

In addition to a large number of her friends and family from Dover-Foxcroft, a sizable group of her fellow Odinists from across New England attended the service. The media was there in force. Reporters from the Bangor and Portland papers, and several television trucks with their tall telescoping antennas were clustered at a respectful distance away in the parking lot. Astrid's murder, along with the earlier two killings, had now reached serial killer status, and the New York tabloids had adopted the "Ice Maiden Murders" headline. The press had not yet picked up on Beth's disappearance but it was only a matter of time until they did. Doug fully expected the case to be taken away from them within the next several days unless they made an arrest.

It was a simple ceremony, with people stepping forward to share memories of Astrid- her vitality and energy, and her warm, loving spirit. When the turn came for her Odinist friends, an attending Odinist priestess consecrated a drinking horn identified as a "Cup of Remembrance." Some of the mead it contained was first poured into the lake and it was then passed among the assemblage. People would take a small sip from the cup before passing it on, and if they wished, offer a personal pledge or statement regarding Astrid.

Dressed in a dark suit and looking exhausted after a sleepless night, Doug sat in the back row with Anne and Jim Torben, and frequently checked his phone for messages and glanced toward the parking lot, hoping to see Beth arrive. As the service was ending he got a text from Tom saying that Beth's car had been located at the Bangor airport. The driver's door was slightly ajar, her purse and cell phone were on the ground under the car, and her suitcase was in the trunk. CCTV camera footage from the back corner of the Four Points Sheraton Hotel adjacent to the airport parking lots provided a grainy image of her appearing to be pulled into a dark colored van, which then drove slowly away. There was no CCTV coverage at the parking lot payment booths, however, and the attendant had only a vague memory of the van and its driver, who she thought might have been a white male.

Several nights after Beth's abduction from the Bangor Airport parking lot a Monson man was driving home late from karaoke night at the Bear's Den in Dover-Foxcroft. He was always nervous before stepping up to the mike and had consumed a few too many beers. But he was driving OK. He drove west into Guilford from Dover-Foxcroft, and when he reached the intersection with Route 150 he turned right. Continuing straight on Route 6 would have involved crossing the Piscataquis River Bridge and then up through the small town of Abbot to Monson. By turning right, he had decided, like a lot of people that summer, to take a short-cut across the North Guilford Road in order to avoid delays on Route 6 due to bridge construction.

Just after turning onto the North Guilford Road off of 150, he saw what looked like a road kill on the left shoulder of the road. It was big, probably a deer he thought, and he turned around and drove back for a closer look. When he illuminated it with his headlights he saw it was a human body, partially submerged in the standing water in the ditch. He put on his warning flashers, called 911, and then approached the body on foot.

It was Beth. She was wearing a filthy sweatshirt, her hands were bound in front of her with a zip tie, and she was barefoot and naked from the waist down. Lacerations crisscrossed her face and legs, her feet were badly cut, and her left eye was swollen shut. But she was alive.

The Monson man belted her into the passenger seat of his truck, turned the heater on full blast, and called 911 again to tell them he was taking a badly injured woman to the Mayo Regional Hospital in Dover-Foxcroft, and was about 30 minutes away. As he came up to the intersection in Guilford he saw the flashing blue lights of an ambulance coming toward him. Flashing his headlights he was able to stop them. Beth was transferred to the ambulance for the remainder of the trip. She was still unconscious upon arrival but her vital signs were stable.

Beth regained consciousness early the next morning, and just before noon Anne and Doug were allowed in to interview her. Taking her hand, Doug asked her to just start at the beginning and tell them what she remembered.

"I remember being irritated that that stupid van was parked so close to my car. And then the hood was jammed over my head and I was being pulled into the van. Someone called me a bitch, punched me hard in the face, and tied my hands. I felt a needle pushed into my butt, and when I came to I was still hooded, my hands were tied, and I was bound to a bed. I had the hood on all the time I was there. How long was I held?"

"Forty-eight hours or so," answered Anne. "How did you manage to get free?"

"I was drugged most of the time, I guess, but it must have worn off when they weren't watching me too close. I managed to squirm out of the ropes tying me to the bed, pulled off the hood, and kicked my way out a window in the small bedroom I was being held in."

Doug picked up the questioning.

"They checked your urine and you were drugged with ketamine. It's a widely used anesthesia, but should be cleared from your system by now. There are no lasting effects, other than some possible memory loss, which isn't all that bad, considering what you've been through. What do you remember about your abductor?"

"I don't remember a lot. Just fragments. Doors opening and closing, a car starting up, cars passing on a nearby road, and someone with a deep voice screaming at me. He called me a whore and a cunt and slut, and said that I would be punished for my sins. It sounded like he was masturbating while he yelled at me."

"Were you sexually assaulted?" Anne asked.

"I don't think so," Beth replied. "I was naked from the waist down, and it was always cold. I think I remember a second man, small with bad body odor, climbing on top of me, whispering my name like a lover, and then ejaculating on my leg. It was disgusting."

They asked a few more questions but Beth couldn't add anything to what she had already told them. Her memories seemed to be coming back a little at a time, she thought, and promised that she would call if she remembered anything else. Doug kissed her forehead and smiled encouragingly.

"Get some rest. Don't worry. We'll catch them. You'll be out of here in no time."

Working west along the north Guilford road and both ways along Route 150 from the intersection, sheriff's deputies were searching for the cabin where Beth had been held. So far they hadn't found anything. Back in their courthouse office, Anne and Doug had started to go back over the abductions of Astrid and Beth to see if they had missed anything. Anne was reviewing the Center Theatre CCTV footage of Astrid's abduction when she froze the image and called Doug over.

"Look at the dark blue panel truck parked across the street along the fence close to the bridge, by the gas station – doesn't it look like the van from the Bangor airport parking lot?"

"Sort of, I guess," Doug replied skeptically. "Can't be the same van though. That's the Toad's van. He always parks it there by the fence."

"But it's worth checking out," Anne responded.

The gas station was dark when they pulled into it, and apparently had been closed all day. The Toad's van was missing. They next checked the Toad's home. He lived out of town toward Milo with his uncle Lem in a ram shackled old farmhouse with a collapsed barn and overgrown yard. The house was dark and there were no vehicles in the driveway.

Doug put out a statewide alert for Vern's van and Lem's car when they got back to the office. Expanding their search for Vern and Lem, they checked the local bars that the two frequented and questioned everyone they could think of who might have seen them. Lem had been at the Central Maine Model Railroad Club right across from Pat's Pizza the day before, looking for the Toad, but seemed nervous and didn't stay long. No one else had seen them since.

Grace Heinemeyer was opening the Sebec Corner Grange Shop the following morning when she noticed something different about the dilapidated "Christmas Village" building across the road. It had been closed for more than five years and was another memorial to the declining economy in central Maine, where it was often said, "dreams come to die." Once festooned with cheerful Christmas decorations, including a line of life-sized toy soldier cutouts on its west wall, the building was now overgrown with weeds and the soldiers were faded and forlorn.

It looked like someone had added another soldier to the line, but this one wasn't wearing a uniform, and was holding his arms out straight from his sides. Setting down her package of quilts and girls dresses to be added to their inventory, Grace walked across the Old Stagecoach Road for a closer look, and then rummaged around in her purse for her cell phone to call 911.

The Toad had been added to the line of soldiers. He was secured to the side of the building with roofing nails that had been nailed through his shirt and pants. Larger spikes had been driven through his hands, holding his arms out horizontally in a crucifixion pose. Judging from the mass of pellets imbedded in the wall behind his head, and the radiating pattern of skull fragments and brain matter, a shotgun had been placed in his mouth after he had been nailed up, and the back of his head had been blown off. A ragged cross was carved into his forehead.

When Anne and Doug arrived, sheriff's deputies were just about to drape a sheet over the Toad's body, shielding it from the stares and photographs of a growing crowd of onlookers. Social media was soon carrying grisly images of the crucifixion, and Doug was sure that TV trucks would show up long before the crime scene team out of Augusta arrived. Looking up at the Toad's corpse, Doug speculated out loud to Anne.

"Looks like you were right. I think the Toad's van was used to abduct Beth, and he could well have been the one who climbed on top of her, whimpered, and then couldn't follow through. He'd probably been fantasizing about that since high school and finally got his chance. Someone then killed the Toad, maybe because he was supposed to be watching Beth when she escaped. Vern's uncle Lem is still missing, and his role, if any, in all of this is unclear. But how about this – maybe the deep-voiced man who screamed at Beth while she was captive is our crazy preacher up at Onawa – Francis Grollig. They both used the same curses, and "whore" and "slut" also appeared prominently in the communication from the killer. The promise made to Beth that she would be punished for her sins also fits the killer's profile. And we have the cross that was carved into the Toad's forehead. I think we should pay Grollig a visit – maybe we'll get lucky before they yank us off the case."

Doug received an agitated call from Stan Shelter on their way back into town, and Sheriff McCormick was waiting for them in their courthouse office when they arrived. Both were angry about the accelerating body count and demanded a major break soon or they would be taken off the case. Doug assured them both that they were following up on a solid lead and could have something by the end of the day.

After McCormick stormed out of the office, Doug took a deep breath and smiled at Anne.

"Let's hope we get lucky."

Anne called Jim Torben, who was heading up the search north of Guilford for the house where Beth had been held captive, and asked him to take his team over to Grollig's place in Onawa, which was not that far away from their search area. Doug and Anne would meet them there. Jim called Anne back as she and Doug were just coming into Guilford.

"This guy Grollig is freaking out. He came barreling out of the front door with a shotgun as soon as we pulled in the driveway, fired several shots into the air, and told us to stay the fuck off his property. He's nuts."

"Seal off the area and block the driveway. We should be there in 20 minutes."

By the time they arrived Grollig had retreated into the house but could be heard screaming and breaking things. He was in an uncontrolled rage. Doug called Tom over in Orono and asked him to let Shelter know they had a suspect in the case barricaded and to call out the state police tactical team and crisis negotiation team. They then settled back to wait, hoping that Grollig would stay inside and not initiate a confrontation. A small crowd started to gather and soon social media was carrying the barricade situation that was unfolding in Onawa, with speculation that it might be related to the recent string of killings in the county.

The tactical and negotiating teams drove into Onawa just before noon, accompanied by Stan Shelter, who assumed command on the scene. The mobile command center of the Maine State Police Incident Management Assistance Team arrived soon after. TV trucks from the Bangor and Portland television stations were next to appear, and began broadcasting live from the scene, with their feed being picked up by the Boston stations and national networks. Shelter and Sheriff McCormick, looking professional in their starched uniforms, held a brief news conference for the assembled reporters and identified the barricaded individual, Francis Grollig, as a person of interest in an ongoing investigation. By nightfall CNN and MSNBC had joined the live broadcast stream and a full-blown media circus was well under way.

Once it was dark the tactical team closed in on the barn and positioned themselves around the house. A search warrant for all structures on the premises had been issued that afternoon and the tactical team cut a padlock on the barn and searched it. They gained access to the interior room that was also padlocked and which appeared to be a specimen preparation room for large animals. A partially mounted black bear was positioned on a table in the center of the room and several large freezers and cupboards lined the walls.

As soon as the barn was secured the evidence response team was called in and began a search, starting in the large animal prep room. It didn't take long for them to find evidence that linked Grollig to several of the killings. Under animal carcasses stored in one of the freezers they recovered zip lock bags containing what looked to be large squares of human skin, one of which carried a tattoo similar to the "tramp stamp" Candace Gray was known to have had on her lower back. In a second freezer, hidden in a shoebox, they found an ice cube tray containing four human eyes. When all of the cabinets were cleared out several Pope's pears and other torture instruments were discovered hidden behind boxes of taxidermy supplies, along with a number of books dealing with the Spanish Inquisition. Illustrations and descriptions of *auto de fé* victims had been earmarked, and inserted between the pages of one of the volumes they found photographs of the first victim, Angeline Bouchard, that had been taken during her torture.

By 3AM the negotiating team had made some progress in their conversations with Grollig. He was still fading in and out of rationality, but was no longer raging, and had put the shotgun down. Shortly before sunrise, however, Grollig unexpectedly came out through the front door onto the porch, brandishing the shotgun and reciting Psalm 23 into the gray dawn:

"Even though I walk through the valley of death, I will fear no evil, for you are with me; your rod and your staff, they comfort me."

He stammered for a moment as he was suddenly illuminated by the floodlights set up during the night. Raising his arms to shield his eyes, he continued:

"You prepare a table before me in the presence of my enemies. You anoint my head with oil; my cup overflow…"

Grollig's recitation was cut off mid-sentence and a bright red bloodstain blossomed across his white shirt. He fell backward against the door before sliding to the porch. A few seconds later they heard the crack of a high-powered rifle.

None of the assembled law enforcement personnel had fired the shot, and ballistics analysis the next day established that it had most likely been fired from the Onawa railroad trestle, a local landmark situated about 750 meters southeast of the Grollig porch, and on a clear line of sight. An impressive shot, but well within the range of a trained sniper.

Grollig's appearance on the front porch and the shooting happened so quickly that none of the assembled media caught it on video. After Grollig's body had been bagged and carried to a waiting ambulance, Shelter emerged from the mobile command center to announce that a press conference would be held at 7AM, just in time for the morning news cycle.

By all accounts the news conference was a huge success. CNN, MSNBC, and several network stations covered it live, and it was carried on the national news that evening. Standing in front of a bank of microphones, and flanked by Sheriff McCormick, Shelter outlined the brilliant investigation that had involved close cooperation between the state police and the Piscataquis County Sheriff's Office that had led to the eventual identification and capture of the killer.

Grollig was directly linked to the torture and murder of the three young women and was suspected in the killing to two additional individuals, Eric Bateman and Vern Rodgers. Shelter added that Grollig was also suspected in the kidnapping of Beth Bateman, who was currently recovering at The Mayo Regional Hospital. Doug and Anne stood behind Shelter and the sheriff, along with Tom Richard and Jim Torben, and all four looked tired and eager to escape the attention. Shelter also acknowledged that the individual who had shot Grollig was still at large, but would be brought to justice.

Doug and a number of other people in Dover-Foxcroft knew that Astrid Ragnarson's father had been a highly-decorated sniper in the Vietnam War, but the investigation into the death of Grollig petered out after a few weeks, and Ragnarson was never considered a person of interest. Further evidence linking Grollig to the Ice Maiden murders came a few weeks later when his DNA was matched to the sample recovered from the robe that the killer had worn in the Sebec Lake Webcam footage of the first killing and then discarded in a nearby ice shack.

The story continued to gain considerable media coverage for the next week or so before fading away, and Dover-Foxcroft and surrounding communities experienced a surge of tourism that summer. Attendance at the annual Woopie Pie Festival dramatically exceeded the previous record.

20.
THE KISS

It was late morning and warm on the municipal basketball court on Moosehead Lane, tucked away behind the Congressional Church in downtown Dover-Foxcroft. The pickup game had ended a half hour ago and Anne was alone, working her jump shots around the key. She was tired but not willing to stop just yet. Ashlee Torben, one of the six girls who had shown up for their Sunday game, had just left. It had been a lot of fun, playing ball with the Lady Ponies. Lots of trash talking and high fives. The girls were beginning to develop an easy rhythm to their game and a good appreciation of each other's tendencies and strengths. Ash Torben, in particular, was developing into a confident three-point shooter and was working on a deceptive stutter step drive to go with it.

Anne reveled in the simple joy of playing ball with the girls, and had developed an easy rapport with them. She had been invited to dinner by most of their families, and was enjoying getting to know more people in town. In the four weeks since they had closed the Ice Maiden case she had become a local celebrity of sorts. People had been going out of their way to wave and greet her on the street, and often thanked her for her service to the community. They also appreciated her self-depreciating response to the many media interviews and stories and her quickness to credit the sheriff's office and the state police. Careful to always mention the leadership of Sheriff George McCormick and the role of Jim Torben in the case, Anne was no longer considered "from away" but a local.

Chasing the ball down after a shot, Anne noticed Doug Bateman leaning against the fence at the other end of the court. She hadn't seen that much of him in recent weeks but had heard from June Torben that Beth had gone back out to Santa Fe and was in no hurry to return. Anne waved to him and continued shooting, wondering how long he had been there.

Doug had been watching her for maybe ten minutes. At first he was struck by her athleticism, her seemingly effortless movement, remarkable vertical height, and her ability to unerringly find the basket with her jump shots. But she also had a remarkable body, he realized. Long tapered legs, without the thick thighs he had somehow expected. Anne was sweating freely, and her red formfitting shorts showed off her slim hips and firm butt. She had muscular, well-toned arms and her sweaty white t-shirt clung to her small, perfect breasts as she continued practicing her jump shots and chasing down the ball.

Anne turned and started to slowly dribble toward him, switching the ball from hand to hand. Doug seemed to be hypnotized by her approach. Without really thinking about it, she dribbled right up to him, found his mouth with hers, and gave him a soft, lingering kiss. He felt loose tendrils of her blond hair brush his face, and the warmth of her body. She never stopped dribbling the ball with her left hand, and stepping back from him, she offered a shy smile, turned and dribbled the ball down the court before tucking it under her arm and walking over to her car.

Doug seemed stupefied, struck dumb, but managed to return her wave as she drove out of the parking lot. Anne hadn't meant to kiss him, but she didn't regret doing it. Now, she thought, it was out in the open. It was Doug's move now.

Neither Doug nor Anne realized that they were not alone. Hidden in the trees along the west side of the court, down toward the Piscataquis River, someone had been watching the game, and stayed to spy on Anne. He saw her kiss Doug, and as the hidden watcher slipped away toward his car, he whispered angrily to himself.

"The cunt, the whore, the fucking slut."

The next morning, Doug was up early. The phoebe that had nested just outside his bedroom window started off the morning chorus just before five, and putting a pillow over his head couldn't shut out the incessant repetition of its call. After breakfast he carried his coffee down to the dock, wiped the morning dew off one of the Adirondack chairs before sitting down, and looked southwest across the lake, past Pine Island and the two young eaglets perched on the edge of the nest, testing their wings and making quite a racket. They would soon be taking their first tentative flights, he thought, and trying their first clumsy landings.

Doug could just make out Anne's dock on the south shore, and her bright orange Nelo racing kayak, which she had been taking out for an hour each morning for the past few weeks before heading off to work. She would paddle west until Borestone Mountain came into view, and then back to her south shore cottage. Doug kept checking his watch and waiting for Anne to launch her kayak for her morning paddle. He thought he would watch her launch, then check back to see when the orange kayak reappeared on the dock, indicating she had returned. He planned on waiting a half hour or so after that and then calling her to see if she'd like to go to dinner. He was nervous and the time seemed to drag by. Seven o'clock came and went and she hadn't appeared on the dock. Then 7:30. At eight he gave up, walked back up through the dense forest to the house and started getting ready for the drive into Orono.

He was still adjusting to being back at work at MCU-North, and missed the easy drive into the courthouse offices in Dover-Foxcroft. He also missed working with Anne and the close friendship that had developed between them. But the Ice Maiden investigation was closed, and she had moved on to other cases. He couldn't stop thinking about her, though, and realized yesterday, watching her at the basketball court, that he needed her in his life. Since they were no longer working the same case there was nothing now to keep them from seeing what their friendship might develop into, and Anne's unexpected kiss indicated she was similarly inclined.

It was busy at work, and Doug didn't get around to calling Anne until almost noon. She didn't pick up, and his call went to voicemail. He tried again right after lunch, with still no answer. Getting concerned, he called Jim Torben at the Piscataquis County Sheriff's Office, only to learn that they hadn't been able to reach her either. She hadn't showed up for work that morning and had failed to make a scheduled court appearance. Ending the call, Doug told Tom he had to take the afternoon off, and started the hour-long drive back to Dover-Foxcroft.

Driving straight to Anne's camp, Doug was relieved to see her Toyota Land Cruiser parked in the driveway, next to the stack of lumber for boathouse renovation. He knocked on the front door and when he got no answer, went around to the side door and knocked again. Still, there was no response from inside. He walked down to the dock, but her kayak hadn't been moved and nobody was in sight.

Returning to the cottage, he looked in the window and saw her car keys, phone, and bag sitting on the kitchen counter. Charlie her cat was standing next to his empty food bowl, mewing loudly. On the upper shelf of one of the kitchen cabinets Doug could see her baton and the butt of her Walther 9mm

CCP semiautomatic pistol. He smelled something burning, and with alarm saw a blackened teakettle over an open flame on one of the burners of the kitchen stove. Something was definitely wrong here, and Doug had a strong feeling that Anne had been abducted. Turning back to his car, he called Sheriff McCormick, told him what he suspected, and sat on the deck to wait for him to arrive.

————

Anne had showered the previous afternoon when she got home from the basketball session and had just put the kettle on the stove for some tea when she heard a knock at the side door. Patty Griffin was playing softly on the sound system as she crossed the kitchen, surprised to see Steve Alexander wave at her through the window. He had never been to the house before, and Anne didn't realize that he knew where she lived. She hadn't talked to him in several weeks and was avoiding returning his calls and emails, hoping he would get the message that she wasn't interested in seeing him. Steve had started to become a little creepy since the case closed, acting possessive and turning up at odd places during the day – almost like he was stalking her.

Anne opened the door, thinking it was time to tell him straight up to leave her alone. Steve smiled broadly, stepped toward her, and jammed a 9.2 million volt stun gun against her stomach, just above the waist of her jeans. Pressing forward, he held it firmly against her bare skin as she collapsed to the floor, her entire body convulsed with muscle spasms and pain. Once she was down he tightened heavy-duty cable ties around her wrists and ankles and put a gag in her mouth, securing it with duct tape wrapped around her head. Lifting her over his shoulder, Steve carried her out to his car, popped the trunk, and dropped her inside. He smiled in at her dazed expression before slamming the trunk lid. It had taken a little under 30 seconds from his knock on the door to the slamming of the trunk lid. He also was a big fan of Patty Griffin, and quietly hummed her classic "Burgundy Shoes" as he locked and closed the side door to Anne's cottage and then drove slowly away.

————

There wasn't that much traffic up and down the gravel road that led to Anne's camp, and as soon as the sheriff arrived a door-to-door search turned up a middle-aged man who had been splitting wood for the winter the previous evening and had seen a car drive down toward Beth's place and then back up the road maybe ten minutes later. He didn't recognize the driver, but thought he looked familiar. The car, he said, was white, one of those late model Japanese models, the ones that were boring and all looked the same.

Doug called Tom to let him know about Anne's disappearance and both admitted that they had harbored lingering doubts about Grollig being the killer – it was just too neatly tied up with all the evidence in the garage and his convenient killing before being taken into custody. Almost as an afterthought, Tom mentioned a weird factoid that he had just run across as he was finally getting around to sorting through the background research that had piled up regarding the locals who had attended Grollig's Sunday get-togethers.

"Here's something curious, Doug. Steve Alexander hasn't always been Steve Alexander. Just before moving from Fort Kent down to Dover-Foxcroft he changed his name. He used to be Stephen Papineau."

Tom waited for a response, and finally broke the long silence.

"Doug, are you there?"

"Yeah, I'm here. Steve's our killer, not Grollig. Get over here as soon as you can, we have to find this guy fast."

———

Anne was groggy and confused as she regained consciousness, feeling like she had when she woke up from surgery for a torn ACL back in her college playing days. At first she thought she was dreaming about being in a small country kirk or chapel. She smelled incense and there was a low background murmur that sounded like a Gregorian chant. She was lying semi-reclined in a vintage Koken barber chair – leather, chrome, and porcelain, which was centered in a sizable rectangular room – measuring maybe 30 by 20 feet. Her arms and legs were fastened to the chair by cushioned restraints, and she was naked. A fire crackled in a Jøtul wood stove in one corner of the room and it was pleasantly warm. The pine floor was brightly polished and gleamed in the soft indirect lighting. Anne saw two large operating room type lights right above her chair, but they were not turned on.

Directly in front of her, on the far wall, Anne recognized what looked to be an ornate altar with multiple candles and an elaborate lace cloth. Centered between the candles, in the place of honor, was a large oval hand tinted photograph of a plain, plump woman in her twenties wearing a pastel blue pantsuit.

Turning to her right, Anne focused on a long waist-high table that was also covered with an elaborate lace cloth. The cloth, however, was protected by a sheet of clear plastic. On top of the plastic a series of tools of various kinds were carefully lined up. Anne recognized a roll of gray duct tape, a set of bolt cutters, several box cutters, variously sized forceps, a large and small pair of pliers, several syringes, a small hammer, a soldering iron, and chillingly, what looked to be branding irons and a Pope's pear.

A steady rhythmic slapping sound was coming from behind her and she tried to see what was making it. She couldn't turn her head far enough to see, but the sound ceased and Steve Alexander came into view on her left side. He was shirtless, barefoot, and wearing a stained pair of faded jeans. A large complex tattoo extended from his sternum down below the waistband of his jeans, depicting a martyred Saint Sebastian like figure with multiple bleeding wounds and arrows protruding from his chest and neck. Steve was sweating, holding a cat o' nine tails in his right hand, and Anne could see a series of lash marks curling around his rib cage. He smiled broadly at her and spoke in a relaxed, friendly tone of voice.

"Ah – sleeping beauty awakens. I gave you a strong dose of K so you would get some sleep. I have just been purifying myself with the lash, but have finished now, and so we can begin."

Blinking his eyes and swaying slightly, Steve looked down at himself.

"Oh – sorry for my appearance – just let me dry off and change."

Humming softly to himself, he disappeared from sight behind her for several minutes. She could hear him drying off, and then the bright overhead lights came on. Steve came back into view as he walked naked over to the wall on her left and put on a pair of bright red shoes, a red bishop's cassock, and a biretta, a small three peaked red hat surmounted by a red tuft. Arranging the cassock until it was comfortable, Steve walked back over to Anne's side.

"Now where were we? Oh yes. I'm sure you are wondering why I have brought you here, and we will get to that, but first – how long has it been since your last confession?"

Anne looked at him, dumbfounded, and noting her reaction, he asked.

"You are Catholic aren't you?"

Anne shook her head, unable to speak.

"Well, that complicates things," he replied, frowning and looking across her to the table of waiting instruments.

"Not Catholic, and certainly not pagan – that pretty much opens the door wide in terms of how to proceed with the questioning. Maybe we can start with a finger amputation – how does that sound?"

Moving around her, he picked up a blunt-ended branding iron and carried it over to the wood stove. Inserting it into the coals, he turned and smiled at her.

"We'll need that to cauterize the stump. I think we should skip the anesthesia – that way you can experience the full joy of the pain – what do you think?"

———

Doug had called the Foxcroft Academy to get Steve Alexander's address but the woman who handled employee records was refusing to provide the information. She had recently been hired from out of state and cited the school's privacy policy, saying that she would have to check with Mr. Alexander before releasing that information. Doug angrily hung up and decided to drive down to the school and sort things out. After talking to the School Head, and following him down to meet with the staff records person, Doug learned that the school did not have a current street address for Steve.

Like several of the other teachers, Steve had indicated that he was concerned about potential hacking of school records and harassment from disgruntled students or their parents and had opted against providing a home address. All they had for him was a post office box address. The School Head promised to call around to see if anyone knew where Steve lived, but was doubtful they could help. Steve was apparently a very private person and didn't socialize much outside of school functions.

Doug drove to the courthouse in downtown Dover-Foxcroft and after finding the right office was told that the registry of deeds didn't show any property in Piscataquis County owned by Steve Alexander or Stephen Papineau. The clerk suggested he try Penobscot County, which bordered Piscataquis on the east and southeast. Doug checked in with the Sheriff's Office and used their phone to call the courthouse in Bangor. After putting him on hold for several minutes they came on the line back to tell him they also had no record of a Steve Alexander or Stephen Papineau owning any land in Penobscot County. With mounting frustration Doug next tried Somerset County, which bordered

Piscataquis on the southwest. Calling the Somerset County courthouse in Skowhegan he reached a recorded message indicating that the registry of deeds had closed for the day at 4:30, and would reopen at 8:30 the following day.

Slamming down the phone in frustration, Doug turned to see Tom Richard coming in the door. He explained the problem to Tom, who immediately went over to a computer on a nearby desk.

"There is a state-wide registry of deeds that is accessible on the web. Let's see what it has."

Tom worked through the deed listings for Piscataquis and Penobscot Counties and turned up nothing. Checking Somerset County, he found what they were looking for.

"Looks like he's got a place in Ripley – where's that?"

"It's southwest of here. South on 7, then west out of Dexter on 23. It's just over the county line, maybe a half hour away."

21.
BROWNVILLE JUNCTION

On the drive down to Ripley, Doug explained why he was convinced that Steve Alexander was the killer.

"It happened my sophomore year at the University of Maine. I took a clinical Psych course during spring semester. We called it 'rat lab.' It was all about designing experiments. We had to try to get our white lab rat to perform certain tasks like running a maze, by using positive and negative reinforcement, food and electric shock. I was assigned a very unpleasant coed named Denise Papineau as my lab partner. She seemed weird right off – always wore heavy perfume and pastel pantsuits and sucked up to the prof. At first she was belligerent and suspicious toward me, really paranoid. But then for some reason she decided that we should be a couple, and started inviting me to do stuff with her. Finally I just told her I wasn't interested in her that way, and she went ballistic – accusing me of sexually harassing her and forcing myself on her. About that time I also became convinced that she was fabricating research results – the rat was doing just amazingly well when it was her turn to run the maze experiments. I was afraid that the prof would find out and think both of us were in on it, so I told him what I thought was going on. He started monitoring our lab sessions, caught her red-handed, and flunked her. It turned out that she was already on academic probation and her getting caught cheating resulted in her dropping out of school. I never saw her again after that.

She was from a devout Catholic family in Fort Kent and they took her back home at that point. I breathed a big sigh of relief, thinking it was over, but then she started stalking me and claiming I had raped her. She got pregnant, although I can't imagine how, and claimed it was my baby. Given her religion there was no question of an abortion. She had the baby, still claiming it was mine, and I was pressured into a paternity test, which of course proved that I wasn't the father. A year or so later she ended up drowning her child in the bathtub and then hanging herself in the basement of her parents' house. It hit all the papers, and was a big scandal up in Fort Kent."

"So who's this Steve Papineau guy?" Tom asked.

"I don't know for sure – maybe a brother? He's about the right age. One thing for sure – insanity runs in that family."

About the only indications Doug and Tom had that they had reached the town of Ripley as they drove west on Route 23 out of Dexter was a scattering of homes on both sides of the road, a reduced, 35 MPH speed limit, and American flags mounted on the power poles. Ripley was centered on the south end of Ripley Pond, which was about 3 miles long, north to south, and maybe a half a mile wide at its widest point. Steve Alexander's place was on the east side of the pond, about halfway up – one of the last houses on Deer Run Lane, just before it dead-ended. They parked a hundred yards or so away and approached on foot in the fading light of early evening.

It was a well-kept cedar shake shingle cabin with an attached garage and a large screened porch facing the water. There were no cars in the drive and no one appeared to be home. They crossed the neatly mowed front lawn, past a bathtub Virgin Mary shrine, several flowerbeds, a vegetable garden, and bird feeders. No lights were on inside but a motion sensor light turned on as they reached the front of the house. Looking in a garage window Tom could see an ATV and snowmobile but no other vehicles. Going around to the back of the house they entered the screened porch, weapons drawn, and Doug tried the door. It was unlocked.

Entering the kitchen they moved quickly through the house but found nothing suspicious or out of place. There was no basement and no second floor, and the house was tidy, with a full refrigerator – mostly microwave dinners and beer, a single plate and glass in the dish drainer, and fresh flowers on the kitchen table. A thorough search didn't turn up anything – he looked like a normal guy leading a normal boring life.

They left by the screened porch, making sure everything was as they found it. Doug called Sheriff McCormick and asked if Jim Torben and another deputy could come down and take over surveillance of the house. As they were walking back across the front lawn Tom noticed a second building in the trees some distance away from the house and down toward the water. They approached it carefully, redrawing their weapons, and after setting off another motion sensor light, listened at a locked, reinforced steel door centered on the wall. They couldn't hear any sounds from within. Doug picked up a piece of firewood from the pile stacked along the wall of the building and smashed a small window high up on the wall. Climbing on the woodpile, he looked inside.

"Nothing. A stored canoe and a beat-up aluminum boat."

———

Anne watched Steve as he moved over to the table holding the instruments and picked up the bolt cutters and several zip ties.

"It won't be long – I'm just waiting for the iron to get good and hot."

After checking the iron heating up in the stove, Steve nodded in satisfaction and came over to Anne's left side. Grabbing her left hand he wrapped the zip tie around her pinky finger and pulled it tight. The pain was sudden and sharp, and Anne cried out. Taking the loose end of the zip tie, Steve pulled it forward, out away from Anne's body, straining on the arm restraint, and secured it to the front of the barber chair. Anne's left hand was now stretched out over the chrome end of the arm of the chair, and her pinky was rapidly turning a deep blue. Steve paused and explained.

"The zip tie is my own invention. It immobilizes the hand, and also serves as a pre-positioned tourniquet."

Stepping forward, he slid the bolt cutters over her left little finger, just above the midpoint of the second phalange, paused, and said.

"Enjoy."

An incredible pain, like nothing she had ever felt, shot up Anne's arm, and she screamed in agony before losing consciousness. Steve quickly reached down and caught the finger before it hit the floor. He dropped it on top of the wood stove, where it sizzled, took the branding iron over and cauterized the end of Anne's finger. Replacing the iron in the stove, Steve crossed to the table and picked up one of the syringes. As he injected the anesthesia, he spoke softly to Anne.

"That's enough for today I think. No need to rush things. Now we need to let you get some sleep – we've got a big day tomorrow."

———

Doug and Tom had hit a dead end. They knew that Steve had Anne somewhere – likely within a half hour of where they sat in the county sheriff's office in downtown Dover-Foxcroft. But they had no idea where, and no good way to find out. About the only option open to them now was an appeal to the public for information. But if Steve was monitoring media outlets and learned of their efforts he likely wouldn't hesitate to kill Anne and disappear. After discussing it with Stan Shelter and Sheriff McCormick, they contacted local TV and radio stations and released appeals on social media asking for assistance in locating Steve and his kidnapping victim, Anne Quinn, and offering a sizable reward for information leading to apprehension of the suspect. Doug also was able to reach Anne's brothers in Manistee, Michigan, to let them know of Anne's abduction, and both said they would be flying out on the first flight they could catch, and would contact him as soon as they arrived in Dover-Foxcroft.

Calls started flooding in early the next morning from as far away as Texas from people claiming to have seen the couple, often in Alexander's late model white Toyota Corolla. Most were dead ends. Doug was convinced that Steve was holding Anne somewhere close by. One of the calls, however, which came from an unlikely local source, immediately jumped out at them. Dwayne Benz, the warehouse worker at Ace Hardware who had been a suspect early on due to misleading DNA evidence, called from work to say he remembered delivering a load of lumber the summer before to the guy he had just seen on TV – Steve Alexander. It was pine flooring, and he thought it was strange at the time. The guy had met him in Milo and led him way up Route 11 past Brownville Junction, then off on a lumber road to a small cinder block building out in the middle of nowhere. Alexander told him it was a hunting cabin he was fixing up.

"Can you find it again?" Doug asked.

"Oh sure, I used to hunt up toward South Twin Lake – should be able to figure it out."

"We'll pick you up in 10 minutes."

———

Anne swam back into consciousness, feeling a throbbing pain in her left hand. Steve was sitting in a chair next to the altar in his bishop's getup, watching her. When he saw her stir, he smiled, and picking up the bolt cutters and another zip tie, walked over to her side.

"You're awake. Excellent. I thought I would start today's questioning by snipping off a bit more of your finger, and then we can go right to the carving of the crucifix."

Anne looked down, and could see that a magic marker had been used to outline a large cross down the front of her torso. About two inches in width, the vertical part of the cross went from her suprasternal notch down to her mons veneris, and the horizontal axis extended across her chest and encompassed both nipples.

"But first," Steve said, "You deserve an explanation for why you're here. It's my sister Denise – there on the altar. That's her high school graduation picture and that urn next to it contains her ashes and baby Doug's ashes. She was a good girl. She was a few years older than me, and took care of me. I loved her. We went to church together and prayed together, and she would let me crawl into her bed at night when I was scared. My dad would come at night sometimes and hurt us. Then she went away to college, leaving me alone, and Doug Bateman raped her. It was terrible when she came home and then had the baby. We were disgraced. We couldn't go to church. We were outcasts in the community and our father was humiliated. He blamed it all on Denise. She got into drugs then and made some bad choices in boyfriends. Finally she took the only way out for her and our baby I guess, but what she did was a sin – worse than having a baby outside of marriage. So she can't get into heaven now."

Pausing, Steve reached down and tightened another zip tie around her left little finger, this time midway on the first phalanges. He then continued.

"I prayed for years, and asked for divine guidance. And then God heard me and told me what I had to do so Denise could get into heaven. I had to destroy Doug Bateman. Just killing him wasn't enough. First I needed to take the people he loved most away from him while also humiliating him. I wanted to expose him as a complete fool, an incompetent loser. Then I would kill him, and Denise would be allowed through the gates of heaven.

Everything was going just like I planned it. I took Eric first, and then the three women – the lost Catholic girls and the pagan, and made Doug and the others all out to be fools. Beth was supposed to be next. I had that fool Grollig all set up to take the fall once I killed Beth. I had planted the evidence where they would find it, and was ready to call in the anonymous tip once Beth and Doug were taken care of.

I was waiting at Beth's sister's house to grab her that night, but that fool Grollig and the two other idiots decided on their own to kidnap her, and snatched her at the airport. The Toad wanted to be her boyfriend and Grollig decided that she could satisfy his needs too. Fucking fools.

I thought they had ruined all my careful planning. But then God intervened on my behalf. The Lord freed Beth and he guided me to Toad the retard, and uncle Lem. Toad got crucified and Lem's at the bottom of Sebec. Then everything else fell into place. Grollig snapped under the pressure and got credit for the killings, just like I planned, and then one of God's angels ended the story with a sniper's rifle.

I was going to have to kill Doug and settle for that, since Beth left town before I could get to her. But I wasn't sure that would be enough to get Denise into heaven. Then I saw you kiss him at the basketball court and I realized that God was giving me another chance. I could take you away from him. You meant something to him, and could take Beth's place."

Steve paused again, raised the bolt cutters, and snipped off another segment of Anne's little finger. She screamed from the pain and Steve jammed a rag in her mouth and taped it in place with a strip of duct tape. He then wrapped a second strip of duct tape around her forehead, securing her head to the back of the barber chair.

"There, that will keep you from squirming too much while I carve a cross into your chest."

———

Doug's Jeep pulled slowly up the dirt track toward Steve's hideaway, stopping behind a clump of bushes. Dwayne stayed in the car while Jim Torben, Doug, and Tom Richard silently stepped out of the vehicle and slipped into their body armor vests. Hearing Anne's scream, Doug pushed past the other two, but Tom grabbed his arm and pulled him roughly back behind him.

"This is my deal Doug. I go first. Stay close behind me. Don't worry, you'll be first through the door."

Leading them across the open weedy area toward the cinder block structure, Tom was crouched and scanning for sensors and trip wires. Low to the ground he carried one of his newest toys – a Rapid Entry Solutions FX6 pneumatic powered battering ram that could easily breach steel reinforced doors. With his Glock 9mm drawn and ready, Doug tucked in behind him, and Jim Torben followed close behind, armed with a Tristar KSX tactical shotgun.

Red squirrels in the nearby trees began scolding them loudly as they got closer to the cabin, and they could smell wood smoke from the stove inside. The afternoon had turned warm and they were sweating beneath their body armor by the time they reached the only door to the cinder block structure. From inside, they could hear Steve talking quietly against a background of low muffled sobs. Glancing at Doug to make sure he was ready and in position, Tom grinned and swung the FX 6 in a gentle arc against the door handle. The door blew inward, and Doug stepped inside, Glock at his side.

Anne was looking straight at him, eyes wide open, her whole body straining against her restraints. Steve had just finished using a box cutter to slice through Anne's chest on both sides of the vertical part of the cross, and was just beginning to make the horizontal cuts across her breasts. Blood was flowing freely from the wounds and pooling on the floor under the barber chair.

Moving with surprising speed, Steve ducked behind Anne and snarled from his hiding place.

"You can't save the slut – she's mine."

Doug could see him repositioning his feet and realized that he was going to reach up with the box cutter and cut Anne's throat. As he raised his Glock and pointed it directly at her head, he looked into her eyes and jerked his head to the right. Anne understood, and abruptly moved her head to the side in that direction as far as she could, exposing the right side of Steve's head as he raised up to slash at her throat with the blood-covered box cutter.

The enclosed space reverberated with the crack of Doug's weapon. Anne felt the puff of air as the round passed a few inches from her right ear. It entered Steve's head just above his right eye, making a small black hole. He dropped to the floor as if he had fallen from a great height, the box cutter still clenched in his right fist. A few drops of blood seeped from the thin shallow cut Steve had managed to make in Anne's neck before Doug's shot blew the back of his head off.

EPILOGUE
THE LAKE

Anne lay on a chaise lounge positioned at the end of her dock, soaking in the sun and watching a boat pull two small girls on a tube, their shrieks of joyful terror carrying across the water to the south shore. It was a beautiful summer day, with a slight breeze riffling the water, and the fledging eagles filled the air with their raucous cries from their nest on Pine Island. Two weeks had passed since her rescue. Her stitches had come out a week ago, and the twin red raised ridges on her torso where she had been cut were beginning to fade. Her little finger was also healing well, and she was thinking about getting a silver replacement like the one Holly Hunter wore in the movie "The Piano."

Her brothers had been stranded overnight in the Detroit Metro Airport and didn't arrive until the day after she had been rushed to the Mayo Regional Hospital in Dover-Foxcroft. Doug sat by her bed throughout that first night, calming her when she woke, and talking to her until she fell back asleep. He was surprised the next day at how much she had remembered of his exhausted rambling narratives of the night before, including his discussion of the four quite different calls of the common loon.

Her brothers burst into her room just before noon the next day, frustrated at their delayed arrival and relieved to find their sister safe and in good spirits. Anne drifted off to sleep after a few minutes and Doug took Jonathan and David to lunch at Allie-Oops, where Tom joined them. The two tall imposing outsiders were met with curious stares as they entered, but people returned to their conversations and their meals when David caught the bartender's eye and called out.

"Four PBRs, long necks if ya got em."

They sat in the window booth and both smiled when the waitress recommended the cheeseburger, mentioning that it's what Anne always ordered. Doug gave them a long detailed account of the case leading up to Anne's abduction and the shooting of Steve Alexander. Jonathan and David relaxed as they heard the story and they realized that Doug was no fool and that he hadn't carelessly put their sister at risk. After asking for details about the shooting and being assured that Doug took the risky shot only because Anne was seconds from death, they wanted to see where she had been held. Tom volunteered to show them, and after visiting Steve's torture house, and checking in on Anne again, they spent several hours with Tom trying out his battering ram, and then insisted on seeing Doug's Chris-Craft. The four of them had dinner at the Bear's Den, and sitting on either side of Doug, and to Tom's great enjoyment, Anne's brothers made it quite clear that he had better have honorable intentions toward their sister or he would answer to them.

Lying in the sun, Anne looked down the lake toward Doug's camp on the north shore and smiled at what her brother Jonathan had told her as they were saying goodbye to her in the hospital before heading to the Bangor Airport.

"Sis, I am not getting much use out of Dad's old Chris-Craft, and you have the perfect lake for it here. I'm going to have it shipped out here to you at the end of the summer."

Down the lake, Anne heard the deep growl of Doug's boat, the Otter, as he started her up, and her smile broadened.

View other Black Rose Writing titles at www.blackrosewriting.com/books and

use promo code **PRINT** to receive a **20% discount** when purchasing.

BLACK ROSE
writing™